PRA... MALL'S

Passionate Pleasures

"Small delivers a marvelously sexy story . . . that's smart, sassy, and definitely sizzling . . . a great love story that just happens to be filled with erotic love scenes."

—*Romantic Times*

"A fun, well-written romantic fantasy."

—Genre Go Round Reviews

Dangerous Pleasures

"A pleasurable erotic tale. . . . Fans will enjoy Bertrice Small's fine character study." —The Best Reviews

"The queen of sensual romance has done it again . . . sizzling." —*Romantic Times*

"Erotica has never been done more tastefully or been more captivating." —Romance Junkies

Sudden Pleasures

"Arranged marriages are nothing new but the spin that Small puts on her contemporary version is hot and different . . . definitely scorching." —*Romantic Times*

"Full of emotions and unruly feelings . . . an entertaining read. . . . Ms. Small writes every character realistically and with realistic faults." —Romance Junkies

continued . . .

ALSO BY BERTRICE SMALL

The *Pleasures* Series

Passionate Pleasures

Sudden Pleasures

Dangerous Pleasures

Forbidden Pleasures

Private Pleasures

BERTRICE SMALL

GUILTY PLEASURES

NEW AMERICAN LIBRARY

New American Library
Published by New American Library,
a division of Penguin Group (USA) Inc.,
375 Hudson Street, New York, New York 10014, USA
Penguin Group (Canada), 90 Eglinton Avenue East, Suite 700, Toronto,
Ontario M4P 2Y3, Canada (a division of Pearson Penguin Canada Inc.)
Penguin Books Ltd., 80 Strand, London WC2R 0RL, England
Penguin Ireland, 25 St. Stephen's Green, Dublin 2,
Ireland (a division of Penguin Books Ltd.)
Penguin Group (Australia), 250 Camberwell Road, Camberwell,
Victoria 3124, Australia (a division of Pearson Australia Group Pty. Ltd.)
Penguin Books India Pvt. Ltd., 11 Community Centre,
Panchsheel Park, New Delhi - 110 017, India
Penguin Group (NZ), 67 Apollo Drive, Rosedale, Auckland 0632,
New Zealand (a division of Pearson New Zealand Ltd.)
Penguin Books (South Africa) (Pty.) Ltd., 24 Sturdee Avenue,
Rosebank, Johannesburg 2196, South Africa

Penguin Books Ltd., Registered Offices:
80 Strand, London WC2R 0RL, England

First published by New American Library,
a division of Penguin Group (USA) Inc.

First Printing, August 2011

 REGISTERED TRADEMARK—MARCA REGISTRADA

LIBRARY OF CONGRESS CATALOGING-IN-PUBLICATION DATA:
Small, Bertrice.
Guilty pleasures/Bertrice Small.
p.   cm.
ISBN 978-0-451-23339-4
I. Title.
PS3569.M28G85   2011
813'.54—dc22   2011009675

Printed in the United States of America

For Laura Cifelli—
It was brief but you were a lovely editor,
and you always made me laugh.
Thank you.

CONTENTS

Author's Note

For those of you who have not previously read one of the *Pleasures* books, a brief explanation of the Channel is in order. The Channel is a secret interactive network known only to women. It is obtained through a cable or satellite provider. It allows you to live out your wildest fantasies between the hours of eight p.m. and four a.m. daily. Men have no idea it exists. If they did, they would want it for themselves, or regulate it, or, worst of all, take it away from us.

The five previous novels in the *Pleasures* series have each dealt with the story of one woman and her involvement with the Channel. They have all taken place in the small town of Egret Pointe. This work of fiction, however, while still set in Egret Pointe, will tell you five short stories about five different women, four of whom have appeared in the previous books. The fifth is a new character employed by a previous heroine.

I hope you will enjoy reading *Guilty Pleasures* as much as I have enjoyed writing it. But remember: This is a work of fiction. So please don't call your cable or satellite providers and ask for the Channel. But . . . maybe one day.

CARLA AND
THE PIRATE KING

C arla Johnson had been married for more than thirty years to a good man. They lived in a large comfortable house on Ansley Court in the small town of Egret Pointe. Their children were grown and not a problem. Rick had a thriving law practice with his best friend, Joe Pietro d'Angelo, in the village. Carla had gone back to nursing at the local hospital. And together they had a fun social life and a regular sex life.

But all that didn't mean a girl couldn't long for something a wee bit more exciting, which was precisely the purpose of the Channel. With a special remote from the Channel, you could program your wildest fantasy and actually live it. Nowadays the Channel remote could program two fantasies, so you could switch from one to the other if the first bored you. You could delete your fantasies and replace them with new fantasies whenever you wanted.

Carla Johnson, however, had only one fantasy programmed in her remote. The year was 1680, and she was

Captain Raven, a dangerous and feared pirate queen. When she had originally programmed her fantasy, Carla had sailed her vessel out of Jamaica. Recently she had created a small island called Amorata Cay, belonging to her alone, that served as her home port. It was a hilly landscape with cliffs that fell into the sea but for a half-moon cove bordered by a small sandy beach.

She had created a house high in the hills that gave her a 360-degree view of the sparkling turquoise sea surrounding Amorata Cay. This was where Captain Raven came for refuge when she was bored with the excesses of Jamaica and her pirate world. The only other humans on Amorata Cay were her servants. Captain Raven didn't keep slaves, and her servants were available only when she inhabited the island. When she wanted her privacy, her crew would leave her on Amorata Cay and return to nearby Jamaica for their own amusement. A carrier pigeon kept her in touch with Jamaica.

In the fantasy, her alter ego, Captain Raven, would sail the Caribbean, taking fat merchant vessels for their cargo and wealthy passengers for ransom or whatever else they might offer her, but she never deliberately sank a ship or killed. That wasn't a part of her pirate fantasy, although the other captains peopling her secret world mocked her for it. And oddly the bounty on her head was greater than that for any of the other seagoing outlaws. A woman who captained a pirate ship, could use a sword as well as she did, and commanded the respect that Captain Raven did was not to be tolerated.

Carla had enjoyed her fantasy for several years now, but of late it hadn't seemed quite as exciting and fun as it once had. She suspected that was why she had created Amorata Cay and the beautiful home, which she seemed to prefer inhabiting rather than slumming in the waterside taverns of Jamaica, fighting, drinking, and getting screwed by various handsome men. There was no excitement in it any longer.

"Hey, babe!" Her husband, Rick, came through the kitchen door from the garage and planted a kiss on her cheek. "How were things in the ER today?"

"Quiet, thank God," Carla replied. "One kid who fell out of a tree and broke his arm, an early labor, and an old-ster with a small heart incident. The kid got a cast and went home. The other two were admitted. What's new with you?"

"I'm going to Europe with Ryan Mulcahy," Rick said in a rush.

"I thought Joe took care of his legal business," Carla said.

"He's Ashley's attorney. I'm Ryan's," Rick replied. "They didn't want a conflict of interest with their two businesses."

"I don't see how there could be a conflict between a guy who does restorations and reproductions and his wife who sells sexy underwear and nighties," Carla noted.

"Neither do I," Rick admitted, "but they wanted sepa-rate lawyers."

"So why are you going to Europe?" Carla wanted to know. "And how long will you be gone?"

"A week, ten days. Ryan is buying a controlling inter-est in a small company that makes perfect replicas of sev-enteenth- and eighteenth-century furniture hardware. They have the original molds. The company is in Austria. Then we're going to England on our way home. He's got another small group of artisans there making replicas of antique clock corners, hands, and dials. He's debating about buying them up," Rick told his wife.

"Well," Carla responded, "I guess that's why you took those new courses in international law last year. This has been in the works for a while, huh?"

Rick nodded. "Yep," he said. "Ryan asked me almost two years ago if I would represent him. I told him that I didn't have enough of a background for what he wanted, that I was just a garden-variety country lawyer. While I could be there for him nationally, international law was a whole different thing. You know how he is. Just shrugged and told me to go get what I needed. Joe agreed. So I did."

"You are something else, Richard Johnson," Carla said admiringly. "I know how hard you studied so you could do this." Then she chuckled. "You're going to make a lot of money out of this. I want that superdeluxe cruise next winter. We can do a half round the world. Be gone for six weeks. First-class all the way!"

Rick laughed. "You know what, babe? You plan it, book it, get the tickets. We haven't had a *real* vacation in years. We're due. As soon as you have the dates set, I'll let Joe know, and he can cover for me while we're away."

"You mean it?" Carla was delighted.

"I mean it," Rick told his spouse. Then he said, "You going to be all right while I'm gone? Maybe you should have one of the girls come home to keep you company."

"God, no!" Carla exclaimed. "I'll be fine by myself. I'm on the seven a.m.–to–seven p.m. shift this month. It will be light when I leave in the morning and light when I get home at night. Rina, Joanne, and Tiffy are all home too, so I'll have plenty of company in the neighborhood."

"And you have your programs in the evening," Rick said with an indulgent smile.

"Yep," Carla agreed. "I do love my telly."

He was relieved she wasn't upset about the trip. Rick didn't think in all the years of their marriage they had ever been apart for more than two or three days, and that had been when their girls were born. "I'll call you every night," he promised her.

"No," Carla said. "Call me when you arrive so I know you're safe. Then call me on Sunday. Remember the time difference between here and there. Besides, I don't relish being called in the middle of the night, sweetie. Every time the phone rings that late, I think someone has died. Where are you going first?"

"We're flying to Vienna. A car will meet us and stay with us until we fly to Paris, and then London," Rick told his wife.

"Vienna, Paris, and London? Wow! Do you need an assistant?"

Rick laughed. God, he loved this woman! "Wish I did," he teased, "but then I'd have to take that hot new paralegal we recently hired."

"Over my dead body!" Carla said. "I think I had better take you upstairs and remind you just where your loyalties lie, sir."

"Yes, ma'am!" her husband said, grinning. "I love your reminders, babe. I do!"

Why did some women whine about their empty nest?

Carla wondered afterward. Having her husband all to herself, knowing some kid wasn't going to burst in on them, was wonderful as far as she was concerned. And Rick, considering he was past fifty now, was still an enthusiastic lover. But having him away would not be such a terrible burden. She had some time coming to her at the hospital, and she would take a nice long weekend so she could enjoy the beautiful home she had created on Amorata Cay. And who knew? Maybe she could come up with some new exciting adventure and end her ennui with her pirate fantasy.

Two days later she kissed her husband good-bye, but it wasn't until he called her from Vienna that Carla felt free once more. Rick's absence was really quite an opportunity for her. She didn't have to hide out in her craft room, where she usually accessed the Channel from her recliner. She could do it from their bedroom. The day after Rick had told her he was traveling on business, Carla had put in for a four-day weekend. Since she rarely asked to take any of the time she had built up, her request was granted. Friday, Saturday, Sunday, and Monday were hers.

Rick had left on a Thursday. He called her on her iPhone as soon as he and Ryan Mulcahy reached their hotel. It was just after four in the afternoon in Egret Pointe, but after midnight in Vienna. "Call me Monday instead of Sunday," Carla told him. "I think I'm going out to dinner at the club with the gang on Sunday." He agreed and rang off.

When Carla got home, she didn't bother cooking for herself. She had eaten a salad at the hospital. She hurried upstairs and quickly undressed, then got into bed naked. It was almost eight p.m., and the Channel opened at eight p.m. sharp. Grabbing her remote, she pointed it at the television in the media center across the room and pressed the A button on it to access her fantasy.

And there she suddenly was. Naked, in her big four-poster mahogany bed with its delicate white netting, which during the day was tied back but now was loose about the bed, keeping her safe from insects. The French doors to the second-floor balcony that surrounded the house on all sides were open. Carla could see the blue sea beyond and the sunrise now dappling the sky with a rainbow of strong colors. A light knock sounded on her bedroom door. "Come in," she called, and the door opened to reveal her personal maidservant, Violetta.

"Good morning, madam," the bondwoman greeted Carla as she stepped into the bedroom. "Shall I prepare your bath for you?" She carried a small tray with a cup and saucer upon it. "I have your chocolate, madam." Violetta offered the delicate china to Carla.

The mistress took it and sipped slowly at the brew, which was sweetened with her own sugarcane. "Aye, a bath would be perfect. I have accounts to do today. I think it may be time to go hunting again soon, although frankly I enjoy just being here on the island."

Violetta smiled. "It is a pleasant habitat, madam," she agreed. "I'll have the bath set up immediately." Then she bustled out to marshal the male servants to bring the water to madam's bathing chamber, where the beautiful white porcelain tub with its high back, decorated with delicate rosebuds and edged in real gold, was installed.

Carla sat up in her bed enjoying her chocolate as a warm trade wind ruffled the sheer bed curtains. She had just finished, setting the cup and saucer on the nightstand, when Violetta came to announce that her bath was ready. The mistress of Amorata Cay rose from her bed and walked across the chamber and into her bathing room. Steam, fragrant with the scent of night-blooming lilies, arose from the tub as she stepped into it and slid down into the water to enjoy it. "It's perfect as always, Violetta," she called to her maid. Servants should always be praised for a job well done, Carla believed.

She enjoyed soaking in the exotic oily water, but then as the water eventually cooled, she picked up the cake of fine milled soap containing the matching fragrance and began to wash herself. "Violetta, put out a simple gown for me today. I do not have to dress elegantly to peruse the accounts."

The servant did not answer.

"Violetta?" Carla called. Hellfire and brimstone! Where had that damned woman gotten to now? Was she with one of the men again? Violetta did have a rather strong libido. "Violetta! Violetta!"

"I'm afraid, dear madam, that Violetta is not available to you at the moment," a deep masculine voice said. "She is far too busy servicing my first mate."

And then a man stepped into the bathing chamber. Actually, he had had to duck as he came through, for he was at least half a foot over six feet in height. His hair, which was pulled back and obviously held by a ribbon, was bleached golden by the sun, and his piercing eyes were a startling sea blue. He was dressed in traditional pirate garb: breeches held up by a wide belt, boots, and an open linen shirt that revealed a smooth, well-muscled expanse of perfect pecs. In his left ear was a small, round golden earring.

Now where the hell had he come from? Carla wondered. She certainly hadn't ordered him up, but she had to admit he was a yummy specimen and quite new to her. Still, she had created this island so she might have her privacy. "How dare you enter my home uninvited?" Carla said angrily. "Who are you?"

"The name is Hawke, Captain Raven. Lord Julian Hawke, and 'tis you who are trespassing, not I," the big man said. "Amorata Cay belongs to me."

"It most certainly does not," Carla said vehemently. "I won it in a card game in Jamaica several years ago. I built this house as my refuge."

"The man who wagered it had not the right," Hawke answered her. "Had he lost heavily to you?"

Carla nodded. "He wanted one more hand, but had no coin. He told me he owned a small island, Amorata Cay, and he would wager it against all I had won that evening."

"But he lost," Hawke said.

"He lost," Carla replied as she considered just how this man she had never imagined had ended up in her fantasy. He had moved farther into the room, and as he did, she looked past him and saw Violetta upon her bed, her legs wrapped about the torso of a rather beefy man who was fucking her for all he was worth. Well, the wench was no virgin. Carla had caught her several times with the men servants. "Get out of my home," Carla said again. "And take that randy pig fucking my servant woman with you."

"Nay, Captain Raven, 'tis you who must leave," Hawke told her in a hard voice.

"This is *my* house!" Carla said angrily. Damn! The water in her tub was practically cold now.

"And 'tis *my* island," he responded. "It would seem we are at an impasse, madam. I suppose we shall have to take this matter to Governor Morgan in Jamaica to be settled, but I cannot see him awarding you my property."

"Where were you these last three years?" Carla demanded to know. "Why would you think I would believe you just because you have said that Amorata Cay belongs to you? Where is your proof? And aye! We will take this to the governor in Jamaica. He is a dear friend of mine despite that ridiculous but flattering bounty he put on my head."

"Would you like to get out of that tub?" Hawke asked casually. "I'm of a mind to follow my first mate's example." He turned his head. "Nestor! Take your wench somewhere else. There have to be other bedrooms in this big house. I want some privacy when I do her mistress. When you're through, make certain the men have secured everything and send back to the ship to come around to Half-Moon Cove and anchor."

"Aye, Captain!" Nestor called. Still buried deep in Violetta, Nestor picked her up and walked slowly from the bedchamber.

Hawke handed Carla a large towel. "Dry yourself off," he said. "I'm not of a mind to fuck a woman who is so oily she keeps slipping out of my grasp."

"Go to hell!" Carla snapped. She hadn't ordered this man up—or had she when she had hoped for something more exciting in her fantasy? Well, she would tolerate him as long as he amused her. Would he amuse her? She glared up at him.

"You're a disobedient wench, aren't you?" he said drily.

"I am not a wench," Carla protested. "I am Captain Raven of the good ship *Venus*. I am very well respected here along the Spanish Main. As for you, I have never heard of a Captain Hawke." She snatched the towel from him and stood to wrap it about her as she stepped carefully from her tub.

"I've been gone back to England for several years," he said, "which is why some thief was able to lose *my island* to you in a card game."

"Possession is nine-tenths of the law, sir," Carla told him. "And I am in possession of Amorata Cay; *and* 'tis I who built this house. If this island belonged to you, why was there no sign of human habitation, or at least a caretaker to protect your interests, sir? No person with their wits about them runs off, leaving their land unattended." She took an edge of the towel and slowly dried her arms.

"Was the fellow who played cards with you a short, plump man with a face like a cherub's and a bald pate?" Hawke asked.

Carla nodded.

"He was my caretaker. I imagine he went to Jamaica for a bit of recreation, drank too much, and got in over his head with the cards. Perhaps you even cheated him," Hawke said insultingly. "You are a notorious pirate, after all."

"I don't have to cheat at cards," Carla told him as she

bent to rub the excess moisture from her legs, all the while attempting to keep the rest of her anatomy covered. "Luck seems to follow me. Anyone can tell you that. What were you doing in England that took you so long to return here?"

"Inheriting a dukedom," Hawke told her. "My uncle died of plague, along with his sons, his grandsons, my father, and my elder brother, who had two daughters but no son. I became the heir to the dukedom of Falk—much to my distress, I might tell you. I far prefer pirating to dancing attendance at court and siring an heir on a suitable virgin. However, having done what was expected of me, I have now returned to the Caribbean to tie up some loose ends. I mean to sell Amorata Cay before I go back to England."

"You are wed?"

"Aye, and sired one son. Venetia is pregnant with another child. She is a sweet if dull girl, but I promised her I would be home before she whelps her second," Hawke replied sanguinely. "I've actually become quite fond of her."

"If you can prove to me that Amorata Cay is actually yours," Carla said, "I will buy it from you. I am in no mood to be dispossessed. However, I will not be gulled into giving you gold unless you can produce a document of ownership that will withstand the scrutiny of Governor Morgan's judges. And if it does, we will conclude the sale then and there in Jamaica with the governor witnessing the deed."

"On one condition," Hawke said.

"Conditions? You wish to set conditions?" Carla was beginning to become annoyed. "You admit that I have been cheated by a man in your employ, and now you would make conditions with me?"

"I can prove my claim, madam," he said quietly. "And when you have been satisfied that my claim is just, I would remind you that I can dispose of Amorata Cay in any fashion I see fit. I can auction it, sell it to the highest bidder, even destroy it. So aye! I will make the conditions by which you, and you alone, will be allowed to purchase my legal property for yourself, Captain Raven."

Carla was intrigued by this unexpected situation in which she found herself. She had the feeling that she should probably end this fantasy right now for good and all. She had wished for a little danger, but this man was not of her making. Where had he come from, and how had he invaded her fantasy? Yet despite her instincts she couldn't seem to resist following this story line to its conclusion, if indeed there was a conclusion. "Name your terms," she finally said. "I will meet them."

"You will give yourself to me in whatever manner I desire," Hawke began, "and you will remain mine until this matter is settled. My deed for Amorata Cay will be sent to Governor Morgan in Jamaica for a decision. While his judges debate the matter, you will remain a slave to my lustful nature. When my deed is proven legal and true, I will allow you to purchase the island from me for one thousand pieces of eight. Then I will leave, and you will never see me again. It is a fair and reasonable bargain."

"It is, unless of course you are lying and your deed proves to be false," Carla said. "And if it does, I have allowed you the privilege of my body for naught."

"My deed is not false," he told her with assurance.

"But if the court rules against me, you may have your revenge on me in whatever manner you choose."

Carla smiled a slow and wicked smile. "In that case I would make you my slave," she said, "and use you to satisfy the lust of any man who desired you."

His handsome features darkened briefly with anger at her words, but then he held out his hand to her. "I will agree to your conditions if you will agree to mine," he said.

One hand clutching her towel, Carla took his hand in a firm shake. "Agreed!"

A wolfish smile touched his thin lips. With a sudden quick movement, he snatched the towel from her. "On your knees, bitch!" He snapped the command.

Carla gasped, surprised to have been taken so off-guard. A little cry escaped her lips as his big hand grasped a handful of her short, dark curls, his fingers tightening about the silken hair, slowly forcing her to the required position. Her knees touched the bare mahogany floor.

"Now," he said in a hard voice, "I will go into the bedroom, and you will crawl after me until you are at my feet. I want you flat upon the floor, wench, abasing yourself to me. Remember, you have agreed to do all I command."

"A little fucking, aye, but this?" Carla protested.

"Disobedience will be punished," Hawke promised her. "Do you want Amorata Cay or not, wench? If you want it, you will earn it, not just pay for it. Now, crawl!" And he turned to walk back into the bedroom, going to stand before the open French doors.

Carla was angry, but at the same time, she was intrigued by what was happening. She had never heard of anyone being killed or otherwise harmed while in the Channel. That being the case, she decided to follow this through, because he obviously had something that she wanted: a little excitement in her old program. Flattening herself to the floor, she crept after him.

Upon reaching the French doors, Hawke turned to see if she was obeying him. He had gotten a good look at her naked body when he had taken the towel from her. She wasn't very tall, standing no more than five and a half feet in height. She had full round breasts, a tiny waist he wagered his hands could span, and shapely limbs. He watched through narrowed eyes as she crawled toward him. Her nicely rounded bottom wanted attending to, and that would be his first order of business. He seated himself on an upholstered pale blue settee next to the doors, and when she reached him, he said, "Put yourself over my knees, wench, so I may punish your earlier disobedience. Be quick now! I'll not tolerate any further refusal to obey my directives."

Ohhh, Carla thought excitedly. *He's going to spank me. I've never included spanking in this program, unless it was me doing the deed.* She rose slowly, letting him see her naked form at his leisure. "Do not be cruel, Hawke," she said to him as she draped herself gracefully across his lap.

"You will refer to me properly, wench, as 'my lord,' or 'your grace,'" he told her. The plump white buttocks before him were bold in their stance. Captain Raven needed a good hard spanking. One hand descended to meet her delicate flesh as the other held her firmly by the back of her neck to prevent any serious struggle.

Carla squealed as the big hand delivered its first smack.

It stung. The hand continued without ceasing as her tender bottom grew pink and hot with his blows. Despite the hand on her neck, she found herself able to wiggle a protest at the length of his punishment. Finally he stopped, the big hand rubbing her burning flesh soothingly.

"I expect you will now remember your place, wench," he said to her. "Now, lie still, for I have a little something for you. His hand wedged between her legs. She was wet. "You're a lusty little thing," he approved. A single finger scooped some of her sticky cream, and then he thrust that finger up her arsehole to the knuckle.

"Whoooo!" Carla exclaimed, very surprised.

"I have heard it said that you enjoy a manly cock in your ass," he told her. "Is it true, wench? Answer me honestly or you'll be smacked again."

The long, thick finger moved back and forth within her tight passage. "Aye, I do, now and again," Carla admitted.

"Good!" he told her. He reached into his breeches pocket and withdrew a small ivory dildo the size and shape of his thumb with a round handle. Wetting it with his own spittle, he slowly withdrew his finger and carefully replaced it with the little dildo. "You'll keep that there until I'm ready to give you a taste of cock, wench."

"Oh, yes, your grace," Carla murmured as he tipped her from his lap and onto her feet. She swayed dizzily, a hand reaching out to steady herself.

He stood up, towering over her as he did. "Undress me, wench, and do it properly, or next time, I'll take my riding crop to your bottom," Hawke threatened.

Carla had been so used to dominating the men in her

fantasy world that she had never considered the fun a girl could have being dominated. This man was tough and he was strong. Her fingers unlaced his shirt, and she drew it from him. His chest was broad, smooth, and golden with the sun of the Indies. Unable to help herself, she began to lick his skin, tasting a mixture of sun and salt on him, but when she nipped at his nipples, his hand grasped her short curls, pulling her away.

"I did not give you permission to do that," he said and slapped her lightly. He sat down again on the settee. "Get my boots off, you savage little bitch!" he snarled.

"I thought you liked me lusty," Carla replied, but she knelt quickly and took his boots from him, setting them aside. Then she rolled down his knit stockings and put them with the boots.

He stood, but kept her on her knees. "The breeches and drawers," he commanded.

Oh, this is going to be fun, Carla thought. *How big is his dick?* Given his height and bone structure, it had to be a goodly size. Her fingers undid his belt and set it aside on the settee. His breeches had buttons, quite rare for the time period, but then he was obviously a rich man. She unbuttoned them and pulled them down. Beneath he was wearing a pair of linen drawers, unusual for a pirate. Most wore just breeches. As she drew them down, she turned to face his penis.

Her mouth fell open briefly. Hawke's cock hung at least ten inches in length against a mat of tight golden curls. Behind it she could see the man's heavy, pendulous balls. What would he be like aroused and dangerous? Carla licked her lips, which suddenly felt dry, and a small moan escaped her throat. Leaning forward, she gave him a quick lick from stem to tip.

"Not yet, wench," he said, his tone hard. "You haven't yet earned the privilege. Now, get over to the bed and spread yourself for me."

"You're not ready to fuck," Carla said, standing and looking up at him. "It's an impressive length, but you're soft as pudding."

"It isn't time to fuck," he told her. "Are you always in such a hurry, wench? Now, do as you have been bid, else I take your attitude for more misbehavior."

"Aye, your grace," Carla said, and then she lay down upon her bed again.

"Arms spread wide," he instructed her, and when she had obeyed, he clamped a thick silk cord about each of her wrists, the other end of which was attached to the two carved bedposts at her head.

Carla was startled. She had no such cords. From where had they come? She was not in the habit of entertaining lovers in her home, let alone her private bedchamber. She was even more surprised when Hawke took each of her legs, raising them up high to attach them with the silken cords to the bedposts just above her wrists. "What are you doing?" she demanded of him.

"I want you properly displayed and immobilized for my pleasure," he told her in a matter-of-fact tone.

Carla was astounded. She was trussed up in such a manner as to fully display her mons, her cunt, and her arse. He sat cross-legged on the bed, solemnly observing her formerly hidden treasures.

"Your mons is nicely plump," he noted, "and your

cunt lips well shaped." He reached forward, his fingers fastened about the dildo ring. He moved it back and forth, briefly twisting it in so she might wring a small bit of pleasure from it. When she moaned, he stopped. Then he ran a single finger down the groove where her nether lips met. It was already sticky with moisture. Sliding a finger between the fleshy folds, he found her clitoris and played with it, the ball of his thumb encircling it over and over again. When she gave evidence of her rising excitement, he pushed a finger into her vagina.

"Not enough!" Carla almost sobbed.

A second finger joined the first, and he smiled as she rode his hand in a desperate attempt to gain her pleasure. Laughing at her, he withdrew the fingers. "I can see that you will need something more for the interim, wench. You will not last the next few hours unless you are satisfied, and you are too delectable a treat to gobble quickly." He looked about the bedchamber; seeing a bowl of fresh fruit, he arose and went over to it. He stood before the bowl for a moment or two before choosing. When he sat before her once again, she saw that he had a long, thick green banana in his hand. "I think this will do," he said to her.

Carla's eyes widened. He wouldn't! He couldn't! But he did. Slowly he pushed the lengthy fruit into her heated sheath. She gasped as he began to fuck her with the long, thick banana. But to her shock she couldn't help herself. She met the banana's inward push with an upward thrust of her hips. Her breath was coming in fierce little spurts as her carnal desires overcame her. "More! More!" she begged him, and laughing once again, he thrust the banana faster and faster until she cried out and her creamy juices flowed down the leathery skin of the fruit.

"Did that help, little pirate whore?" he asked her.

"You're horrible!" Carla told him. "And I'm not a whore. I am Captain Raven, queen of the Spanish Main."

"Who just allowed herself to be fucked with a banana by the king of the pirates," he replied. "That's what they used to call me, you know," Hawke told her. He frigged her briefly with the banana, leaving it in her vagina.

"Take it out!" she said.

"Nay, wench, I won't. At least not yet. It will keep you nice and primed for my cock. The banana was just to take the edge off your lust. My cock will give you more pleasure than you've ever attained."

"The king of the pirates," Carla said slowly. "Aye, I have heard talk of you, but not a great deal, and certainly not by name. When you leave these environs, you are quickly forgotten. Did you come back just to sell the island?"

He smiled an amused smile. "Nay, I came back for my treasure, wench. A dukedom requires gold if it is to survive." Then, to her surprise, he withdrew the banana from her vagina. "I have had second thoughts," he said. "If I allow the banana to keep you open, you will not be as sensitive to the thickness of my cock when I fuck you. Now I am of a mind to taste you, wench." He knelt before her, and his tongue snaked forward as his two thumbs peeled her nether lips apart.

Carla's head spun as he tongued her sensitive flesh. She had never known a lover like this man. He was mysterious, and he was frightening, yet she couldn't wait to have his big cock buried deep inside her. She didn't think she had the imagination to have brought such a man into her fantasy, but she wasn't unhappy to have him here. "Oh, yes, your grace," she moaned. "I'll do whatever you desire," Carla promised. She was close now to perfection, and then he suddenly stopped.

"I find that I am hungry," he remarked. Reaching up, he began to free her from the restraints. "Nestor should be long finished with your maidservant. Call her, and send to your cook for a hearty meal."

"Finish me!" Carla begged him. "I am desperate with my longing for you!"

"And I am desperate for some food, wench. More so than my need to fill your eager cunt with my cock," Hawke said.

"You are a bastard!" she practically screamed. He had aroused a fierce sexual need in her, and now was more interested in a good beefsteak than satisfying her?

His hand flashed out, grabbing her short dark curls again. His mouth pressed cruelly against her in a punishing kiss. "You will be fucked, wench, but in my good time, not yours. Have I not satisfied you already twice?"

"Nay! Nay! It was not enough!" Carla protested.

"Well, it will have to be for now, wench," he told her. "Now see to my food!"

Ping! Ping! Ping! The Channel is now closed, the syrupy voice cooed.

"Shite! Shite! Shite!" Carla almost shrieked as she found herself once more in her own bed, the television screen filled with snow. She was so hot to fuck right now, she was close to screaming. She got up and went to her dresser, then dug down in the bottom drawer beneath the underwear she rarely wore and pulled out her old vibrator. Its batteries were dead, and though she searched throughout the entire house, there wasn't a D cell to be found. Flinging herself back on the bed, Carla cried with her frustration, but there was nothing for it. Aching with her need, she curled up and finally found a restless sleep.

"You look like hell," her friend Tiffany Pietro d'Angelo said the next afternoon when she stopped over to see if Carla needed anything from the grocery store. "What's happened?" She plunked herself in the den's oversized chair. "Talk to me, Carla!"

"It's my Channel fantasy . . . ," Carla began.

"Yeah?" Tiffany looked curious. She knew about Carla's pirate fantasy.

"All I ever wanted to do was play pirate queen," Carla started. "I grew up watching those old Errol Flynn pirate movies on television. For years I've been a female version of those parts that he played while in the Channel. Gallant. Honorable. A great lover. Always eluding the authorities, yet always in the right. A couple of months ago I began to get bored with the whole scenario, but there really was no other fantasy with which I wanted to replace it. So I added something to my fantasy. A small uninhabited secluded island I named Amorata Cay.

"I even created one of those beautiful Caribbean dwellings with open porches going around all four sides of the house. I have a small staff of bondmen and -women as servants. I didn't want slaves. And instead of sailing the Spanish Main taking merchant ships, I've been going to my house on my island just to relax. But then last night *he* showed up claiming that Amorata Cay was *his*, not mine."

"Who is he?" Tiffany was intrigued.

"His name is Julian Hawke, and he used to be called *the king of the pirates*. A couple of years ago, according to him, he inherited a dukedom back in England, so he cleaned up his act. He went home, took a wife, and sired an heir, and his duchess is expecting a second child. He came back to the Caribbean to sell Amorata Cay. Being a duke, he says, is expensive. He says he has a document to prove his claim," Carla said.

"Just how did you think up this island?" Tiffany wanted to know.

"I won it in a card game in Jamaica," Carla said. "The guy who said it was his had lost everything that night. He wagered the island in a last bet. Hawke claims the guy was his caretaker. He's willing to take his documents to Governor Morgan to have them authenticated. Then he's going to sell Amorata Cay to the highest bidder."

"So buy it," Tiffany said in a practical tone. "What's the big deal? It's your fantasy. He wants to sell. You want to buy. End of story."

"Tiffy, I did not imagine this guy in my fantasy. He is definitely not of my creation, so how the hell is he there? Did anything like this ever happen to you?"

Her companion shook her head in the negative. Then she said, "Maybe altering your fantasy after so many years screwed with something. Are you certain you didn't think up this guy, Carla? And even if you didn't, you can get rid of him by purchasing the island from him. Isn't that easy enough?"

"He insists his papers be proven real," Carla said. "And when they are, he did say I could buy the island from him, but only under one condition. I have to do everything and anything that he wants until the deal is concluded."

Tiffany's eyes lit up. "Ohh, sounds kinky and fun," she opined.

"You have no idea," Carla said. "You cannot begin to imagine."

"Tell me everything," Tiffany replied, leaning forward, an avid expression on her pretty face. "If it's as good as some of the adventures you've shared with me before, then it has to be terrific. Don't leave out a single detail, girl-friend."

"Well," Carla began, "you know how my pirate queen persona has always been the dominant? Not this time, sweetie. He is the master, and he is obviously expert at it." Then she went on to explain in detail to her friend what had happened the previous night while she was in the Channel.

Tiffany's blue eyes grew wide with surprise and then glazed with shock. "A banana?" she gasped. "He screwed you with a banana? Omigod! Omigod! Omigod! What did it feel like? Did you come?"

"It felt smooth, a bit leathery, and while firm, not the hard sensation of a stiff cock," Carla answered her. "And yeah, I came."

"What did it feel like when he did you?" Tiffany inquired.

"He hasn't yet," Carla said, "but frankly, I can't wait

till he does. He is hung like a bull, Tiffy. His dick has got to be between ten and eleven inches in length. He's got self-control down to a science. He never lost it. He remained long and soft while he was teasing me. He's thick to begin with, so I can only imagine what he's going to be like fully aroused." She sighed. "I don't know if I can take much more of his torture."

Tiffany sighed too. "He sounds yummy," she said. "I love a dominant. All my sultans and caliphs are very dominant." Then she sat up straight. "You're going back tonight, aren't you? You can't not go back, Carla."

"Of course I'm going back," Carla said. "I want him out of my fantasy, and if that means I have to play his game until he lets me purchase Amorata Cay, then so be it."

"Do you think he'll fuck you tonight?" Tiffany wondered.

"He'd better! I woke up just burning for it. My vibrator was dead in the water, so get me some D cells at the store," Carla replied.

Tiffany giggled. "I'm sorry," she said. "But it really is funny. The Channel closes for the night. You're hotter than a firecracker, and your vibrator won't work. Could it have gotten any worse?" She giggled again, throwing Carla an apologetic look.

"Yeah, in retrospect it was funny," Carla said, "but the reality at the time was very unpleasant, Tiffy, so get me those D cells so I can at least remedy any lack on the part of the king of the pirates," she said and chuckled. "I still would like to know how the hell this guy turned up in my fantasy. I swear I never imagined anyone like him."

Tiffany stood up. "I'll get your batteries," she said.

"Tiffy, not a word to anyone about this," she warned her friend.

"Hey, the only time they've heard of your pirate fantasy was from you," Tiffany responded. "I only talk about my fantasies to you." Then, with a wave of her hand, she was gone off to the market. When she returned an hour later, she left the bag with the batteries on the kitchen counter for her friend, as she saw Carla was sleeping soundly on the couch in the den, which was off the kitchen.

It was the house phone that woke Carla. Dragging herself up from sleep, she fumbled for the land line they kept connected for emergencies. " 'Lo?"

"Hey, babe, greetings from Paris," she heard Rick's voice say.

Carla was immediately awake. "It's not Monday. Are you all right?"

"Hey, can't a man call his wife from Paris?" Rick teased. "I miss you."

"I wasn't expecting you to call," Carla responded.

"You got a hot date?"

"I was taking an afternoon nap," she admitted, glancing at the wall clock and seeing it was close to eight p.m.

"No ER today?"

"I decided to take a couple of days off," Carla told her husband. "No ER. No husband. Just a nice empty, quiet house, some wine, and all the Mallomars I can eat."

"So that's why you didn't want company?" he replied.

"That's why," Carla said. "I've got so many days racked up now, they've been asking me to jettison some of them. This trip of yours came at the perfect time. So how's Paris, and how was Vienna? Did Ryan complete the transaction?"

"Paris is French, the food too rich, and the wines good. Vienna was Viennese, the food too rich, and the wines good. Ryan got his little company bought. Everyone was happy. Now he's talking with a guy here who makes reproductions of old porcelain knobs and handles. We're off to London in two more days."

"You're sure getting the grand tour," she told him. "I think I'm a little envious."

"Don't be. It's all very dull business, but I will say Ryan travels first-class, and he doesn't waste any time. Hates being away from Ashley and the kids, especially that little girl of theirs. Why is it that men are such mushes over daughters?"

"Don't know," Carla answered. Then she said, "Hey, it's way after midnight in Paris. Don't you have to get up and do business tomorrow?"

"I couldn't sleep," Rick said. "I needed to hear your voice, babe."

"Awww," Carla said as she felt her heart expand. "Well, you've heard it. Now get into bed, and go to sleep, sweetie. You'll be home in a few days, and I'll take a day just for you then, okay?"

"Okay," he agreed, and she could hear the happiness in his voice. " 'Night, babe!" He made a couple of kissing noises.

" 'Night, sweetie," Carla replied, and kissed back.

Then the line went dead, as the tall clock in the front hall struck eight p.m. Carla considered, and then she decided that she was hungry. She was going to eat and take a shower before she went upstairs to enter the Channel. Given her adventure last night, who knew what would happen tonight?

She fixed herself a nice rare burger, topping it with cheese, tomato, and Indian relish. She sat down in the den with it, a small plate of endive, and a glass of red wine. Turning on *Headline News,* she caught up on the day's events. An improving economy with the stock market up just enough, and decent weather nationwide. Finished with her meal and the news, Carla washed the frying pan, stored it away, and put her glass and dishes in the dishwasher. After checking to be sure everything was locked and secure, she went upstairs to shower.

The warm water sluicing over her body felt good. She was so far from being a kid that it had begun to hurt. And even the perfect form she took in the Channel wasn't immune afterward to aches and pains in her real world. She lathered shampoo into her short dark curls. She was lucky. Neither her mother nor her grandmother had ever gone gray or white. Both had always had hair as black as the day they were born, and she seemed to have those same genes. There wasn't even a hint of a light hair on her head.

Refreshed from both her meal and her shower, Carla toweled off before getting into her unmade bed. *Well,* she thought, *let's see if we pick up where we left off.* Her thumb pressed down hard on the remote's A button, and she immediately found herself back where she had been when the Channel had closed the previous night. Arms and legs bound again to the posts of her bed, she focused on a naked Hawke, who was just finishing his meal at the little round mahogany table across the bedroom.

He was certainly a good-looking specimen of masculinity. Broad shoulders and chest. Sturdy arms and legs. Big feet and hands. Flat belly. That lovely long dick with its pendulous companions. Carla wondered what delicious torture he had in mind for her tonight. She hadn't decided yet if she should be thrilled or frightened of his presence. After all, he was not of her creation, so what exactly was he? *I can always say 'Fantasy end,'* she told herself. *If it gets too rough for me, I can stop it. That's the rule in the Channel.*

Then she felt his icy blue eyes on her.

"You have stopped complaining, wench," he said, standing up and coming over to sit on the bed. Reaching out, he pinched one of her nipples hard. "My vessel is now in Half-Moon Cove. I sent Nestor out to bring back a lovely selection of toys for us to play with, my pretty. I think you will like them." He twisted the little dildo in her asshole. "I think we shall replace this with something a bit sturdier," Hawke told her.

"How about that fine cock of yours?" Carla suggested to him.

"Nay, wench, we are not quite ready for that yet, but I am pleased to see how eager you are for me." He withdrew another dildo from the velvet-lined basket that had been placed on the nightstand. It was ivory, as was the smaller dildo, but ridged and at least four inches in length. "This one, I think." Then he dipped the instrument into a bowl of scented oil, coating it lavishly as he used his other hand to withdraw the little ivory thumb.

"Ohh." Carla's dark eyes widened. "That looks delicious, your grace."

"You are too eager for it," he said and chuckled. "First that tempting bottom of yours needs a bit of priming, for I see its color has faded. Just a bit though, wench." He stood up, and she saw a thick hazel switch in his hand. He began to whip her vigorously with it, the blows regular and spaced apart just enough so that her flesh began to quickly tingle.

"Oh! Oh! Oh!" Carla shrieked as the stinging and burning spread across her skin.

"Tell me you want to be punished," he demanded. "Tell me that you are a very naughty girl and need the chastisement that I can give you."

"Ohh, I am very naughty, your grace, and I thank you for teaching me how to behave with my betters," Carla said, knowing it was exactly what he wanted to hear from her. The look of satisfaction in his cold eyes told her she would now be rewarded.

Hawke smiled, dropped the switch, and, taking the second dildo from the bowl of oil, slowly inserted it where the first had been. He twisted it several times, and she gasped with surprise at the sensation. "There, wench. Does that please you?"

"If it pleases you, your grace, aye!" she told him.

"It does please me," he responded. "In fact, you please me far more than my duchess. She does not like to be whipped, and she has not taken to the cock well at all, I fear. I got her *enceinte* on our wedding night. After that, she avoided her duty to me unless I forced the issue. When she proved fertile so quickly, I let her be until two months after my heir was born. Then I locked her up with me for three days, pleasuring myself mightily while she wept and prayed. But I got her with child again. A man needs an heir and a spare at the least.

"Her reluctance to keep me content is why I decided to come back to the Caribbean to sell Amorata Cay. I will find myself a mistress when I return home. I don't suppose you would be interested in filling that position, wench? We haven't fucked yet, but you have pleased me well so far. I suspect you will be a most glorious fuck, for you are quite a delicious little whore."

"I have told you once, *your grace*, that I am no whore. Because a woman enjoys coupling and playing with a man doesn't mean she is a whore," Carla said irritably.

Ignoring her, he leaned over to take something else from his basket of toys. Then he sat down next to her again. "Your arse is quite pink again," Hawke remarked. "I believe it is now time to attend to your cunt once more."

Carla could now see the object he had drawn from the basket. It was a long feather with a sharply pointed tip. He ran it slowly down her slit, and she shivered.

"Oh, yes, wench, you will enjoy this, I promise," he said as he skillfully plied the feather across her cunt lips, as well as back and forth along the shadowed slit. She could feel moisture beginning to rise. Then, with the thumb and forefinger of his free hand, he spread her open and began to tickle her clit, slowly at first, and then with quicker strokes and flicks of the feather.

Carla's lust exploded. Despite her trussed-up position, she attempted to squirm away from the feather that was so skillfully torturing her. Her juices were flowing, and she screamed with her desire. Carefully he inserted the feather into her vagina, teasing the sensitive walls of flesh. "I want to be fucked!" Carla moaned desperately. "I want to be fucked, you bastard! Aren't you man enough to do it to me? Can you only tantalize me, your grace? I want to be fucked, damn it!"

He withdrew the feather. "Woman!" he declared in bored tones. "Either you can't bear being fucked or all you want is to be fucked. There is more to passion. You will be fucked, wench. You will be fucked until you are breathless and unconscious, but I am not yet of a mind to give you that. I am enjoying torturing you with desire." But then he thrust three fingers into her vagina, jamming them back and forth several strokes until she came with a shriek. "There! Are you satisfied for now, wench?"

"Unbind me," she begged him. "I am beginning to lose feeling in my extremities." And she was.

"Of course," he said in reasonable tones. "It's time for you to tease me a bit." He reached up and undid the bonds holding her legs and arms, massaging each limb for a few moments so that the feeling came back into them.

Carla lay flat on the bed, breathing deeply. "Can I do whatever I want?" she asked him.

"You can't bind me," he said.

"Just your arms," she begged him. "I want free reign over your body."

"You want to slit my throat, wench, and I am fully aware of it. I will let you have your way as long as it pleasures me." He stretched out next to her.

Carla knew she had to be satisfied with that. "No touching me unless you simply can't bear it," she warned him. Then, getting onto her haunches, she looked him over carefully. He was definitely lickable, and so she decided that she would lick him. First she bent to kiss him, her tongue shooting into his mouth to find his tongue. The two digits intertwined and stroked at each other for several long minutes. Then Carla broke the embrace, her tongue licking the side of his face.

The tongue moved slowly, at a leisurely pace, to his throat, his neck, his shoulders. It lapped across the broad chest, tasting him, savoring the scent of salt and sun, sensing the muscles beneath his flesh. She moved to his belly. It was hard and smooth. Her tongue dipped into his navel and out again.

"You are not permitted my cock yet," he warned her.

"Very well, your grace," Carla agreed. But then she moved across the bed so she might see what was in his basket. With a smile she drew out a small leather tawse. "Get on your hands and knees," she commanded him, and was delighted when he obeyed. Admiring his round, firm, and tight butt, she smacked him with the tawse. To her surprise he didn't protest, so she began to lay several hard blows on him. His buttocks quickly bloomed crimson, and his cock, which had hung beneath him, now stiffened, shooting straight forward. Carla hit him harder. "You are a very bad boy," she told him.

"More than you can imagine," Hawke replied, and then he sprang off the bed. Yanking the tawse from her hand, he pulled her from her place. "On your knees, wench! You know what to do, and I expect you to do it well or you'll suffer the consequences."

Kneeling before him, Carla began to lick the thick

length, but she was excited by what she had done and couldn't resist taking him almost immediately into her mouth. She could barely contain him, but she began to suck him, harder and harder, drawing him deeper into her mouth until his cock tip was touching the back of her throat, causing her to gag. She felt his hand on her head, kneading it, and heard his harsh breath.

"Ah, wench," he groaned, "your skills are to be commended. Suck harder!"

He was going to come in her mouth, Carla knew, and she wanted him in her cunt. How long would it take him to renew his vigor? Well, it was her fantasy, wasn't it? She wasn't sure right now, but if she still had some kind of control, he would come and still be hard. That was just what she wanted. *Make it so,* she prayed silently.

And then he came, spurting his creamy, salty juices down her throat so hard and fast, she could barely swallow quickly enough. He groaned loudly with the act. "By God, wench, I have never had better," he told her, "but alas, I am not yet satisfied." He yanked her up. "On your back," he said, pulling her onto the edge of the mattress, pushing her legs up to her shoulders. Looming over her, he moved closer, thrusting into her cunt with a sigh and another groan of distinct pleasure.

Then he began to piston her hard and deep with an energy that both surprised and astounded her. Carla's head spun with delight. This was what she had been waiting for, and she was not disappointed. She couldn't ever remember entertaining a cock of such length and girth. His performance was incredible, and while at first it had felt as if he was splitting her in two, the sensation quickly gave way to a feeling of unbelievable rising pleasure. Unable to contain herself, she screamed with delight, and before she could stop herself, she climaxed, shuddering over and over again until she finally ceased quivering.

He withdrew his sated cock, slowly nodding with open satisfaction. "Wench, you know well how to please a man. I am content for now."

"I'm not," Carla finally managed to say. "Is that all you are good for, your grace? One small fuck? I will not believe that!"

"You are too bold," he said, his handsome face darkening. "I will fuck you again when it pleases me, and not a moment before."

She smiled sweetly at him. "Well," she said, "you are hardly a youth. I suppose I was fortunate to gain one good poke from you. I had, I will admit, hoped for better."

"Do you think me incapable?" he demanded.

"You said you would do me when it pleased you," Carla answered him. "That certainly means you are not capable of fucking me again. How typical and how selfish. You have satisfied yourself but care not if I have been satisfied."

"You screamed with your pleasure, wench," he said.

"I did. But do you mean to ration my pleasure? If that is so, then just let me pay you for the island now, and you can be gone back to England."

"I haven't sent the documents to Governor Morgan yet," he said. "Are you telling me that you believe my claim is true?"

"Whether 'tis true or not, you would in a pirate's fashion have gold from me. Take it then, and leave me to find a lover who can satisfy me fully," Carla told him. She suddenly felt better. She had been well fucked, and felt she was about to regain control of this unexpected fantasy she was enjoying. Then, casting a scornful glance at his groin, she saw that his cock was more than ready to do battle with her cunt once more. "*Ohhh,*" she murmured, and a wicked smile touched her lips as she scrambled from her precarious perch on the edge of the bed back into its middle.

He said nothing, instead climbing atop her to push slowly into her vagina again. "Is that better now, wench?" he growled at her.

Carla wrapped her legs about him. "Ohh, yes, your grace," she purred into his ear.

The day beyond the bedroom's French doors began to fade into late afternoon, but neither Hawke nor Carla tired of their sexual play. But then she fell asleep, and when she opened her eyes again, she was in her own bed—the bed she shared with her husband. A contented smile touched her face, and then Carla fell back to sleep. When she awoke again, it was raining outside. *What a night,* she thought. She might not have imagined someone like Hawke, but she had to admit she was not dissatisfied with him. He was every woman's dream. Tireless and skillful.

The rain stopped by eleven, and Tiffany called just after noon. "Did you survive last night?" she asked, giggling.

"Barely," Carla answered. "He whipped me. I whipped him. I sucked. He fucked. And oh, let me tell you about the pointed feather."

"A feather?" Tiffany almost whispered. "Pointed?"

"Yep, and a most devastating weapon, I might add," Carla said as she explained how he had used the wicked tickler on her clitoris.

"God, he sounds like a perfect brute," Tiffany said. "I am sooo jealous."

Carla laughed. "Create a brute of your own. Your sultans don't all have to be civilized and gallant. Certainly the real ones weren't."

"I couldn't," Tiffany replied.

"Why ever not?" Carla wanted to know.

Tiffany hesitated.

"Tiffy! You have a secret," Carla accused. "Tell me! Don't I tell you everything? Come on now. Spill it!"

"The men I fuck with all look like Joe," Tiffany finally said. "Oh, they have better bodies than my husband, but they all have the same face. If I'm going to screw them without guilt, they have to look like Joe."

"Oh. My. God!" Carla said. Then she laughed. "If I put Rick's face on any of my playmates, I couldn't do half the naughty stuff I do. And I wouldn't want to, Tiffy. Rick is a sweet and tender lover. He always was. But adventurous and wicked isn't in his character. If I put Rick's face on a lover who whipped me and ass-fucked me, I wouldn't believe it at all. I'd get a fit of the giggles."

"I love my romance novels, especially the harem ones, as you well know," Tiffany admitted, "but I have never been able to see myself making love to anyone else but Joe. I can't help it. I'd feel guilty. Don't you ever feel guilty?"

"No," Carla said. "The Channel is fantasy, nothing more. You don't think married guys dream about screwing other women? I'll bet Joe does now and again."

"I can't do it," Tiffany said. "Here I am, a smart woman who raised her twins, got her training, and now works in a law office. But I can't imagine loving anyone but Joe."

"The Channel isn't about loving anyone," Carla said. "It's just fantasy. I would never consider being unfaithful to Rick in real life, but the Channel isn't real."

Tiffany sighed. "I guess I'm just different from the rest of you," she said. "I can't help the way I feel."

"You're sweet," Carla told her friend. "Rick called from Paris last night."

"He's in Paris? Wow! Maybe Joe should have taken Ryan as a client and left Ashley to Rick," Tiffany teased.

"Rick's in Paris, not me," Carla said drily. "And if it were Joe, you wouldn't be in Paris any more than I am."

"Hey, I'm the firm's legal aide," she said.

"I would still wager no Paris," Carla said and chuckled. "Are we going to the club this weekend for dinner?" she asked. "I told Rick I was going."

"How about Sunday?" Tiffany responded. "With Rick away you don't want to have to cook for just one."

"You could invite me for dinner," Carla teased.

"I don't want to have to cook either," Tiffany said with a laugh.

"What time? Not too early. I'll need to recover from Hawke's playfulness," Carla said with a grin. "Hey, it's Saturday night, after all."

"You are going to be exhausted by the time Rick gets home," Tiffany said. "He's going to think you're coming down with something."

Carla chuckled, and then she grew serious. "I'm still

concerned about how this guy got into my fantasy. I did not think him, or anyone like him, up, Tiffy."

"But you were thinking that you wanted more excitement in your fantasy," Tiffany reminded her friend again. "Maybe that translated into your pirate king."

"I didn't think such a thing could happen," Carla said. "With events maybe, but with people? I've always micromanaged my fantasy carefully. Pirates weren't the nicest people in reality, as I've told you. I absolutely did not think up this Hawke character. So where did he come from, Tiffy?"

"You got me, Carla," Tiffany admitted. "Maybe you should call the Channel's customer hotline and ask."

"Yeah," Carla replied slowly. "Maybe I should." She paused and added, "Just not yet. Since I didn't program this, I'm curious as to how it's going to play out."

"You're braver than I am. I think when that pirate walked in, you should have said 'Fantasy end.' If you aren't in control like you're suppose to be, then something is wrong, Carla."

"I'll call customer service after the weekend," Carla promised. "It's Saturday afternoon, and no one will be there anyway."

"They have service twenty-four-seven," Tiffany said.

"But what if they had to take me off-line until whatever is wrong could be fixed?" Carla murmured. "If I thought there was anything seriously wrong, I just wouldn't access it, Tiffy. Who knows? Maybe my subconscious wanted an adventure with a bad boy, and the king of the pirates is certainly a very bad boy. Besides, I'm back in charge now, and I have some serious payback to deliver to his grace."

Tiffany shook her head. "As I said, you're braver than me. Nora's home, by the way. Why don't you ask her if something could go wrong? She works for the Channel Corporation, and she's pretty high up in the organization now."

"She's the CEO of their development division," Carla said proudly. "Who would have thought a woman who had the mind-set of a fifties housewife just seven years ago could have wised up and come so far? Yeah, I'll go over and ask her if she's ever heard of something like this happening."

"Good," Tiffany replied. "I'll feel better about it then. You going to the Blairs' barbecue today?"

"Yeah," Carla answered. "I can't get over how love found Kathy, and it's all so perfect for them. See you there?"

Tiffany nodded. "Ride with us," she suggested.

"Nah," Carla responded. "I might want to leave before you do."

Tiffany shook her head. "You mean you want to get back to Amorata Cay and your big bad boy."

"Yep," Carla agreed cheerfully, "but I promise to speak to Nora before I do."

When Tiffany hung up, Carla did just that, crossing the lawn in midafternoon to Nora Buckley's big white Colonial. Despite her rise in the corporate world, Nora kept the house she had lived in for so many years with her unfaithful deceased husband and their two children.

She called it her refuge.

"Hey," she said as Carla came in the kitchen door and walked into her den. Nora was an elegant, attractive woman with red-blond hair and gray-green eyes.

"Hey, yourself," Carla said, plopping down on the den couch. "I got a question for you. It's about the Channel."

"Shoot!" Nora replied.

"Did you ever hear of someone popping into a fantasy who wasn't created by the customer?" Carla asked.

"No," Nora said from her recliner. She sat it up and put her wineglass down. "Why? What's happened?"

"Well," Carla began, and then she went on to explain.

Nora Buckley listened carefully; then she said, "You're certain you didn't create him, Carla? Maybe once you thought of someone like this."

Carla shook her head in the negative. "I'll admit I've been bored lately being the pirate queen. That's why I added Amorata Cay and my house. Actually, I go there to relax when I'm stressed out from the ER at the hospital."

"And this Hawke, who calls himself the king of the pirates, just walked in on you?" Nora was thoughtful. "I'll have to check this out, Carla. I have never before heard of something like this, but you never know, and the Channel isn't my division. I will, however, call Mr. Nicholas about it."

"Thanks. While I'm curious about how this happened, it's Tiffy who worried," Carla said. "The guy is a sexual master, so for now I'm just enjoying myself."

"As long as you don't feel you're in danger," Nora replied.

"Hey, I'm the queen of the pirates," Carla said and chuckled. "I fear no man!"

Nora laughed, but she was considering the possibility that whoever this Hawke who called himself the king of the pirates was, he was no man. When Carla left, Nora picked up her cell and punched 1.

Mr. Nicholas immediately answered. "Yes, Nora?"

"I apologize for interrupting your weekend, sir, but we may have a problem relating to the Channel." Then she went on to recount her conversation with Carla.

"I will speak with Julian immediately," Mr. Nicholas said. "I feared he was too young to be put in charge of the Channel. I had been informed that he allows some of his friends to play in fantasies to which they have not been invited, but he assured me it wasn't so. Obviously he lied. It isn't a wise thing to lie to *me*."

"No, sir," Nora responded.

"Thank you, my dear, for informing me of this breach. Please tell Mrs. Johnson that she is perfectly safe."

"Well, frankly, sir, I got the idea that while she was startled by his appearance, she was enjoying herself," Nora told her employer.

"Then we shall allow her one more night. I am told Julian is quite adept at naughtiness, which is why I gave him the Channel to oversee. Obviously he could not resist partaking of the wickedness," Mr. Nicholas replied. "Thank you, Nora." And then the head of the Channel Corporation hung up.

At the Blairs' barbecue that evening, Nora spoke with Carla. "Just a slight glitch in the system, Mr. Nicholas told me," she said. "He assures me you are safe. They should have it fixed in another day or two. If you're worried, just don't access it for a few days. Or program another fantasy," Nora suggested.

"Oh." Carla sounded mildly disappointed. "Well, if it's

going to be fixed, then I suppose one more night with the king of the pirates won't hurt." She left the Blairs' house shortly after eight. She was feeling very pleased to learn the pirate king's tenure on Amorata Cay was about to end. It gave her a sense of power over him, and in the Channel, she had always been the dominant lover. While she had to admit to enjoying having the tables turned on her, she had had enough now. Well, almost enough, Carla thought and chuckled to herself as she pulled into her driveway. She wanted her island back.

The message light on the phone was blinking. She picked up the receiver and pressed the PLAY button to hear Rick's voice. "Cheerio from London, babe!" Carla smiled. "Call me back if you get in soon. It's just after two a.m. here. Can't sleep again." Carla erased the message and hit REDIAL.

"The Dorchester," a woman with a plummy British accent answered. "How may I help you?"

"Richard Johnson's room, please," Carla said.

"Babe?" Rick's voice answered. Despite his claim he sounded sleepy.

"Just back from the Blairs' barbecue," Carla said. "Everyone is fine. The baby is adorable, and Tim is a fool over her. Everything okay?"

"Yeah," he answered. "We're flying back Monday morning. We'll be into Kennedy by midday. Tomorrow Ryan is taking me sightseeing."

"Then you'll need some rest, sweetie," Carla told him. "Two calls in just a few days. I think you miss me, Mr. Johnson," she teased.

"I do!" he said with such sincerity that she was touched.

She had always taken Rick's love for granted because she loved him back. Now, hearing the deep emotion in his voice, Carla realized that she loved him more now than when they had married all those years ago. And she missed him too. "Want me to sing you a lullaby?" she said. "Or can you go to sleep now like a big boy?"

"I'll sleep now," he said, and she heard the smile in his voice.

"Travel safe, sweetie," Carla said. *Kiss. Kiss.*

"I will. See you Monday," he replied. *Kiss. Kiss. Kiss.* And the line went dead.

Somehow she didn't feel like accessing the Channel now. Carla went straight to bed. On Sunday she had dinner at the Egret Pointe Country Club with Tiffany and Joe.

Tiffany got her aside in the powder room just before they were leaving. "So? Last night? Did it rock your world?"

"Rick called while I was out and wanted me to call him back. I just didn't feel like dealing with the king of the pirates after that. You know, Tiffy, I'll go back tonight, but then I think I'll delete that pirate fantasy. I'm going to get myself a chalet up in the Austrian alps, where I can go and relax when I need a break from the ER."

"And . . . ," Tiffany queried, grinning.

"Welllll, maybe a ski instructor now and again, but *only* now and again," Carla said with an answering grin.

Could she really delete the pirate fantasy she had enjoyed for so long? Yeah, Carla thought as she showered before getting into bed, she could. Like anything too delicious, a surfeit of it could become dull and/or sickening. One more wild ride with Lord Julian Hawke, the king of the pirates, and she was through. Climbing into bed, she picked up the Channel remote and pressed the A button to find herself alone in her bed.

Beyond the French doors, the sea sparkled. There was a ship just sailing into Half-Moon Cove. It wasn't hers, but it did fly the Jolly Roger from its topmast. Her bedroom door opened and Lord Hawke strode in and out onto the porch without a word. "Is it your ship?" Carla asked.

"Aye, just back from Jamaica. They'll be carrying a letter from Governor Morgan confirming my claim to Amorata Cay."

Carla sat up. She didn't bother to hold the sheet to her bared bosom. "You're very certain," she said. "But if your claim is just, I will have one thousand pieces of eight counted out from my treasure room for you. You will then sign the island over to me, your grace, and leave. I shall have to go a-pirating now to make up my loss."

Turning, he stared fixedly at her full, generous breasts. "I want to see you being fucked by another man," he said bluntly. "I want to hear you scream with passion, my pirate queen. My first mate, Nestor, wants a go at you."

"He's worn my poor servant Violetta out with his enthusiasm," Carla noted to Lord Hawke.

"She hasn't satisfied him in the weeks we've been here," the king of the pirates said. "He needs to lodge that cock of his into a woman filled with fire as you are."

"And if I say nay?" Carla asked him.

"If I say aye, there is no nay, my pretty little bitch, and I say aye!" he told her. "That defiance of yours has earned you another spanking, wench!"

"Will you fuck me before you depart with my gold?" Carla asked him boldly.

A slow smile lit the face of the self-proclaimed king of the pirates. "It will be my last act before I leave you to sail away to England."

"Then how can I refuse you, your grace?" Carla murmured seductively.

"You can't!" he replied with devastating surety. "Nestor! Come in. The lady is ready to receive your attentions."

Nestor sauntered into the bedchamber.

"Can we all be naked?" Carla asked.

"A grand idea!" Lord Hawke replied enthusiastically. He nodded to his first mate, and the two men quickly stripped their garments off.

Carla smiled as she eyed them both. The king of the pirates stood at least six inches over his mate. He was golden all over from his wavy hair to the curly bush between his legs. Nestor was perhaps an inch or two over six feet. He was a stocky man with dark brown hair pulled back and tied. The bush beneath his flat belly was thick, and the cock nestled there was more than impressive, perhaps a tiny bit longer than his master's, but Carla could see it would not be as thick. She held out her hands to the two men. "Do you mean to stand there preening, and leave me alone with my need for you both? Come, sirs! Join me at once."

They complied immediately.

"Take the lead, Nestor. I want to watch for now," the king of the pirates said.

Nestor smiled. "Those are a fine pair of tits you have there, lass," he told her.

Her back supported by several pillows, Carla sat straight. She slipped her hands beneath her breasts and held them up and out to him in invitation. "Help yourself."

He chortled, pulling the sheet away so her entire body was available to him, then pushed her legs apart and knelt between her thighs. Leaning forward, he availed himself of her breasts, kissing the nipples, licking them, then sucking the tender flesh hard so that the tips grew hard and pointed. He bit down sharply on one nipple.

Carla squealed and smacked his head.

Nestor laughed heartily. "By God," he exclaimed approvingly, "you're a feisty one, lass. I like a woman with a lot of pepper and spice. Your Violetta was too tame for me, but his lordship swears you'll give me a good ride." Then suddenly he yanked her legs over his shoulders, burying his face between her thighs with a growl. "Lock your ankles about my neck, lass. I'll need my hands to play. I've never seen a mons plucked smooth as silk. 'Tis a pretty sight, I must admit." When she had complied with his command, he peeled her nether lips apart, his tongue beginning to forage amid the sensitive flesh of her cunt, licking its walls first, and then finding her clit with the very tip.

Lord Julian Hawke, the king of the pirates, watched as his first mate satisfied his lusts on the woman known as the queen of the pirates. He had thought to be dispassionate about it, for other than his wife, he had always shared his women. But watching Nestor bring beautiful Captain Raven pleasure began to irritate him. Still, having promised the man full access, he could hardly throw him out now. But soon.

Carla pulled the first mate to her, and kissed him heart-ily. She could taste herself on his lips and his tongue. "Fuck me!" she whispered into his ear, and then she nipped the lobe of it for emphasis.

"Aye!" Nestor said and drove his long cock into Carla. He brought her to a satisfying climax after some minutes.

"You didn't come," she complained to him.

"I will," he told her, withdrawing. "Roll over, lass, and raise your arse up so I can get at it. I hear you like a good arse-fuck."

Damn, how exciting this is, Carla thought as she turned herself over and elevated her butt. *"Do it!"* she hissed at him. His fingers dug into the flesh of her plump hips. She felt the tip of his long, slender cock nosing be-tween the cheeks of her ass. *"Do it! I'm dying for it! Do it now!"* she half moaned. "Ahhhhh! Aye! That's it, First Mate!"

Her face was a mask of perfect lust. Watching her, the pirate king felt himself overwhelmed with jealousy. He had expected her to demur at his suggestion that another man fuck her while he watched. Instead she had wel-comed it, and even now he could see that her need for more and more cock was being fulfilled, and not by him. When Nestor finished he was going to be dismissed, and the bold pirate queen's arse would burn with his punish-ment. He watched through half-closed eyes as she came again with a cry. He could see that Nestor was emptying his load into her arse, and when they had both collapsed with satisfaction, he growled, "Well, now, Nestor, are you satisfied?"

Nestor rolled over so he might look up at his captain.

"Aye. Sir, you did not lie. I am drained of all pent-up passion."

"Then get out," the king of the pirates said. "I'll want her to myself for a time."

Nestor scrambled from the bed, then gathered his garments and hurried from the room with a contented smile on his face.

When he had gone, Lord Hawke turned on Carla. "Bitch! You enjoyed every minute of his attentions, damn you."

"Wasn't I suppose to?" Carla said wickedly.

He jumped from the bed, dragging her with him into her bathing chamber. The tub was filled and rose petals floated on the surface of the water. "Wash yourself!" he ordered her. "I want his stink off of you before I fuck you, damn it!" He lifted her and dumped her in the water, which to her surprise was comfortably warm.

Carla washed herself slowly and thoroughly as he watched with burning eyes. She knew every movement she made was a torture for him. It pleased her that it was. She wasn't above enjoying this interloper's sexual prowess, but she would punish him for his bold intrusion. To his credit, he said nothing as she bathed. Just watched. When she finished, she stood and the lightly oiled water sluiced down her petite, lush form. Stepping from the tub, she dried herself carefully. "Satisfied now?" she said in a smoky voice. The look in his eye was dangerous, and she knew what he was going to do.

He didn't disappoint her, half dragging her back into the bedchamber, sitting on the edge of the bed, pulling her over his knees, and smacking her bottom until it tingled and burned. "You. Will. Fuck. Whoever. I. Tell. You. To. Fuck. But you will not enjoy being fucked by anyone else but me. Do you understand me, my pirate queen?" He punctuated his demand with a hard smack to her already hot flesh. Then he turned her over, glaring into her face as he pulled her up.

"If your claim to Amorata Cay is proved true," Carla said, "you will be paid for this property, and gone from here by sunset."

"My claim is true, but I have decided not to sell the island. I shall remain here, and we will go pirating together. I will fuck you in front of every captain and every crew along the Spanish Main so that they all know you are my property, and mine alone," he said angrily.

"What about your wife and children?" Carla wanted to know.

"I've done my duty by my family. I do not need to go back. I don't want to go back," he told her in surly tones.

"I didn't invite you into my fantasy," Carla said. "You intruded upon me. You are, according to Mr. Nicholas, a glitch in the system. You will be removed shortly."

Julian Hawke smiled wickedly. "So you know Uncle Nicholas, do you?"

"My best friend works for him," Carla said. *Uncle? Uh-oh. Does Nora know this?*

"My uncle will be irritated with me for this breach, but I'll reassure him it won't happen again. Of course that's a lie. He'll know it and punish me in his own unique way. So since the jig is up, my beauty, we'll have a final fuck that will leave you breathless, I promise."

Carla laughed. "Then do it, your grace, my lord, king

of the pirates. I will admit that you have one of the finest cocks I have ever encountered in all my time as the pirate queen. Stand up now, and let me take the edge off your lust by sucking you dry." And when he did, she knelt before him, taking the long limp penis and rolling it between her palms. It quivered beneath her touch. She laughed, and then she began to lick him with slow, firm strokes of her tongue from the tip to the root. She twisted her head so she might take his balls into her mouth, her tongue teasing at them, rolling them around the heated cavern. Then she returned to his cock, taking it into her mouth, sucking, sucking, sucking until he was groaning, growing thick and hard with his need.

He attempted to stop her from milking him, from stealing his cream, his fingers tightening about the thick black curls on her head. But he could not force her to relinquish her hold on him. Unable to help himself, he groaned as if in pain, spurting his thick cream down her throat as she eagerly swallowed it, gulping noisily.

His great cock limp, he cursed her, but Carla stood up, her hand stopping the flow of his words. She pushed him back onto the bed and climbed atop him, smiling down into his handsome face. "There is more, sweeting," she promised him. Then, leaning forward, she pushed one of her nipples into his surprised mouth. "Suck!" she told him. "If you do not make me hot with lust, you shall not have me at all."

His hands fastened about the cheeks of her ass, holding her firm. His mouth sucked hungrily upon her tit. "You are such a bitch, and you have turned the tables on me, haven't you? We are a worthy pair, my queen." Then he continued sucking her. His hands gently pulled her ass cheeks apart so she could feel his newly rejuvenating cock settling between the twin halves.

She felt the flesh hardening and pulsing as it grew in length and width. She could hardly wait for him to impale her on it. But she would torture him a bit longer. He deserved it for spoiling her retreat at Amorata Cay, for ruining her longtime fantasy, but then perhaps that was a bit unfair. She had, after all, grown bored with it all until he'd forced himself into her Channel life.

Suddenly he rolled her over onto her back, his cock free of her flesh. He began to lick her as she at once licked him. She purred with pleasure as his tongue moved across her breasts, her belly, and over her plump mons. "Aye," she told him. "Aye!"

"Little whore," he murmured into her ear. "So hot for it, but so careful not to show it. Shall I punish you by not fucking you, my queen? Or shall I bury myself to the hilt within your tight sweet cunt that even now is crying out for me?"

"If you say so, your grace," Carla replied coyly.

"Jesu!" he groaned, and then without another word he rammed himself into her, fucking her lustily until she screamed with delight, her juices crowning the head of his cock. But he was still hard as iron. He began again. And yet again. Each time she came. Each time she howled her pleasure more loudly. "I can't get enough of you," he moaned, fucking her to another climax. "Why can't I get enough of you?"

"Because you have been a very bad boy, I suspect," Carla said, smacking his bottom several hard blows. Then she wrapped her legs about him. "But you will come this time for me, king of the pirates. You will fuck me and fuck me and fuck me. And then you will come. I am going to drain you, king of the pirates."

Her strength and her fierce words stoked his lust. He rode her hard until they were both climaxing together, groaning and crying out with their satisfaction as they came, finally rolling away from each other, wet with their exertions.

"You were magnificent!" he said, sighing with his deep pleasure.

Ping! Ping! Ping! The Channel is now closing.

"I know I was," Carla told him. She had won! "By the way, sweetie, I'm deleting this fantasy." She grinned triumphantly at him.

"No!" the king of the pirates said fiercely.

"Farewell," Carla told him. "You really were a grand fuck, your grace." Then she was back in her own bed. Carla picked up the remote. It had been an incredible night, but such nights were rare, even in the Channel. Could she? Should she? Her hesitant finger lay upon the DELETE button. Carla rolled over in her bed. Even now Rick was flying over the Atlantic. He'd be home in a few hours, and she suddenly realized she couldn't wait to see him. She loved him, and he loved her. And in a few months, they would be taking together the first vacation they had had in years. Carla could hardly wait. She pressed down hard on the button beneath her finger.

Fantasy deleted, the syrupy voice said. And then the television clicked off.

NINA AND
THE MOVIE STAR

"Have dinner with us tomorrow," Ashley Kimbrough Mulcahy said to Nina, the manager of her Egret Pointe shop, Lacy Nothings. "A client of Ryan's is building a house here in Egret Pointe. He'll be staying with us this weekend."

"Are you trying to fix me up?" Nina Parsons said with a smile. She was a pretty women in her midfifties with fashionably short strawberry blond hair and warm brown eyes. "I told you a long time ago I'm not breaking in another husband, and the Channel satisfies my libido."

Ashley laughed. "But you aren't against dinner out with a good-looking man, are you?" she teased her longtime employee. "Besides, a foursome is better than a threesome."

"Oh, I don't know," Nina replied, unable to resist. "I think threesomes are fun."

"Nina!" Ashley said.

"Okay, okay! I'll have dinner out with you, your delectable hubby, and the mystery man," Nina agreed. "Where? And what time?"

"Saturday night at the East Harbor Inn," Ashley said. "We'll pick you up. The chauffeur will be driving, so we can all drink the night away."

"Sounds good to me," Nina replied. "What's he like, the mystery man?"

"Early sixties. Good-looking. Two divorces," Ashley responded.

"Sounds difficult if two women have dumped him." Nina carefully threaded a price tag onto the silk nightgown as she spoke.

"I don't think so. The first was ages ago. The second, from what I gather, is because wife number two didn't want to live in the Northeast. Couple of years ago. No kids from either marriage."

"So he's fancy-free. Does the mystery man have a name?" Nina inquired.

"Bob. Robert Talcott. I actually think you two will enjoy each other's company," Ashley told her companion.

"Well," Nina said, "a free dinner with two people I actually like and a mystery man will make a nice treat tomorrow night."

"Ryan will be tickled pink. He really wanted you to come," Ashley responded.

Nina smiled. "Ryan is hunky sweet. His mama brought him up right."

"She did," Ashley agreed. "Well, I have to jet. Mr. Hunky has been watching the kids while I came into the village. Car will pick you up at seven."

"I'll be waiting," Nina promised as her employer hurried out the door. Then, as it was close to five thirty, she prepared to close Lacy Nothings. Late summer wasn't their busy season anyway, but the autumn wedding season and the holidays loomed ahead. Already the special orders and Christmas items were beginning to arrive. After emptying the till into the night deposit bag, she locked up, made the bank run, and headed home.

Nina Parsons had been widowed for ten years. Her husband, Charlie, had owned Egret Pointe Insurance along with his younger brother, Ralph. When Charlie had died suddenly of a massive coronary, Nina had learned to her distress that while she owned her late husband's half interest in the business, it was Ralph who was to be in charge. She would be given Charlie's share in the profits quarterly. If Ralph sold the company, she would have half of the sale price.

And that was exactly what Ralph Parsons had done. He had, at the urging of his hysterical wife, found a buyer for Egret Pointe Insurance. May Parsons didn't want her husband to end up like his older brother. She had convinced him that selling and taking an early retirement in Arizona was the right thing to do. Nina, who had managed the business, found herself out of a job. Her half of the sale wasn't nearly what it might have been if Ralph had been patient and waited for the right buyer. She had attempted to advise him, but spooked by May, he took the first offer he got.

May complained about Nina getting half, but Nina held firm. It was Charlie's money that had started the business. He had brought his brother into it because Ralph could never seem to hold down a job anywhere else. Nina sat in on the closing of the sale, took the check that represented her half of the proceeds of her late husband's hard work, bid her in-laws good-bye, and looked for another job. She put her small profit from the sale with Hallock St. John's investment firm in town for her old age.

She couldn't help but feel a small twitch of satisfaction when three years later Ralph Parsons choked on a piece of steak and died. She reasoned that if he had stayed in Egret Pointe and run the insurance agency with her, he might be alive today. Or not. She briefly wondered how May was surviving. But other than informing her that Ralph had died, her sister-in-law didn't seem inclined to renew their acquaintance, and neither did Nina.

Because Egret Pointe Insurance carried the policies of just about every business in the village, Nina had known that Ashley Kimbrough was looking for a shop assistant. Although she knew nothing about fine lingerie, she was willing to learn, and Ashley liked the stylish older woman. Now, ten years later, it was Nina who managed the flagship store of the Lacy Nothings growing empire, which now consisted of five shops and a mail-order business. Ashley Cordelia Kimbrough, now Mrs. Ryan Mulcahy, telecommuted from an office at home, where she could also manage to look after her two young children, without ever leaving Egret Pointe. And Nina Parsons was, as all employees of AKM Enterprises knew, the boss's right-hand woman, not just a shop manager.

Nina liked her life. She had enough money to assure herself a comfortable old age if she ever decided to get old. She had a mortgage-free house and a purpose in life. She had friends, but after Charlie had died, there had been no one to engage her romantic interest. But she did have the Channel, which meant she could have as active a sex life as she wanted, and no one would be the wiser unless she chose to share that part of herself. Ashley, of course, knew. She had once been an enthusiastic subscriber to the Channel, before she married Ryan and started having babies. Despite the almost twenty-year difference in their ages, Nina and Ashley had become best friends. Ashley knew Nina's secrets. And Nina knew Ashley's secrets.

Nina limited her visits to the Channel. She never went on a work night. Having a wild sexual adventure and then having to get up and go to work was too much for her. She limited her forays to Saturday and Sunday nights because the shop was closed on the Sabbath and on Mondays. She wanted to wake up from her adventures and be able to roll over and go back to sleep. And she could always attend either the five p.m. Saturday evening mass at St. Anne's or the noon one on Sundays.

This Saturday, however, she was having an evening out. She might forgo the Channel entirely. *Robert Talcott.* It was a nice name. A youthful divorce was understandable, but Nina couldn't help but wonder why his second wife had divorced him rather than live in the Northeast. What was so bad about the Northeast? Where was better? Well, it wasn't really her business, was it? And it was unlikely she was going to find out on short acquaintance. But she was curious to learn just where he was building a house in Egret Pointe.

Saturday was slow. It was a late-summer beach day, and the local strip of sand would be active. Nina closed at three p.m. and hurried home to get ready. Because they had had no children, Nina and her late husband had lived in a five-room cottage on Maple Lane. It was almost two hundred years old, but they had modernized the kitchen and the bathroom. They had even enclosed a small alcove in the center hall, turning it into a half bath for guests, installing a commode, a pedestal sink, and a skylight. Nina's creative side loved designing and decorating. She was good at it—everyone said so.

Looking through her closet, Nina decided on a short-sleeved wrap dress in a silky pale green material. She showered, and then lay down for a brief nap. By six fifty she was dressed, summer sandals on her feet, a cream-colored pashima shawl over her arm, a small clutch in her hand containing her reading glasses, lipstick for repairs, and a handkerchief. And at exactly seven p.m., her doorbell rang. The Mulcahys' chauffeur was always prompt. But opening the door, she found herself face-to-face with a stranger.

"Nina, I'm Bob Talcott." He held out a hand. "Nice to meet you. The kids are waiting in the car, but Ryan thought I should come and get you."

"It's lovely to meet you, Mr. Talcott," Nina said, looking past him to the Town Car at her curb. "I understand from Ashley you're building a house here in Egret Pointe." She stepped out of her cottage and pulled the door closed behind her. Nice manners, Nina thought as he offered her his arm and escorted her to the car, helping her in and then joining her. Ashley was on her other side. "Hey," Nina said. Then, leaning forward, she teased Ryan. "You should have just honked. I could get used to having handsome men come to my door, sweetie. You have to stop spoiling me."

Ryan Mulcahy guffawed.

Nina turned to Ashley. "I closed up at three. Didn't even have a looker today."

"Weather is too nice," Ashley responded, "but that will change soon enough."

The car sped through the village and out onto the coast road. They arrived at the East Harbor Inn and were seated immediately at the best table in the dining room, a bow window overlooking the bay. They could already see the moon above the water.

"God, this is perfect," Bob Talcott said with a sigh, then took a sip of the Glenfiddich on the rocks that he had ordered. "It's paradise to me."

Nina smiled. "It is, isn't it?"

"Are you a native like Ashley?" he asked her.

Nina shook her head. "No," she replied. "I was born and raised in Albany, New York. I came to Egret Pointe as a bride when I married my late husband. But once here I didn't want to live anywhere else."

"That's how my last wife felt about Southern California. She didn't want to leave it, and so when I came east again, she didn't," he told her.

Nina sipped her daiquiri. Then, unable to help herself, she said, "I'm sorry. I think if you love a man you go with him whenever and wherever he goes. Guess I'm old-fashioned, but I won't ever have to worry about leaving Egret Pointe."

"Yeah," Ashley murmured with a wicked little chuckle, "Nina says she's not going to break in another husband."

"How long were you married?" Bob Talcott asked.

"Twenty-six years," Nina answered. "I've been a widow the past ten years. How long were you married?"

"I married first when I was nineteen. It was a mistake. We divorced quickly. I remarried when I was in my thirties, and we hung in for twenty-three years," he told her. "No kids. So when I decided to come back east—I was raised in New England—she was quite frank to admit that she preferred Southern California."

"But if she loved you . . ."

He laughed. "She obviously didn't," he admitted candidly.

"I'm sorry," Nina said, realizing as she spoke that the longer she looked at Bob Talcott, the more familiar he seemed to her. "Have we ever met?" she asked him.

Ryan snickered.

"If we had, I would have remembered," Bob said, smiling into Nina's brown eyes.

Wow! Nina thought. *The single ladies at the country club are going to be all over this guy.* The beautiful silver hair. No trace of yellow in it, so he hadn't been a blond when he was younger. Gorgeous blue eyes. Tall, maybe just six feet or an inch under, and he looked to be in pretty good shape. He reminded her of someone, but she couldn't quite put her finger on it.

They ordered. The specials tonight were filet mignon with Bordelaise sauce and a large boiled lobster with all the trimmings. In Egret Pointe that meant the crustacean would be accompanied by some steamed clams and corn amid a bed of dark seaweed on an oval platter. The men ordered the lobster. Nina ordered a Cornish game hen stuffed with wild rice and apricot. Ashley had the filet.

"I'm not much of a fish person," Nina said.

Bob ordered a bottle of wine, a Pindar Winter White.

"What did or do you do?" Nina asked the Mulcahys' guest.

"I worked in Hollywood," he answered her.

Ryan snickered again.

"I've never been to Hollywood," Nina said, "but I'm sure I know you." Then she laughed. "Has anyone ever told you that you look just like the movie star Lyon Roberts? He was always a favorite of mine. He used to be the guy who was the hero's best friend in all those cute comedies. He never got the girl, but I thought he should have. I always liked him better," Nina said.

"Yeah, I get that a lot," Bob said.

Ryan Mulcahy began to laugh now. "Tell her!" he said to Bob.

"Tell me what?" Nina asked. What the hell was the matter with Ryan Mulcahy tonight? He'd had only one drink, and she'd never known him to be affected by booze.

"I look like Lyon Roberts because I am Lyon Roberts," Bob said. "At least I was once upon a time. Lyon was my mother's maiden name. Now that I'm retired, I prefer to use my own name which happens to be Robert Lyon Talcott," he told her. His blue eyes twinkled at her. "I'm glad you liked me best."

Nina colored becomingly. "Oh, my!" she said softly. "Of course. You left Hollywood and came back to do Broadway."

"It's where I began my profession," he explained. "I'll end it there, but I'm still a little too young to retire entirely. I'll be starting rehearsals on a new play opening in early March. It's a comedy."

"You were always so good in those cute movies. You have a terrific sense of timing," Nina told him admiringly.

"A must for the second banana," Bob said.

"You were a star!" Nina exclaimed. "None of those pictures would have been as successful without you."

He laughed. "Ryan said you were a fan," he teased her. "I was the last of my kind. Back in the day there were some pretty good second bananas in those light and frothy comedies. Van Johnson and Tony Randall, to name a few, but by the time I got to Hollywood, that kind of movie wasn't being made very often. Still, I came from Broadway, had a good career in the movies and television, and have been back on Broadway for the past few years. While it's flattering, I'm just a working actor, Nina. You don't have to be impressed."

"You're just an ordinary guy building a house in Egret Pointe," Nina responded drily. "Yeah. Sure. Is it going to be a McMansion? I imagine you'll be entertaining."

"It's going to be cozy and small," he told her. "I never hung out in Hollywood, and I live in a one-bedroom pre-war in the city. I'll only keep the apartment as long as I'm working in theater. My home is for me."

"I'm intrigued," Nina told him. "Where are you building?"

"I bought some property near Ryan and Ashley's place."

"The old Oliver property," Ashley interjected. "Remember, the house burned down years ago, but the road in from the main road is still there."

"It's all wooded," Nina remarked.

"And it's going to stay wooded," Bob told them. "I'm building on the bluff over the bay."

"Back far enough, I hope," Nina said.

He nodded. "I'm aware of the erosion problems," he acknowledged.

Their meal came. The food was good as always. East Harbor Inn was noted for its cuisine. They finished the bottle of white wine, then ordered dessert, unable to resist the warm homemade peach-and-raspberry cobbler with fresh churned vanilla ice cream. Outside the bow window, the moon was now bright and high over the bay. They lingered over their fresh brewed coffee.

"You folks going to close up for me this evening?" Felicity Clarence, the inn's owner, was tableside. "Don't mean to rush you, but it's ten o'clock."

"Oh, my," Nina said. "It's been such a pleasant evening. I can't believe it's so late." She smiled up at the innkeeper. "Sorry, Felicity."

"Haven't seen you out on the town in quite a while," Felicity noted. She turned to look straight at Bob Talcott. "You're a nice-looking gentleman," she said. "Where did Nina find you? And about time she had a fella. Charlie's been gone forever."

"Oh, he's not my fella, Felicity," Nina quickly said. "He's the Mulcahys' guest, and they invited me to dine with them this evening."

"Too bad," Felicity Clarence said tartly. "'Bout time you had a fella again, Nina. Now go home, please, so I can close up."

They rose, laughing. The tab had already been paid, so they went out to the car, where Bill, the Mulcahys' chauffeur, was waiting for them. He helped them into the vehicle, and then began the drive home.

"Is there somewhere in Egret Pointe where you can get breakfast?" Bob Talcott asked as the car sped through the moonlit night.

"Mrs. Byrnes fixes a great breakfast," Ryan said. "Whenever you get up."

"I know she does, but if you don't mind," Bob said, "I'd like to invite Nina to breakfast." He turned to her, inquiring, "Do you go to church?"

She was surprised. "Yes," she managed to say.

"Do you want to eat before or after?" he asked her.

"I suppose we could eat around nine, and I'll go to noon mass," Nina heard herself say. Was this a date? Did breakfast count as a date? She honestly didn't know. Oh, damn. If she was going to meet him at nine for breakfast, there could be no Channel tonight. It was already after ten, and the Channel closed at four a.m. At her age she didn't want to meet a man with only four hours' sleep. Even for breakfast.

"Then you'll come. Great! I've got my own car. Bill can give me directions to your house, and you can navigate me to"—he paused—"where?"

"The luncheonette," Nina said, laughing. "The place to go for weekend breakfast is the Egret Pointe Luncheonette."

"It's a date then," Bob Talcott said.

A date! Breakfast obviously did count as a date these days. When was the last time she had had a date? Before she and Charlie were married, and that meant not since the 1970s. She almost gasped aloud. She wasn't used to thinking of time in such huge chunks for herself. "I'll look forward to it," Nina replied, and to her surprise, she was looking forward to it.

They reached her cottage on Maple Lane, and Bob got out to escort her to the door. "Do you have your keys?" he asked.

"Door's open," Nina told him. "We don't lock our doors in Egret Pointe." Then, giving him a smile, she said, "It was the nicest evening I've had in a long time, Bob. See you tomorrow morning." With a final smile she opened her door, slipped inside, and closed it behind her. Oh! My! God! She had just had dinner with her favorite movie star. "How about that, Charlie?" Like all widows, she often talked aloud to her deceased husband. "Lyon Roberts in the flesh. I think he's better-looking in person, and he is certainly aging well. Guess I better hit the sack if I'm going to look decent in the morning. I've got a date for breakfast before mass. Good night, dear."

At two minutes after nine the next morning Nina opened her door to greet Bob Talcott. "Good morning," she said. God, he really was good-looking. He was wearing a pair of khaki chinos and a blue windowpane-checked shirt that brought out the blue in his eyes. Nina stepped out of the house. "I'm not certain I'm hungry after last night's wonderful dinner at the inn," she said.

"We could go to mass first, then," he said. "Is there a nine thirty?" The blue eyes swept over her. Damn, she was one pretty woman! The strawberry blond hair, the warm brown eyes, and that trim figure. He was surprised to feel his dick twitch with interest.

"Yes, there's a nine thirty," Nina answered him. "Are you a Catholic?"

"I used to be," he told her. "I'm a little bit lapsed."

"Everyone, or almost everyone, goes to church in a small town. It's not just the religion—there's a social aspect to it as well," Nina explained. "It's how you make friends and contacts."

"Let's go, then," he said, escorting her to his car, which was parked at her curb.

Nina was surprised to see the vehicle he drove was a Chrysler PT Cruiser. "I thought you'd have more elegant transportation," she said as she got in.

He laughed. "I bought this when they first came out. It's not the kind of car anyone wants to steal. I garage it, but those fancy cars have been known to disappear from even the best garages in the best neighborhoods. I go for my car, and I know it's going to be there."

"A practical man," she replied, fastening her seat belt. "Take a left at the corner. St. Anne's is just three blocks down. I usually walk it, but since we're going to eat afterward, it's good to have the car right there. You'll see the church parking lot."

Robert Talcott thought the church charming. It looked like something out of an English village. The stained-glass windows were very old, their colors rich, each portraying a moment in St. Anne's life as imagined by the artist. The brief mass was conducted by an elderly priest Nina introduced afterward as Father Sullivan. She explained to him that Mr. Talcott would be moving to Egret Pointe eventually.

"Then we'll expect to see you regularly," the old man said. "You appear to be at an age where you'll be wanting to begin making your peace with God."

Nina swallowed a giggle as Bob manfully agreed.

"Your priest doesn't mince words, does he?" her escort said as he helped her back into the waiting car.

"He's really a dear man," Nina said, defending Father Sullivan. "I have no idea what possessed him to say such a thing."

"He's got a sharp eye. He saw I didn't come up for the host," Bob replied.

"Turn left out of the parking lot," Nina directed him. "Then right at the next corner onto Main Street. The luncheonette is on the right, and if we're lucky, we'll get a parking space right in front." They were.

Inside, they had to wait a few minutes for a table. He was surprised, and remarked it was just like trying to get a table at a trendy restaurant in the city or Hollywood. They were finally seated in a comfortable booth.

"Coffee?" the waitress asked, slapping down two menus in front of them.

"Tea and a large cranberry juice for me," Nina said.

"Coffee," Bob said.

The waitress hurried off.

"What's good?" he asked Nina.

"Blueberry pancakes," she answered. "With sausage."

"Done!" he told her, and when the waitress returned, he ordered for them both.

"I'm curious," Nina said, "and it's really none of my business, but I'm so surprised your wife could just let you come east alone. You were married to Sallie Blair, weren't you? She's a fantastic actress."

"She is, isn't she?" he agreed. "The studio wanted us to marry," he explained. "My first wife and I met at a cattle call. That's when a show puts out a casting call, and every young actor and actress in town comes. It was fun. It was the seventies. We were still old-fashioned enough to get married when we decided we wanted to have sex and share an apartment."

"Did you love her?" Nina wanted to know.

"To this day I'm not quite sure," Bob admitted. "She was a terrific girl. But then I got my first big break in a Broadway show. I was the hot new young actor. Lots of publicity and parties. Then Hollywood beckoned. She got scared because she realized it wasn't the kind of life she wanted after all. We divorced after two years."

"Do you know what happened to her?" Nina asked.

"We stayed friends," he said. "She eventually married a nice businessman. They live in the suburbs of the city and have three kids, all grown now. I stayed a bachelor in Hollywood, the man about town with this starlet and that up-and-coming actress on his arm at all the important parties and events. That's how I met Sallie. We did a few movies together, and then she began to get bigger and bigger roles. Suddenly she was a star of the first magnitude with a capitol S, but she had a secret, and the moneymen controlling the studios by then didn't want her secret revealed.

"Since I was considered a nice guy in a not-so-nice town, I was approached. If I would marry Sallie Blair and remain a good husband, at least publicly, my career would continue to bloom. If I didn't, my career would be in the toilet, and my reputation would be smeared so that I couldn't get work anywhere on either coast. I said I would agree if my physical needs could be met discreetly. You see, Sallie Blair is gay. I knew it because we had become friends.

In fact, it had been she who suggested I would make her an excellent husband.

"Everything was worked out so that she kept her lover, who was her personal assistant, by the way, and I got what I needed when I needed it. We staged a two-month courtship. The columns got planted with all kinds of items about it. And then we eloped to Vegas, where we were married in one of those amazingly tacky wedding chapels. Several paparazzi were tipped off, and we were caught coming out of the chapel."

"Ah, now I understand a little bit better," Nina said as the waitress arrived with their breakfast, plunked down the plates, and retreated. "That's why she didn't come with you when you returned East."

"She had her own life," Bob replied. "She and Nancy had been together for years. Her career is still booming. She likes living in Malibu. The roles offered me were becoming fewer and fewer. My agent told me that the playwright Arthur Billings had a new play going into production and wanted me for the lead. I took it. We obtained a quiet divorce, to which her people didn't object. The publicity about it simply said we had grown apart and would remain the best of friends. No scandal. No story. The end."

"It sounds so dispassionate and chill," Nina said softly as she cut a piece of blueberry pancake.

"I'm a New Englander and a practical man. I never fell in love, so it never mattered. With Sallie's proclivities, there was no chance of a child. We were the perfect professional Hollywood couple. Two actors. Talented. Well liked. Well groomed. Well matched. We made money for the studios we worked for, we caused no trouble, and unlike so many of these young actors today, we didn't end up in the middle of unsavory scandals. Our marriage was a business arrangement first and foremost."

"And here I thought you were the perfect Hollywood couple," Nina said with just a hint of sarcasm.

"Hell," he said and laughed, "we were. Old school, of course."

"How long have you been back in New York?" she asked him.

"Eight years now," he said. "I've done five plays in that time. Only one of them bombed. But straight drama and comedies are becoming rarer. It's those odd musicals like *Les Miz, Phantom,* and *Cats* that bring in the dollars today. Those and the revivals of the fifties and sixties musicals. There's a chance they may do a revival of *Kismet* next year, and if they do, I'll be playing the role of the wazir." He laughed. "There would have been a time, and it doesn't seem that long ago, when I would have been asked to play the role of the young caliph. Now it's the villainous older man."

"I think you would be a great wazir," Nina said. "You've always been a terrific character actor." She set her knife and fork down and began to sing softly, "'When they caught the seven hundred men, and hung them in their prison pen. Who said suspend them by their fuzz? Was I wazir? I was!'"

He chuckled. "You know the words to that song?"

"*Kismet* was one of my favorite musicals," Nina admitted. "I know the words to all the songs in that show. Some of the lyrics are seriously meaningful and poetic."

"I'll have to give you house seats, then," he said.

"Opening night," Nina replied with a sassy grin, "and I'll expect an invite to the cast party afterward."

"Are you flirting with me, Mrs. Parsons?" he asked her mischievously.

Nina laughed. "I think I might be," she said. "It's been so long since I flirted with anyone, I'm not quite certain. Do you think I am?"

"Yeah, I do. And it's nice," Bob told her.

"Tell me about the house you're building?" Nina said, turning the subject back to him. Her cheeks felt warm, but she couldn't believe she was blushing at her age.

"I don't know what I'm building yet," he said. "Want to drive out to the property and tell me what you see there?"

"I'd love to," Nina answered.

He paid the bill, leaving their taciturn waitress a generous tip, which had her calling out, "Thanks!" behind them as they exited the luncheonette. Bob helped Nina into the car, and they drove off. He knew his way from Egret Pointe's Main Street to the old Oliver property, driving two miles down the town's major road, finally turning off onto a narrow paved path that led through a thick wood. Nina knew the Oliver property bordered the main road. It was a lot of property.

"You're keeping it wooded," she said.

"I like the woods, but I may clear some saplings and brush so the big trees stay healthy," Bob replied.

"We have a lot of deer," Nina told him. "They do have rather gourmet appetites for plants like hostas and day lily buds."

"Duly warned, but the truth is, I like the deer. What's

that saying by Confucius? If God made them, there must be a use for them." He brought the car to a stop. "We have to walk from here, Nina."

"No problem. I don't wear heels," she told him as she got out of the car.

They walked about a hundred feet before coming out into a large clearing that overlooked the water. The sun was sparkling on the waves and the bay was full of boats.

"Well," he said, "what do you think? What suits this property? A mansion like the Mulcahys' or something else?"

"I would build low to blend into the natural landscape," Nina said without any hesitation at all. "It doesn't have to be small, but this piece of property is different from Ashley's home, which has stood on her hill for over two hundred years."

"There was a house up here once," he reminded her.

"It was in the woods," Nina said. "It was big, dark, and gloomy. You want to take advantage of the spectacular view, but you don't want your home sticking out like a sore thumb. 'Oh, look! There's the McMansion that actor built,'" she trilled.

"Single level, then?" Bob asked, thinking as he had earlier how pretty Nina Parsons was. Especially standing here with the sunlight touching her hair.

"I would, but then I'm not you, and this isn't my property," Nina replied.

"Know any local architects?" What was it about her? She was normal, he thought. In Hollywood few people were normal, and in New York everyone he knew was in the theater or an allied industry. But Nina was a nice normal woman, and he found himself very much at ease with her. He wanted to know her better, he decided. "I have to go back into the city later today," he said, "but could I see you when I come back?"

"Of course," Nina answered. The movie star wanted to see her again, and this wasn't one of her fantasies. This was reality. He drove her home, parking in front of her cottage. Nina leaned over and kissed his cheek. "Thanks for a lovely day," she said. Then she gave him a mischievous smile. "Now I can say I kissed a movie star."

His hand reached out to cup her face, and his mouth closed over hers in a deep, warm kiss. When he finally released her, he said, "*Now* you can say you've kissed a movie star, Nina Parsons." Then he got out of the car and went around to open the door for her.

When he had touched her face, she had been startled, but when his lips pressed against hers, Nina had practically swooned away like some Victorian maiden being kissed for the very first time. But now she had to swing her legs out of the car, stand up, smile, and let him escort her to her front door. How she did it without collapsing amazed her.

"See you next week," he said casually, turning to go.

Nina opened the door and stepped into her foyer, then leaned back against the wall, breathing deeply and slowly. She hadn't been kissed since Charlie died. And she hadn't been kissed like that ever. Wow! His kiss was everything she had ever imagined it would be. Did he realize he had just turned her life upside down? She doubted it, but he had. It was only early afternoon. She had at least six hours until the Channel opened. She could hardly wait. Nina decided to take a nap. But she couldn't sleep. She took a long bubble bath in her claw-foot tub. She fixed herself a sandwich and salad since she hadn't eaten since breakfast, and that was now hours ago.

The phone rang. It was Ashley. "I can't stand it, Nina. How did it go?"

"He kissed me!" Nina blurted out without meaning to, and felt the heat rising up in her cheeks. "Do you know how long it's been since I've been kissed?"

"I take it this wasn't a peck on the cheek," Ashley said, a hint of laughter in her voice. "And yes, I know how long it's been."

"Mouth to mouth, hot, sweet, lingering," Nina replied.

"Any tongue?"

"No! I would have fainted dead away if he had used his tongue," Nina admitted. "The kiss was more than enough to leave me weak in the knees. Frankly, I don't know how I walked up the path and into the house. He wants to see me again, Ashley."

"Wonderful!" Ashley Mulcahy said. "Ryan really likes him."

"He wants a local architect," Nina said.

"I'll tell Ryan," Ashley replied. "Now, calm down, Nina, and I'll see you at the shop Tuesday morning." She rang off.

Finally it was eight o'clock. Nina got into her bed, picked up the special Channel remote, and pressed the A button. She was immediately in a gazebo set within a garden. It was an early-summer evening. The stars were beginning to twinkle one by one in the sky above. She was twenty again, and it was 1891 in Egret Pointe. Nina smoothed her bell-shaped skirt down, her hand going to her throat as she heard his footsteps crunching down the gravel path. "Lyon? Is that you?" she asked.

He sprang into the gazebo, grinning. "Of course, darling. Who else would it be?" Sweeping her into his arms, he kissed her, and Nina recognized the kiss as Robert Talcott's. There had been no identity to it before. His hand went to her bodice and fondled a breast. "Have you thought about what we talked about, Nina?" His fingers were unbuttoning the front of her dress.

"Oh, I don't know, Lyon, if we should be so naughty."

"We're going to be married, Nina," he protested.

"Shouldn't we wait until then?" she questioned him.

"Everyone who gets engaged fucks, Nina. Oh, what a good girl you are," he praised her. "You didn't wear a chemise, just as I instructed you." He began to fumble with the laces of her corset so he might completely free her breasts.

"But what if Papa finds out?" she worried.

"He won't," Lyon said. "We're engaged, and he doesn't want to know anything." He got the corset open and, bending, began to suck on her nipple.

"Ohhhh," Nina squealed softly. "That is so naughty!"

He lifted his head briefly so she might see his face. "But you like being naughty, Nina," he said. "And I want to be naughty with you." He drew her into the shadows of the interior of the gazebo, pulling her down onto the velvet love seat. Then, pressing her back, he allowed himself full access to her glorious titties. They were big with large nipples he enjoyed sucking and rolling between his thumb and forefinger. She murmured as he paid the twin orbs extravagant attention.

Nina lay back, enjoying the attentions of the young actor known as Lyon Roberts. He had always been her fantasy, and a Victorian setting was her favorite as she played the reluctant virgin. Some nights she let him have his way. Other nights she did not. Tonight, however, she wanted to be fucked. His mouth sucked hard on one of her nipples, while his hand began to slip beneath the white cotton batiste of her skirt and up her leg.

"Good girl!" he praised her again. "You aren't wearing your drawers."

"You told me not to, Lyon, and I want to show you that I'm going to be a very obedient wife to you," the young Nina simpered. "Ohh, you shouldn't touch me there!"

"Yes, I should," he assured her, his fingers playing amid the thick brown pubic curls of her mons. He ran a digit along her labia, pushing through and finding her little clit. His fingers squeezed the small nub of flesh, and then he began to tease it with his finger. She squirmed beneath his hand, and her breath came in short pants as he roused her to a clitoral orgasm. "Now, wasn't that nice, darling?" he murmured, lifting his head from her tit and kissing her a slow, deep kiss. "Don't you like it when I tease you?" His finger began to push into her, and she bridled beneath his hand but forbade him not. His finger pushed quickly in and out of her wet vagina, frigging her to another small orgasm.

"Don't you want to do it with me, darling?" he whispered. "Don't you want me to fuck you? Here, feel my cock, Nina." He pulled her hand down to where his penis now thrust forth from his trousers.

"Oh, it's big," she told him, wide-eyed. "Surely it won't fit inside me, Lyon."

"Why don't we try?" he purred softly.

"I don't know," she demurred.

He drew her to her feet, and then pushed her gently over the high rolled arm of the love seat. "Let me fuck you, darling," he whispered in her ear as he drew her skirt and her petticoats up, bunching them just above the small of her back. Her bared buttocks were smooth and nicely rounded. Eventually he would introduce her to the fine art of strapping, which he had learned while studying at university in England. He had brought back a fine leather tawse for just that purpose.

"I'm afraid," the virgin Nina said softly. She was now fully bent over the rolled arm of the love seat, her toes just barely touching the floor.

"Don't be," he told her. His hand rubbed her buttocks soothingly. "You have such a pretty ass, darling," he said as he began to nose the tip of his penis beneath her, seeking his way into her vagina. He considered taking her asshole, but he really wanted to pop her cherry tonight, introducing her to the delights of fucking. Finding his way, he pushed just the tip of his dick into her hot, tight cunt.

"*Ohhhhh!*" she cried out as she felt his entry. She had been right. He was much too big. "Stop! Stop!" Nina cried.

He pushed himself another inch inside her, and then quickly another.

"*Ohhhhh! Oh! Oh!* You will tear me asunder," Nina protested.

"Just a moment more, darling, and you will like it," he promised. Then he thrust hard into her cunt, shattering her hymen, claiming her virginity. And having done so, he began to fuck her with long, deep, hard strokes of his cock until they were both moaning.

At first the pain had been fierce, but then as he moved back and forth within her, the pain had dissipated, leaving a feeling of pure deliciousness. She heard his voice slowly and deliberately whispering with each stroke of his penis. *Fuck! Fuck! Fuck! Fuck!* He excited her. The word excited her. "Oh, yes!" she cried as she experienced her first real orgasm. "Oh, yes, Lyon! Do it! Don't stop!" And he hadn't stopped for some time. That was the beauty of the Channel. Tireless lovers.

Eventually their clothing was dispensed with, and they whiled away the evening in an orgy of fucking and sucking. When the Channel finally closed, Nina slept, exhausted but contented. Still, upon awakening, she couldn't help but wonder if the Robert Talcott she knew, a man almost past middle age, would be as enthusiastic a lover as the young actor he had once been, who was now her fantasy lover.

Robert came back to Egret Pointe several days later to meet with the architect that Ryan Mulcahy had recommended. Ashley wouldn't hear of him staying at the local motel. He stayed with the Mulcahys, and at his hostess's insistence came and went as he pleased. Robert Talcott invited Nina to look over the first plans at his architect's office. She made one or two suggestions, and agreed with his final decisions. It was the end of September now, and the foundation was dug and the footings poured. The framing began.

Suddenly her every lunch hour was taken up by Robert Talcott, who would come and whisk her away to check on the progress of the house. They were eating dinner together several times a week. The Egret Pointe gossip mill was beginning to churn, which amused him, although Nina was certainly not used to such attention.

As he brought her home one October evening, he said, "You know, brown eyes, you've never asked me into your house."

And Nina was surprised to realize that that was true.

"Maybe an after-dinner drink?" he suggested softly.

"I might have some brandy," she said slowly. "Or something."

So Robert Talcott parked his car in Nina's driveway this time, and went into the house with her. He found her house charming. All floral chintz, comfortable furniture, and good small antiques. A fire was set in the living room fireplace. "Shall I light it?" he asked her, and when she nodded in the affirmative, he did.

Nina checked in the dining room sideboard and found a small unopened bottle of Grand Marnier. Opening it in the kitchen, she poured two small cordial glasses of the liqueur. "No brandy," she told him, coming into the living room and handing him the glass. "Hope this will do."

Robert Talcott took a sip and smiled. "Grand Marnier will do nicely." He sat down on the striped couch, patting the seat next to him.

Nina joined him. *Oh, Charlie,* she thought, *I hope*

you don't mind I've brought a man into your house. We've been doing a lot of kissing, and frankly, I like it. I think tonight we may do more than kiss. Hope that's okay with you. Nina sipped her cordial. "Umm, it's good. I have no idea where the bottle came from, but it was unopened."

"Somebody gave it to you as a gift. You don't entertain a whole lot, do you?"

"Not anymore. A few friends for a meal now and again," she admitted. Then, seeing his glass was just about empty, she said, "Would you like a tour of my manse? Charlie and I started and ended here. Since we didn't have any kids a larger house really seemed unnecessary." Nina stood up, and he followed as she led. "This is the dining room. When Charlie was alive, we always seemed to be having friends for dinner, for brunch."

"It's nice," he said sincerely, admiring the barn red paint above the chair rail, and the border with the roosters just below the crown moldings. There was a simple pewter chandelier over the long painted table, with its rush-seated high-back chairs. It was very Americana, with a painted sideboard and corner cabinets.

"Kitchen," Nina said, leading him through a small, square, surprisingly modern kitchen. He followed her back into the hall. "Den," she said.

"You have two fireplaces," he noted, peering into the comfortable room at its built-in bookcases.

"That's what sold us on the house in the first place," Nina told him. "And this is the master. She stepped deep into the room and he followed.

After a long, silent moment, Robert Talcott said, "I

think this is the point where I either bid you good night and go or I stay, isn't it?"

Her heart was beating rapidly. *Sex.* The man was suggesting that they have sex, and she sure as hell must have been thinking about it or she wouldn't have invited him into her bedroom. "I haven't had sex in years," she admitted, flushing as she spoke the words.

"It's like riding a bicycle," he told her in an amused tone. "You don't forget. It's been a while for me too, brown eyes."

"What do you want to do?" Nina tossed the hot potato back to Robert Talcott.

"Frankly? Well, I want to put you on your back, and jump your bones. What do you want to do?"

"Same thing," Nina conceded. "But what if we do— Well, what if it isn't good for one or both of us?"

"We admit it, put it down to experience, and stay friends," he said.

"You wouldn't feel used?"

"Would you?"

"Well, maybe a little," Nina allowed.

"Then I guess I'm going to have to make the earth move for you, brown eyes," he said as he reached out and pulled her toward him, wrapping his arms about her. Then he gave her a long, slow, deep kiss. *With tongue.*

Feeling him against her as they kissed, knowing they were going to have sex shortly, made the kiss very different for Nina. He had the sexiest mouth. She danced with his tongue, and when he pulled her even closer, Nina could feel his dick against her thigh. This was reality, and she hoped to heaven she was ready for it. His fingers unzipped her dress, pushing it off of her. Thank God she was still in decent shape and wore sexy underwear. She pulled his sweater over his head, tossed it aside, and began to unbutton his shirt. He wasn't wearing an undershirt, and he had a nicely toned body, she saw as the shirt came off. She ran her hands over the smooth skin of his chest, shoulders, and back.

"That feels nice," he told her as he undid his belt, then unzipped his trousers to step out of them. He was wearing white briefs. His body wasn't buff, but it was surprisingly good.

Reaching around her, Robert Talcott unhooked Nina's bra to reveal her breasts. They kissed again, her breasts crushed against his chest, and while they did, she pulled his shorts down, feeling him step out of them while their lips were still fused together. Then she felt him removing her bikini briefs, and they were both stark naked. They hadn't turned on the lights in the bedroom, the only light coming from the hallway outside the door.

Maybe that was better, Nina thought, as he pushed her back onto the bed. Her heart was pounding wildly. What the hell was she doing? But, oh, God, she didn't want to stop now. She let her eyes stray to his groin. Oh, my! He was certainly well equipped.

"You have beautiful breasts," he told her as his eyes admired them. He trailed the backs of his fingers over the tops of them. Then he bent and kissed each nipple. "I want you to know I'm not in any great rush, brown eyes. I want you to enjoy this."

"I want you to enjoy it too," Nina replied. "Are you sure we're going to remember how to do this?"

He laughed. "I don't know about you, but it's sure as hell all coming back to me now," Robert Talcott told her with a grin.

"I think you could be a bad man," she teased him.

"I can," he agreed. "You like bad?"

"I don't know," Nina said slowly.

"Then let's just keep it simple for now," he said as he began to kiss Nina again.

She let him have his way, meeting him kiss for kiss for kiss until she felt she was going to melt with the heat their two bodies pressing together was generating. God, he felt so damned good against her. It was very different from the Channel, although she had to admit that having that pleasure was a godsend. But this was so much better. She sighed as his lips left hers and began a slow journey across her flesh.

Damn! How long had it been since he had taken the time to enjoy a woman's body? His sexual activity in Hollywood had been confined to very discreet high-priced call girls paid for by his wife's studio. They were pretty and charming for the most part, but it had always been just sex. Nothing more. In New York he had allowed himself one or two dalliances, but he always knew the women involved were hoping to use him as a stepping-stone. Again it had just been about sex, and very discouraging. But with Nina there was something else. Yeah, there was going to be sex. But it was with a woman who seemed to actually like him and enjoy his company. She wanted nothing from him except perhaps his company. They were friends. And if it went well between them, they might even become what was called today "friends with benefits."

Her skin was smooth, and there was a slight floral fragrance to it. It wasn't the skin of a young woman. While toned, there was a softness to it. He kissed and licked his way first across her full breasts, and then down her torso. The curls covering her mons were not quite the color of her hair, but then he'd already figured out that she did something to enhance her hair. Most women her age did.

Nina wanted to scream. The kissing and the licking was just so delicious. Her breath caught in her throat as, kneeling between her spread thighs, he parted her labia lips and leaned forward to lick at her. *"Ohhh!"* The sound emerged from her tight throat. The sensation of his broad, flat tongue stroking her was mind-blowing. When he began to lick with the very tip of that tongue at her clit, she almost screamed.

"You taste so damned good," he groaned. "I just want to eat you up, brown eyes."

"I wouldn't want to spoil your fun," Nina managed to say. Oh! My! God! She was going to explode, she thought, as the small orgasm brought on by his tongue burst. "I want to make you feel good too," she said, realizing she was being selfish.

"Later," he told her. "This first time is just for you, brown eyes." He reached down and lifted his penis up, preparing to enter her.

Nina almost wept at the sight of it. Long. Thick. The kind of cock every girl dreamed of but seldom got. Charlie had had an average dick, but Robert Talcott's was just slightly beyond average. She almost moaned with her excitement.

He leaned down and whispered in her ear, "I want to talk dirty to you. Can I?"

Nina looked straight into his blue eyes. "Fuck me!" she said.

Robert Talcott laughed. "You betcha, brown eyes. I'm going to fuck you until you come screaming, and then I'm going to fuck you again with the same result."

"Promises, promises," Nina taunted him. "*Fuck me! Oh, God!*" she gasped as he pushed deep and hard into her. "*Yes!*" He was filling her, and she could feel every inch of him straining and stretching the walls of her vagina with his thick cock.

He began to move upon her—at first with slow, deep strokes of his penis, again and again and again until Nina was half-conscious. Then he began to move on her with swift, hard thrusts, forcing her to her next orgasm as she screamed with pleasure. But he was a man of his word, and as soon as Nina came to herself again, she discovered that her lover was still hard within her. She looked questioningly at Robert Talcott.

"I told you, brown eyes. Two this first time. Ready to go again? And this time I won't go easy on you. I'm going to fuck you to a stand, brown eyes."

"You are amazing," Nina said.

"For my age?" he teased.

"For any age," Nina told him.

He grinned the Lyon Roberts boyish grin that had won her heart years ago. "Let's get those legs up and over my shoulders now," he said. "Time for me to go really deep, and for you to fly to the moon." His penis still buried deep inside her, he helped her bring her legs up and over his shoulders. He thrust two quick thrusts, sliding deeper into her.

"Oh, my God!" Nina gasped. "Can you die of sexual pleasure?"

"Let's find out," he said, and began to piston her once again.

Nina clung to his shoulders, her nails digging into him as he fucked her. Her heart was pounding in her ears. It was too good. Too sweet. Too perfect. And at their age too. She felt her orgasm building and building until she knew it was going to break and possibly kill her. Robert was groaning loudly now, and somewhere a woman was screaming with her pleasure. They came together and collapsed quickly afterward.

When Nina awoke, the first gray light of an October dawn was coming in through the bedroom windows. Robert Talcott lay sleeping, snoring softly, next to her. She realized that she ached all over. Unaccustomed as she was to real sex, she had forgotten how a body could feel after a wild night of unbridled passion. She was sore, but she felt great. She slipped quietly from the bed, going into the bathroom and taking a quick shower. Then she dressed in a pair of fleece sweats before hurrying to the kitchen to fix them a hearty breakfast. It was a workday for her. She would have to change afterward.

Robert Talcott awoke in a strange bed. For a moment he was confused as he looked around the bedroom, with its peonies on a peach background wallpaper and elegant cherry French Provincial furniture. Then he remembered. He had practically invited himself into Nina Parsons's home, and they had fallen into bed together and fucked each other to a fare-thee-well. He felt terrific. Better than he had in years.

"Good morning, Robert," he heard her say. She was standing in the doorway.

"There are towels in the closet in the bathroom. I'll have breakfast ready for you after you've showered," she told him.

"Thanks," he replied. Damn! She looked so cute in that green fleece outfit. When he had cleaned himself up and put his clothes back on, he found his way to the kitchen. He could smell both bacon and coffee.

Nina was sitting at a butcher-block table, already eating. She looked up and smiled. "Everything's in the oven. Coffee on the counter. Sit down and join me before I head off to work."

"Are you all right?" he asked her. He wasn't certain exactly how she would feel after their wild encounter. He pulled the warm plate filled with fluffy scrambled eggs, bacon, and a blueberry muffin from the oven and sat down. There was juice to drink, and he'd get his coffee in a minute, after he learned how she felt.

Nina looked up. "I'm not sure what to say," she began. "'Baby, you were great'? 'Was it good for you?'" A smile played about her lips. "I've never been in this kind of situation before. And until last night Charlie was the only man I ever had sex with, Robert. I suspect you know more about something like this than I do."

"All I've ever known are high-class hookers and ambitious actresses," he began. "But last night with you was different."

"Different good? Or different bad?" Nina asked him.

Did he regret what had happened between them? It didn't matter. She would have this memory forever.

"Different incredible," he answered without hesitation. "God, brown eyes, you are warm and passionate and caring. I know this sounds a little wussy for a man to say—hell, it sounds a lot wussy for a guy to say—but I felt safe with you, Nina."

Nina blushed at the tender admission. "Oh, I'm so glad that I could do something for you, Robert, because the sex with you was wonderful. Even my Charlie never put me over the top like you did last night, and I mean no disrespect to my husband's memory when I say that."

"Then you're not mad at me for taking advantage?" he asked.

Nina giggled. "I wanted you to take advantage, Robert. I practically seduced you," she said, blushing again. "I hope you won't think badly of me for it."

Reaching across the table, he took her hand and kissed it. "I will never think badly of you, brown eyes. Other than my first wife, I never asked a lady to be my girl, but I'd like to ask you. Will you be my girl, Nina Parsons?" His blue eyes met her brown ones, and he smiled his boyish grin.

"I'd like that," she agreed. Her heart was racing again with excitement. Lyon Roberts had just asked her to be his girl. No! Robert Talcott had, and they weren't twenty-somethings. They were grown and practically seniors.

"Good!" he said, leaning across the table to kiss her.

Nina sighed and kissed him back. Then the clock in the hall struck eight, bringing her back to reality. "I've got to go and change for work," she said, standing up.

"Can I come and help you?" he asked innocently.

Nina laughed. "I'd never get there, and Ashley would wonder why her shop wasn't open. We're extra busy now with the winter weddings and the holiday ahead."

He sighed. "Then I'll just have to satisfy myself with another of these muffins," he said, "and a cup of coffee."

"Muffins are in the warming oven," Nina told him, hurrying from the kitchen.

Back in the bedroom, she sneaked a look at her bed, with its very tumbled sheets and down coverlet. Yes, indeed, someone had had wonderful sex in that bed recently. She stepped into the walk-in closet that served as a dressing room for her and pulled off the fleece pants and top, then pulled on a pair of beige-and-cream tweed slacks and a natural-colored cashmere turtleneck sweater. Cashmere socks and saddle brown ankle boots completed her outfit. She exited the closet and went into the bathroom, where she put on her lipstick, gave her short hair a final look, and, grabbing the elegant little shoulder bag from the top of her dresser, hurried back to the kitchen.

He looked up from buttering a blueberry muffin when he saw her. "I'm sorry," he said. "I should be dressed and ready to go myself, but damn, these muffins taste good."

"No problem," Nina said with a smile. "Take your time. Remember, we don't lock our doors here in Egret Pointe. When you go, just close it behind you."

"Do I need to move my car?" he asked.

"I walk to work on nice days," Nina told him.

"Dinner tonight?" he asked.

"I'd like that," she answered.

"You still want to be my girl?"

"Robert, I've been your girl from the first time I saw

you up there on the silver screen," Nina told him, and then she hurried out the door. She hoped she wasn't dancing as she walked down Maple Lane. She sure as hell felt like dancing. Dancing and singing. She had not been unhappy with her life. Sure, it was lonely sometimes being a widow, but after the initial shock of Charlie's death had worn off, she wasn't unhappy. And yet, suddenly she was filled with euphoria, and it felt as if she had actually been in a holding pattern these last years. She wasn't certain where this sudden relationship with Robert Talcott was going, but did she really need to know?

The builder had promised that Robert's house would be ready by Christmas. Robert had taken Nina's advice from their first dinner together to heart, and the architect had agreed. He had designed a long, low, single-story house with lots and lots of glass to take advantage of both the view and the sun. They had used a lot of green technology and kept the site as pristine as possible. There were solar panels across the roof to heat water and run most of the electric.

The floor plan was simple. A two-sided stone fireplace divided the living room from the dining room. The kitchen was galley style and very efficient. There were two bedrooms and two luxurious bathrooms. The master bedroom had a fireplace too. They had dug a cellar, and it was completely finished, with a storage room, a small exercise room, and a large, comfortable den. Nina had fallen more and more in love with the house as it was built and took shape.

"I can't wait to have sex with you in the bedroom," Robert told her one late November day. "Ryan is building a spectacular bed for me. I'm actually going to start living here this weekend. Trial run of all the systems to make certain nothing needs adjusting, or if it does to do it before all the furniture arrives." Then the blue eyes twinkled. "The workmen are gone for the day," he said, waggling his eyebrows at her.

"There's no bed," she reminded him.

Reaching out, he first pulled her into his arms, then put her back against a wall. "We could do it here," he murmured in her ear.

"*Here?*" her voice squeaked. She had heard that you could do it standing up, but Charlie, bless him, hadn't been an adventurous man.

"*Here,*" he repeated. He unzipped his fly and pulled out his already hard dick, then began pushing her skirt up. "I am so damned hot for you, woman! Just thinking about us here in this room gets me hard."

"You are one adventure after another," Nina told him, laughing softly.

"I've saved all those years of pent-up passions just for you, Nina Parsons," he said, and he pulled her panties down. Then his hand cupped her, and she sighed.

"I have to admit, Robert, I'm enjoying those pent-up passions," Nina said. Then she kissed him hungrily. Her clit was absolutely throbbing. "Do me," she whispered in his ear, the tip of her tongue licking at him.

Reaching around, he slipped his palms beneath her butt, and raised her up. She wrapped herself around him with both her legs and her arms, feeling him, now guiding his penis into her wet, welcoming vagina. The delicious sensation of the thick, sturdy length slowing plunging into her body was so incredible she came immediately, and he laughed.

"What a greedy, bad girl you are," he teased as he began to fuck her.

She clung to him, letting the erotic rhythm of his skilled cock lull her into a semiconscious state. "Don't stop!" she begged. "Don't stop! God! It is soo good, Robert!"

He laughed again, and began moving with increasing speed now. "I'm going to come!" he groaned. "Jesus, you feel so damned good!"

"Me too!" she gasped, and she felt the hard spasms as his come filled her.

They stood entwined until at last Nina's legs fell away from his torso, but she didn't dare loosen her embrace about his neck. She would collapse into a small puddle if she did. She just knew it. Finally she said, "Isn't it illegal for two people our age to be having such wild sex?"

"Is it? Arrest me, Officer," he teased her. His big hand cupped the back of her head. "Move in with me when this place is finished."

Nina was stunned by the invitation. *Yes! Yes!* the little voice in her brain shouted. "I'm not certain that's a good idea," she heard her practical self saying.

"Do you want to get married?" he asked candidly.

"I've been married. So have you. Marriage isn't the point here, Robert. We've only known each other a few months."

"Long enough to know we like each other. Long

enough to have incredible sex," he said. He was a little surprised by her refusal.

"Let's wait a little longer before making any changes to this relationship," Nina advised. "Can't we just remain best friends with benefits for a little while more?"

The cell in his pocket began to ring. "Bridge to Captain Kirk! Bridge to Captain Kirk!" Robert Talcott was a *Star Trek* fan. Automatically he pulled the phone from his pocket. His eyebrows lifted in surprise. "I have to take this," he said, "but this conversation isn't over, Nina." Putting the phone to his ear, he said, "Sallie! Long time." Then his face grew serious. "Slow down, Sallie. Stop crying. I can hardly understand a word you're saying. What? Damn, I'm so sorry, sweetie! Franklin? Is she going to be all right? What? No, I can't. I'm starting rehearsals in a couple of weeks. I'm building a house. No. What part of no don't you understand, Franklin?"

"What is it?" Nina whispered.

"Sallie's longtime lover just got killed in an accident. They want me to go out to the coast and make a show of sympathy with her," he said softly. "You know the kind of stuff they do. Ex-husband rushes to grieving star's side."

"Go!" Nina told him.

"I don't want to leave you until we settle this," Robert Talcott said. "I don't want to be that Lyon Roberts again."

"You won't. You aren't," she assured him. "Look, being widowed suddenly is a horrible thing to have happen. Granted, your marriage was hardly a conventional one, but you were married and together for a lot of years. Go to her. It will be good publicity for you too. The house will be finished, and I'll be waiting for you when you get back. Okay?"

"Promise?" The blue eyes looked anxiously at her.

"Promise," Nina said. "You can count on it!"

"Franklin, my fiancée says I should go, so I'll catch a flight tomorrow," he said. "Yeah, fiancée. Her name is Nina. I love her, and we're going to have a nice normal life together. No, it's not public knowledge yet. Tell Sallie I'll be there." He closed the phone shut.

"I'm not your fiancée," Nina said breathlessly.

"If you expect me to go to California to stand by the side of a grieving star ex-wife, then we are taking this relationship to the next level before I leave," Robert Talcott said.

"We'll deal with a ring when I get back, but I want to know you'll be here waiting for me. And while Egret Pointe might be shocked by the widow Parsons moving in with the semiretired movie star, they will hardly be shocked by my fiancée moving in with me. We can have the longest engagement in the history of mankind, Nina, but we are now engaged. Hell, I've told a Hollywood agent. You can't back out now."

"You are totally insane," she responded. "I'm not giving up my house, even if I do move in with you."

"You don't have to, brown eyes," he said, and then he pulled her close, kissing her very firmly. "Will you marry me, Nina Parsons?"

"Eventually," she agreed, "maybe. I don't want to make you a liar in front of a Hollywood agent," she said, and they laughed together.

He left the next morning for California, promising to be back in a few days' time. Nina couldn't help but check out the television gossip shows in the evening after work. Nancy Kramer, Sallie Blair's longtime assistant, had been killed driving home to Malibu when a tractor trailer had blown two tires and gone out of control, literally running over her small sports car, the gossip mavens reported. Ex-husband Lyon Roberts had flown to her side. There was film of Robert hurrying through LAX to a waiting limo.

And as the days followed, there was film of him escorting Sallie Blair, looking vulnerable, beautiful, and so damned young, into the church where the funeral was held, and then again out of the church. The paparazzi caught them at the cemetery, a weeping Sallie putting a rose on Nancy's coffin as it was about to be lowered into the grave. A week went by. Robert called to say he was going to remain a few days longer. Sallie's people feared she was suicidal, and he seemed to be the only one who could comfort her.

"I can't be certain if she's playing to the balcony or is really that upset," he told Nina. "God, I hate it here! And I miss you."

"Stay a little while longer," Nina advised. "I can't believe anyone would be that coldhearted. After all, she was with Nancy longer than she was with you. If you leave, and she attempts something foolish, you'll feel terrible."

"Thanks, brown eyes," he said. "I'll be back by Christmas. Rehearsals start in January, and I want some time with you before then."

Nina resorted to her Victorian fantasy after a few days. She had simply grown too used to regular loving to be without it. Her twenty-year-old alter ego had slipped away from her family one autumn afternoon to pay a visit to her fiancé, Lyon, in his bachelor's quarters in the town. "You promised me a treat if I would come," she said coyly as he took her cloak to set it aside. "What is it?"

Lyon smiled wickedly at her. "It's something I was introduced to in England, darling." He went to his desk and drew out what appeared to be a broad leather strap, the ends of which were cut into strips. "It's called a tawse, darling, and it is used to warm the bottoms of naughty little girls. Would you like to try it?"

"Will it hurt?" she asked, eyes wide.

"No more than a hard spank," he assured her, "and the sex that follows is quite delicious, I promise you."

"Oh, I don't know, Lyon," the young Nina demurred.

"Come, darling, take off your gown and petticoats. I want you in your corset and stockings," he wheedled her. "I'll tawse that wicked little bottom of yours, and then we will have a lovely fuck. You know you want to fuck."

She did. Slowly, with a pretense at reluctance, she disrobed until she stood only in her corset, her breasts swelling over its top, and her black stockings, which were held up by the corset's garters. Her mons was visible, as was her backside. "What do I do now, Lyon?" she asked him.

Taking her into his arms, he kissed her a slow, deep kiss, his tongue foraging with hers. Then he led her over to the small tapestried sofa with its high rolled arms. He bent her over one arm. Her toes were just barely touching the Oriental carpet. Then, to her surprise, he wrapped a silk cord about her wrists, fastening the end to a hook hidden beneath the sofa's cushions.

"Oh! Oh!" Nina cried out. "You have bound me. I have no escape from you."

He laughed. "Yes, I have tied you down, darling. It will but add to your excitement." He took off his quilted velvet smoking jacket, unbuttoned his shirt at the collar, and opened his fly to pull out his penis so it would be easily available when he was ready to fuck her. Picking up the leather tawse in one hand, he ran his other hand over her smooth plump posterior. Then a wicked light came into his eye.

Leaving her a moment, he went into his bedchamber, then returned with a small jar of lubricant. After swirling his middle finger about in the jar, he parted the cheeks of her buttocks with the thumb and forefinger of his other hand. "A little ass-fuck to begin, darling," he said as he slowly began to insert his thick finger into her fundament.

"Ohhhh!" Nina squealed. "That is too naughty! Take it out! Take it out!"

"You're being a bad girl, Nina," he scolded as he buried the finger to the knuckle. "You will take my finger, then later a dildo, and finally a cock there because it will please me, and as my fiancée, it is your duty to obey me." He frigged her for a few minutes to underscore his point.

"Oh, I hate you! I hate you!" she half sobbed.

He laughed. "Now, my darling," he said, finally withdrawing the finger, his hand smoothing over her rounded flesh, "you are deserving of a good tawsing for your impudent behavior in attempting to deny me my rights." He wiped the lubricant from his finger, then picked up the tawse and brought it down across her bottom.

Nina shrieked, although the truth was, it hadn't hurt

at all. It had just stung her flesh, and as he continued to rain blows on her ass, she began to feel a tingling in her nether regions that seemed to grow with every smack of the leather. "Ohh!" she cried. "Ohh!"

He ceased his punishment briefly to put his hand beneath her, cupping her mons, feeling the heat and dampness. "Another five good ones and you'll be more than ready to be fucked," he told her. His cock was already swollen and eager. He laid the required number of blows across the now hot pink flesh. Then, tossing the leather aside, he grasped her hips with his two hands and thrust into her. "Ahh, Nina, my love," he moaned. "This is so perfect."

"You are a horrible man!" she complained at him as her hips moved in time with his cock. "I hate you! I do! Oh, fuck me, Lyon. Fuck me deep and hard! Ohh, that is sooo good. Don't stop! Don't stop!" And he didn't until the Channel closed for the night. Her fantasy, however, wasn't enough anymore, now that she had come to know passion in the real world again. In the days to come, she punished her fantasy lover for that fault.

Robert wasn't back by Christmas. Instead, Nina began watching the gossip shows regularly. Rumor had it that Sallie Blair was suicidal. Rumor had it that ex-husband Lyon Roberts was staying at her Malibu home. Was a reconciliation possible after all these years? The television gossip reporters smiled into the camera knowingly. Wouldn't all be right with the world again if Hollywood's former perfect couple were reunited?

And when the paparazzi began taking pictures of Robert and Sallie Blair together out walking on the beach, relaxing in her hot tub, and having dinner in some cozy and intimate restaurant in Beverly Hills, Nina found herself beginning to wonder if maybe something was happening. And why not? Sure, he said that the marriage had been one of convenience and that Sallie was gay. But what if she was bisexual? And now, with the loss of her longtime companion and lover, she wanted Robert back?

When he'd called two days before Christmas to tell Nina that he wouldn't be back, her heart sank. "I can't leave her alone this particular Christmas," Robert Talcott said.

"I'm alone," she said softly. She was suddenly tired of being the noble one.

"Oh, brown eyes," he said to her, "don't make me feel any worse than I already do about this. I never liked Christmas in California. I was going to put a tree up in the living room, and we were going to decorate it while looking out at the bay. I wanted to shop for a hundred presents for you and put them all under that tree. I want to go to midnight mass at St. Anne's with you, then come back to the house to drink whiskeyed eggnog, and have wild monkey sex with you."

Nina sniffled. "How soon after Christmas can you get back?" she asked him.

"Sallie has asked me to remain until after New Year's," he said. "It will be a tough one for her."

"And will Valentine's Day be tough too? And the long Presidents' Day weekend, and St. Patrick's Day?" Nina said, suddenly angry. "You've got rehearsals starting at the end of January. Will she let you come back to New York to do the show? Or will she go into her mourning act again and have her people beg you to stay a bit longer? Do you know what I see every night on *Access Hollywood* and *Entertainment Tonight* and *The Insider*? Pictures of you and your ex-wife in one cozy situation or another, with the reporters all twittering that the rumors are that you'll remarry. Tell your ex-wife to suck it up like a big girl. Come home, Robert! And if Sallie Blair is going to kill herself over Nancy's death, then let her do it, and be done with it, damn it!" And Nina slammed down the phone angrily. Then she burst into tears.

She didn't sleep that night, and dragged herself into the shop the next morning.

Ashley was there before her. Christmas Eve was always a busy day, and she knew Nina could use the help. "You look like crap," Ashley said. "Are you all right? Are you coming down with something, Nina?"

"That beautiful bitch has got her claws back into Robert. He called last night to say she begged him to remain for Christmas. I can't be noble about this anymore. Sallie Blair doesn't give a rat's arse for Robert. She just doesn't want to be alone, and he's familiar. Every time he's ready to leave, it's something else. This role in the *Kismet* revival is tailor-made for him, Ashley. He starts rehearsals the end of January, but the way things are going he's never going, to be able to escape her clutches. What the hell is it about nice guys? He was supposed to go out to California a few weeks ago, support her in her sorrow, and then come home, not stay on and on and on."

"Good guys sometimes can't help themselves," Ashley

said. "But what's the matter with you that you're standing here taking all this crap?"

"What else can I do?" Nina wanted to know.

"You could go out to California and get your man back before she swallows him whole. You're not the only one who watches the entertainment shows. The town is buzzing about it. Haven't you noticed the looks you're getting?"

"Oh, my God!" Nina gasped. "I'm an object of pity now? The poor jilted shop assistant? How fast can I get to California?"

"Call Robert. Tell him you're coming to fetch him home. It's the only way you're going to get him back. He hasn't got any real feelings for Sallie Blair. He's just a stand-up guy, and he's being sandbagged."

"But it's Christmas. How am I going to get on a plane?"

Ashley smiled. "I'll take care of it. Now, you call Robert and tell him that you'll be there tomorrow, that Ryan will text him the details so he can meet you. Okay?"

"Okay," Nina said. "Thank you, Ashley. I never thought I'd be seriously interested in another man after Charlie died, but I am. I'm not even really interested in the Channel any longer."

"Ohh," Ashley said with a grin. "The sex is *that* good, huh?"

Nina nodded. "It is! Last night I was so mad after I hung up on Robert that I accessed the Channel, but instead of having my hero seduce me, I made him drop his trousers and whipped his butt raw. I made the poor thing cry. I was so surprised at what I had done that I exited the fantasy."

"Too much information," Ashley said, but she giggled.

Nina blushed. "Oh, God!" she said. "What a mess I am."

"By this time tomorrow, you'll be with Robert, and all will be forgiven," Ashley said, smiling. "Take Christmas week off. I'll see you after New Year's. We don't get a lot of returns or exchanges, and I will love getting out of the house. The kids are off the wall right now. It will be worse after Santa delivers. And you know how generous my mother-in-law is. She's coming today, and she loves having the kids to herself."

"You are the best damned boss," Nina said.

As expected, they had a very busy day. When it was over, Nina drove home to Maple Lane. The Mulcahys' driver, Bill, would pick her up at nine p.m. to drive her to the airport. To Nina's surprise, however, Bill did not take her into the big major airport that served New York City. He drove her to the small private airport about thirty miles from Egret Pointe.

"Mr. Mulcahy has rented a private Leerjet for you, Mrs. Parsons," Bill told her. "Mrs. M. says, 'Grab Mr. Talcott and fly right home.' The jet will be waiting for you. You should be able to escape the press people that way.

"There will be a car and driver waiting for you in L.A. It's yours until it brings you back to the airport. It's all taken care of for you. Mr. and Mrs. M. said to tell you it's your Christmas present."

"Some gift," Nina remarked. "Tell them I thank them." Nina was astounded, but then both Ryan and Ashley had individual fortunes, and they were generous.

When they reached the airport, Bill took her luggage

and escorted Nina through the small, elegant terminal to her plane. The steward hurried down the steps from the plane to take her small bag. As she had no intention of remaining in California any longer than it took to extricate Robert from his ex-wife's clutches, she hadn't packed anything but the essentials.

"I'll be waiting when you and Mr. Talcott get back," Bill said. "Have a good trip, Mrs. Parsons." Then he left her.

Nina lowered herself into a luxurious, soft leather seat. The plane taxied down the runway and took off into the winter night. The cabin was gorgeous. Thick carpeting. Comfortable swivel chairs. She could get used to this, Nina thought, grinning. She was on her way to California to take her man back from one of Hollywood's most beautiful and talented actresses. Nina Parsons. Fiftysomething shop manager. She had to be crazy or in love. Maybe a little of both, Nina decided.

"Mrs. Parsons, I've made up a bed for you"—the steward was at her elbow—"and I've laid out some essentials in the lavatory for you. I understand you've had a long day, and I expect you're tired."

"Why, thank you...." She cocked her head to one side.

"Joseph," he responded with a smile.

"Thank you, Joseph. You're right. I could use some sleep," Nina agreed.

"We get into L.A. after midnight. Since this is your private jet, I imagine you'll want to sleep here until morning. Where are you headed from the airport?"

"Malibu," she told him. "I want to be there in time for breakfast."

"I'll wake you in plenty of time, then, and see your car is waiting, Mrs. Parsons," Joseph said. Then he disappeared.

Nina got up and went down the aisle of the plane. Right behind the wing window, she saw the bed all nicely made up with a silk sheet, pillowcase, and down comforter. She went into the lavatory, which was larger than on a commercial plane, and undressed. Then she put on her nightgown, which had been laid out for her. She washed and creamed her face, and brushed her teeth. Then she exited the bathroom and got into the bed, certain she wouldn't sleep despite the luxurious comfort.

"Mrs. Parsons." Joseph was gently shaking her shoulder. "Mrs. Parsons, it's just after six a.m. western time. If you're ready to get up, I'll get you some coffee and juice."

"Ummm, yes, please," Nina murmured, opening her eyes. Turning, she looked out the portal by the bed. They were on the ground. The sky was very blue, and the sun was slowly coming up. Nina got up, washed, and dressed. She switched the wool slacks she had worn last night for a pair of cream silk slacks and a deep green silk shirt, along with a pair of elegant leather sandals. "Will I be warm enough?" she asked the steward when he brought her the juice and coffee.

"You should be fine, Mrs. Parsons. Merry Christmas!"

"Oh, my goodness, it is Christmas morning, isn't it?"

"Yes, ma'am, it is. The pilot would like to know if you know how long you'll be gone. He'll get the plane gassed up and ready for the return."

"I will be gone as long as it takes me to get out to

Malibu, fetch Mr. Talcott, and drive back," Nina said in such a firm and certain tone that Joseph didn't question her.

"A couple of hours, then," he said. "It's about twenty miles to Malibu from this airport. We'll be ready to go by noon for you, okay?"

"Perfect," Nina agreed. "If we get here earlier, we can leave earlier." She drank the small orange juice. It was fresh squeezed. She asked him to put the coffee in a travel mug. After debarking, Nina walked to the waiting Town Car. "You know where you're going?" she asked the driver.

"Yes, ma'am," the chauffeur said.

"Good, 'cause I sure as hell don't." She fastened her seat belt and sat back. Soon they were driving along the Pacific Coast Highway. Reality began to set in, and Nina asked herself just what the hell had ever gotten her to agree to come to California and take Robert back with her to Egret Pointe. What if he wouldn't go? What if he wanted to stay with Sallie Blair? She sipped the coffee and was surprised to find it was a sweet cappuccino. Geez, being rich certainly had its perks. The car began to slow down. Nina swallowed hard. Her armpits felt damp. She hoped they didn't stink too. What was she going to say? Oh, God! She sipped the cappuccino slowly, then, realizing she would have coffee breath, put it down and scrambled in her clutch for some mints. She chewed furiously as the car swung into a narrow, short driveway lined with greenery.

Her vehicle stopped. The driver jumped out and came around to open the door. "I'm supposed to wait," he said as he helped her out.

Nina nodded silently. There was no going back now,

and she hadn't come all this way to wimp out now. Taking a deep breath, she strode to the heavy wood door of the house, raised the horseshoe-shaped knocker, and pounded on the portal. There was no answer. Nina banged on the door again and then suddenly it swung open.

"Who the hell are you?" Sallie Blair demanded. "Why are you banging on my door on Christmas morning?"

"I've come for Robert," Nina said. Damn! The actress was really gorgeous.

"Who? There's no Robert here."

"Robert Talcott," Nina insisted.

"I'm telling you there is no Robert Talcott here," Sallie Blair said.

"You were married to him for twenty-three years and you don't know his real name?" Nina was astounded. "Lyon Roberts." She was angry now. This selfish woman was horrible. "I've come for Lyon Roberts, then." She pushed past the petite actress and into the house. "Robert! Robert! Where the hell are you?"

"I'm calling the police," Sallie Blair said. "You're crazy."

"Call them!" Nina dared her. "Robert, damn it! Answer me! I haven't flown all the way to California for nothing. You'd better get that cute butt of yours out here right now, or I'm going room to room to find you."

He came into the tiled hallway, and he was laughing. "You are one helluva woman, Nina Parsons! You actually flew out here to get me?"

"Yep," Nina said, walking straight up into his now outstretched arms, and letting him kiss her very thoroughly. When they broke off the embrace, she told him,

"Get your things, Robert. The Mulcahys got me a plane, and it's waiting to take us home."

"Lyon! Who is this woman? What does she mean take you home? We have parties all week." Sallie Blair suddenly looked frail and vulnerable.

God, Nina thought, *she is good.* "I'm Robert's fiancée, Ms. Blair. While you have my deepest sympathies on your loss, you cannot have my man."

"He was mine first." Sallie Blair's voice quavered with what appeared to be genuine emotions. She appeared ready to collapse.

"He was *your beard,* Ms. Blair. You let him go because you didn't need him anymore. And he has a life back east. On Broadway. In Egret Pointe with me," Nina said, not in the least impressed by the other woman's attempts at keeping Robert with her.

"*Lyon!* If you leave me I'll kill myself!" Sallie Blair cried dramatically. She stumbled into the large open living room, which faced the ocean, and flung herself onto a couch. Her hand clutched at her heart. "I can't bear any more hurt and sorrow!"

"Get over yourself!" Nina said sharply. "Robert may be fooled by your histrionics because he's a sweet, caring guy with a conscience, but you're dealing with me now." She turned to the man in question. "Go pack," she said. "Ms. Blair and I are going to have a little talk. Then you and I are heading home."

For some reason, Nina's tough, sensible attitude was getting through to him. Robert Talcott suddenly realized that his ex-wife had been taking advantage of him. He missed Egret Pointe, and he sure as hell missed Nina. He felt like a first-class fool. "I won't be long," he said to Nina.

"*Lyon!* Lyon was a star. I could make him one again!" Sallie Blair half rose, and then fell back on the couch, eyes closed.

"You're good," Nina said with a soft laugh.

The actress's eyes snapped open, and she sat up. "I'm amazed a woman *your* age could attract a man like Lyon," she said nastily. "He's always preferred younger women. I don't think I've ever known him to show interest in an older woman."

"The sex is incredible," Nina said wickedly.

Sallie Blair's mouth dropped open with surprise.

"Now, listen to me," Nina began. "You don't want Robert. You just don't want to be alone, and you want someone familiar around you. I understand. I've been widowed for a number of years. Robert coming into my life was a miracle. Do you have cable or satellite? Tomorrow I want you to call your provider. Tell them you want the Channel. You will not be alone if you do."

"What are you talking about?" Sallie Blair wanted to know.

"The Channel is a secret, Ms. Blair. It's for women only. Any fantasy you want, you can have with the Channel. Men don't know about it because if they did, they would either take it from us or want it for themselves. Certainly you've heard of the Channel Corporation. I believe they own both your studio and the agency that represents you. I want you to trust me on this one. I'm not your enemy. I just want my man back. You wish you could have your Nancy back. Well, you can in the Channel."

"How do you program a fantasy?" Sallie Blair asked, curious in spite of herself.

"Just think about what it is you want the first time you access the Channel, and it becomes reality. You can program two fantasies in your remote with the A and B buttons. Women all over the world use the Channel. As I said, trust me on this one, because I'm taking Robert out of here as soon as he's packed. I'm tired of having to listen to all the rumors about you two getting back together again that your flacks are putting out to keep your name in the headlines. Order the Channel tomorrow, and you won't regret it. If I've lied, you can put a hit out on me, okay?"

Robert Talcott came back into the living room with his suitcase. "I'm ready," he said. "Let's go home, brown eyes." The look he gave her was filled with pure love.

Nina smiled. "Merry Christmas, Ms. Blair," she said, noting even as she said it that there wasn't a speck of holiday decor anywhere in view in the house.

"Lyon, please, I need you," Sallie Blair made a final attempt.

"No, you really don't, Sal," Robert Talcott said. "Go to Aspen for the rest of the holiday. Don't you have a picture beginning to shoot soon?"

Sallie Blair sighed. "You love her, don't you?" she said.

"Yep, I do," Robert Talcott admitted. "It's my turn now, Sal." He put his arm about Nina. "Let's go home, brown eyes. Do we have snow yet?"

Sallie Blair watched them go, thinking as she did, *Now who can I call?*

They walked out to the car. The driver put Robert's

bag in the trunk. Inside the black leather interior of the car, Nina snuggled next to her man. She had done it! She had stolen him back from Sallie Blair! If she had her way, neither of them would ever see the actress again, except maybe on the silver screen. "We should be home before Christmas Day ends," she said to him. "I've got a present for you."

"Do I have to wait until we get to Egret Pointe to get my present?" he asked mischievously. "I kinda thought we could exchange gifts all the way across the country, brown eyes." Then he kissed her long and deep.

Nina's head spun riotously. She broke away from him, laughing. "We have an onboard attendant named Joseph," she told him.

"Well, then," Robert Talcott said, "I'm sure when he realizes the situation, he'll find himself a discreet place to nap for a couple of hours."

"Are you suggesting we initiate each other into the Mile-High Club, Robert?" Nina asked innocently, eyes wide.

"Why, my darling, that is just what I've been thinking," he said.

"It's a long trip home," she said, smiling as she caressed his cheek.

"We've been apart for several very long weeks," he countered.

Nina smiled. "Merry Christmas, Robert Talcott," she said, kissing him.

"Merry Christmas, brown eyes," he told her. "Thank you for coming and rescuing me from the dragon lady."

"You are such a sweet dope. Just like the parts you

used to play. But I'm going to make sure no one ever takes advantage of you again. Except me, of course," Nina said.

"I'm glad I found you, brown eyes."

They arrived home to find it had already snowed in the hours since Nina had left Egret Pointe. But it had cleared, and as the car sped through the night, they sat silently admiring the moon that was lighting up the night and making the snow sparkle.

"What a perfect ending to a perfect day," Robert finally said.

"Just like in the movies," Nina agreed.

"In that case we had better fade to black, brown eyes," he remarked. And then he kissed her a kiss that told her without question that this time the hero's best friend had gotten the girl, and they were going to live happily ever after.

NANNY MAUREEN AND THE CELTIC WARRIOR

E milie Shann, aka Emily Shanski Devlin, Egret Pointe's bestselling romance novelist, delivered her first child—a boy, Sean Michael—fourteen months after her marriage to her editor, Michael Devlin. She delivered a daughter, Emlyn Kathleen, in the early winter of 2010. But then she and Michael had what they later referred to as a "whoops moment" to celebrate her hitting the number-one spot simultaneously on the hardcover, trade, and mass-market lists of both the *New York Times* and *Publishers Weekly*. It was a very big whoops, and Emily delivered twin boys, Liam Joseph and Dermid Aaron, on the last day of February 2011.

Looking after Sean and Emlyn had been no problem, even though she was working. She fit her schedule around them. She could go up to her studio tower and write a couple of hours a day while Essie, her longtime housekeeper, kept an ear open and an eye out for Emily. She worked when her kids napped. She worked at night. It was a matter of honor with Emilie Shann that her manuscripts got in on time. She was proud to have never missed a due date, and her husband relied on that.

She had had it all. A handsome husband. A great career. Children she cared well for, but then the twins were born. It took Emily less than a week to admit that she wasn't a superwoman, and nobody really could have it all. "Gah!" she groaned, joining Mick in their bedroom one evening. Toddlers Sean and Emlyn were already asleep in their rooms. She had just finished nursing Liam and Dermid. "We need a nanny!"

"I know," he replied in that sexy Irish lilt of his.

"You know? Damn it, Devlin, you can be so annoying sometimes."

"You're not a housewife, Em," he continued in that same calm tone. "You're a successful working writer. If you want to retire, I'm behind you, but if you want to keep working, yes, we need a nanny. There's a small nanny school near Dublin. I'd like to look there first."

"We can't go to Ireland," Emily said.

"Ever hear of teleconferencing, my love?" He ducked the blow she aimed at him.

"I've got a month before I have to go back to work," Emily said. "Let's do it!"

"I'll set it up," he promised her.

Two days later Michael Devlin and his wife spoke with the head of the Ballyglen Nanny College at six a.m., which was eleven a.m. in Ireland. Mick had spoken on the phone with Mrs. O'Hara the day before, stating their requirements and setting up this morning's teleconference.

"I have two young women for you to interview, Mr. and Mrs. Devlin," Mrs. O'Hara said. Then she peered at them. "Oh, is that one of your twins?"

Emily had been nursing. "Liam Joseph," she told the woman with a smile.

"Ah, now isn't that just a lovely"—it sounded like *loovily*—"name. And the other?"

"Dermid Aaron," Emily replied.

"Mr. Devlin tells me they are the youngest. You have two toddlers."

"Yes, Sean Michael and Emlyn Kathleen. Sean is four, in nursery school, and Emlyn is just a year, but walking," Emily said.

"And there'll be more, of course," Mrs. O'Hara said without waiting for an answer. "Well, then, you'll want to interview the girls. I'll send them in one at a time." She pressed a button on her desk, then got up and disappeared from their view. "Come in, Brigid. Sit down in my chair so Mr. and Mrs. Devlin can interview you."

A tall, thin girl came into view. It was obvious she was very nervous. They asked their questions, then thanked her for her time. She gave them a faint smile and thanked them for the interview. It was obvious she wasn't enthusiastic.

Their second prospect was a tall, healthy-looking girl with ruddy cheeks, bright green eyes, and a thick head of dark reddish brown hair. "My name is Maureen Flynn," she said briskly. "I'm twenty-four years old and in good health."

"Do you mind living in the States, Maureen?" Michael Devlin inquired.

"Mind? I'm excited about it. I hope you haven't decided on Brigid. She doesn't want to leave Ireland, but if you offer her the job, Mrs. O'Hara says she has to take it."

Emily laughed. She already liked this girl. "Do you believe in discipline and structure, Maureen, and what kind of discipline?"

"I certainly do believe in it, Mrs. Devlin," Maureen answered. "I prefer the time-out, no-dessert method for the wee ones, removal of privileges for the older ones. Children have to learn where their boundaries are if they're going to be good adults."

"We live in a small town, Maureen," Michael Devlin said. "Will you mind that it's not the exciting big city? You will have a day and a half off each week."

"I can go into the city then if I want," Maureen answered him.

"Have you ever looked after a child and lived in before?" Emily inquired.

"No, Mrs. Devlin, I haven't. This will be my first real job."

"There are four children, three still in diapers, or nappies, as you call them," Emily said. "It's a big job. Do you really think you're up to it?"

"Sure, and I'm the eldest girl of thirteen, Mrs. Devlin. I've been changing nappies since I was two," Maureen Flynn said pertly.

Her husband was grinning. "We're going to put you on mute for a moment, Maureen," he said and pressed the button. Then he turned to Emily. "I think she's perfect. She's a big girl with experience who can handle them all, and she's got common sense. Emlyn will take to her, and so will Sean. Liam and Dermid will know her all their lives, Em. And she's not too starchy. What do you think?"

"I like her," Emily responded to her husband's query. "God, changing diapers since she was two. Poor kid! That must have been some childhood. Living with us will be a vacation, I suspect."

"It was an Irish Catholic childhood," he said. "Then we're agreed. We hire Nanny Maureen?" And when Emily nodded, he unmuted the speaker. "Maureen, we would like to offer you the job," he told her. "Will you take it?"

"I'd like to go over all the particulars with Mrs. Devlin first, if you don't mind, sir," the young Irish woman said. "Just the two of us."

He was intrigued, but he stood up. "Of course," he replied. "I'll look forward to meeting you in person, Maureen Flynn." Then Mick Devlin left his wife to continue the conversation with the nanny.

"Your salary will be a thousand dollars a week to start, minus Social Security and your unemployment insurance," Emily began. "You'll have a health insurance policy, and I'll expect a letter from your doctor in Ireland attesting to your good health. I'll give Mrs. O'Hara my fax, phone, and cell phone numbers for you. You'll want Sundays off, I'm sure, and you can have a half day too each week. It doesn't have to be the same day each week if you don't want it to be, but I don't want to be notified at the last minute. You'll have your own bedroom with a television, a large closet, and a full bathroom. You can wear your own clothing, but I do expect respectable attire. Any questions so far?"

"Would you be getting the Channel?" Maureen Flynn looked straight at Emily.

"They have it in Ireland?" Then Emily laughed. "Of course they do. But you can't use it every night, Maureen."

The girl nodded. "Just enough to keep me on the

straight and narrow like a good Catholic lass looking for a good Catholic husband should be."

"I understand," Emily said. "When can you come?"

"I'd like two weeks to say good-bye to my family and friends, and to shop," the girl said. "Oh, one other thing, Mrs. Devlin. Would you be including a signed copy of your book each year in my employment package? I'm a great fan, and especially since you started getting sexier. *The Defiant Duchess* was just wonderful, but I think I really liked *The Wicked Earl's Bride* even better."

Emily laughed. "I was going to ask if you knew what I did. Here in Egret Pointe everyone knows me and my family. You'll get to know everyone quickly, but I do prefer my privacy from strangers, and you'll have to keep people of that sort away from the kids, Maureen. I do work at home, so I'll be there if you need me. And I have a housekeeper."

"We take a course in protecting the children of celebrities," Maureen responded.

"Good. Okay, then, you're hired if we meet with your approval. Mrs. O'Hara will be sent your tickets. Oh, and we're paying her fee. You won't owe her anything."

Maureen Flynn's face registered surprise. "Oh, Mrs. Devlin, that is so good of you," she said. "I certainly didn't expect it."

"I want you to be starting fresh, Maureen. New country. New job. New adventures," Emily replied. "See you in two weeks, then!" She disconnected.

For a long moment Maureen sat in Mrs. O'Hara's desk chair. Then the old harridan came back into her office.

"Well?" she said. "I know they were disappointed in Brigid, but did they hire you, Maureen Flynn?"

Maureen nodded wordlessly.

"You're a lucky girl, then," Mrs. O'Hara said. "When are you to go?"

"I have two weeks to say my good-byes and settle my affairs here in Ireland," Maureen said. "I'll go home, and then come back here. Mrs. Devlin says they'll be sending my tickets to you. *And* they're paying my fee to you! You'll have it all in your pocket in one lump sum, and not be waiting for my money orders every month."

"We're both lucky, then," Mrs. O'Hara said. "Oh, by the way, you've passed all your exams. You and Brigid were at the top of your class, which is why I picked you both to interview. I could tell Brigid didn't make a good impression. They spent little time with her. What's the matter with the girl?"

"I don't think she wants to leave Ireland," Maureen said honestly. "You should ask her about it, Mrs. O'Hara."

"More the fool," the older woman replied. "Working for a bestselling American novelist is a plum assignment. What are the arrangements you made?"

"A thousand each week to begin," Maureen said, and then went on to explain the terms of her employment. She did not mention the Channel.

Mrs. O'Hara nodded approvingly. "They're generous," she noted, "but then there are four children. But, Maureen, if you find you suit, you'll have employment for the next several years, and in this economy, that's nothing to sniff about."

. . .

Maureen Flynn went home to her small village in County Monaghan, bringing her widowed mother a little cell phone. "I'll be calling you every Sunday, Mum," she promised. Her twelve siblings all gathered to see her off to America. She had four older brothers, five younger ones, and three younger sisters. Seamus, the oldest at thirty, was a priest. Her twenty-two-year-old sister, Mary, was in a local convent aspiring to be a nun. Twenty-year-old Bridget was married, with one child and another on the way. The remainder of her siblings—the youngest of whom was thirteen-year-old Rory—were still at home. The family farmed several acres, raising sheep and cattle, along with the grain needed to feed them. Her father had died just two years prior.

"This place has a church for you, I'm hoping," Father Seamus said.

"St. Anne's. Father Porter is the priest in charge. I Googled Egret Pointe."

Her eldest brother nodded. "Good! Good!" he said.

"You'll not forget the holy days," her sister Mary said piously.

"I'll get to church on Sundays," Maureen replied, and her sister shook her head.

"These people you're to work for," her mother said. "They're decent Catholics?"

"Surprisingly, yes," Maureen responded. "Mr. Devlin is from Ireland, born and raised here by his grandmother. I Googled him too. He and his wife are most respectable, Mum. His wife works, which is why they need a nanny."

"She'd do better to remain home and look after her children," Mrs. Flynn noted.

"She works from home, Mum. She's a writer. Writes novels," Maureen said. "Her name is Emilie Shann."

"Oh! My! God! Sorry, Mum," sixteen-year-old Maeve exclaimed as her mother shot her a fierce look. "I just *love* her books. This is so exciting! You're working for my favorite author, Mo! You have to write me all about her! Oh, I wish I had a cell phone!"

"Indeed, and who would be paying for such a frivolous thing, my girl?" her mother said sharply. "Where do you get books that aren't schoolbooks to read?"

"From the library van, Mum. Bridget reads her too. Don't you, Bridget?"

"It's nice you have the time to read with your house, your husband, and your children to look after," Mrs. Flynn said scathingly.

God, Maureen thought. Her mother was such a hard woman. "Give over, Mum." She attempted to defuse the situation by teasing. "Bridget only has one and a half children right now, so of course she has time to read."

Her brothers guffawed. Mary giggled. Bridget and Flora smiled.

"A big family is a blessing," Mrs. Flynn said. "With your brothers here to manage the farm, and Maeve still in school, at least I'm not alone."

"She thinks when I finish school I'm going to stay home and look after her," Maeve told Maureen later, when they were alone. "But I'm not! I want to go to university and study to be a teacher. Let one of the boys marry and bring his wife into the house to care for her. I'm going to make something of myself like you, Mo."

"I'll help you," Maureen promised her youngest sister.

She stayed a week with her family, and then went into Dublin to shop for a few bits of clothing to round out her small wardrobe. Back at Ballyglen Nanny College, Mrs. O'Hara had a large packet for her, but to give the woman credit, she hadn't opened it. However, she insisted it be opened in her office. Maureen complied. Inside the FedEx envelope she found tickets on Aer Lingus, an envelope with five hundred American dollars in it, and a note from her employer saying that it was a signing bonus.

"Very, very generous," Mrs. O'Hara murmured, impressed. "Let me see your tickets." She took them, looked, and gasped. "Glory be to God, Maureen Flynn! These are first-class tickets! You'll be traveling like some swell, and not a plain Irish nanny. I can only hope that you won't get spoiled with all this fine treatment."

"No, Mrs. O'Hara," Maureen said dutifully. She had never flown, but her brother the priest had, and had complained of being packed in like a sardine. A first-class ticket was obviously not sardine class. Secretly she was thrilled. No one in all her life had ever spoiled Maureen Flynn.

The rest of the packet contained a working visa from the U.S. Immigration Service, and a note from Michael Devlin saying that he would pick Maureen up at the airport and drive her home to Egret Pointe. He would be just outside of Customs waiting for her when she came through. A photograph was enclosed with a Post-it note that read, "This is what Mrs. Devlin and I look like."

"Now that was nice," Mrs. O'Hara noted, "and quite practical. You'll not be stolen away by some criminal element." Then, opening her desk drawer, she pulled out a passport and handed it to Maureen. "This is yours. Re-member, I had all the girls in your form get one when you first came to Ballyglen so you would be ready to go when you obtained a job offer."

"I'm glad," Maureen said.

A week later a livery car arrived at the nanny college to take Maureen down to Shannon Airport. She climbed into it and sat back, giving Mrs. O'Hara a farewell wave as the car pulled away.

At Shannon a representative from Aer Lingus came to escort Maureen on board her flight. Maureen pretended that this sort of thing happened all the time to her. When she was seated in her window seat, the stewardess in-formed her that the flight would take off right on time. "I've never flown before," Maureen admitted to the pretty redhead.

The stewardess chuckled. "Well, first-class is certainly a good introduction for you," she said. "What's bringing you to the U.S. of A., Miss Flynn?"

"I've got a job," Maureen said.

"Computer company?" The stewardess was curious. Usually it was the big important companies who flew new and valued employees in first-class.

"No," Maureen said, and she was beginning to see the humor in her situation. "I'm a nanny. I'm going to be working for Emilie Shann, the novelist."

"Wow! She's giving you really special treatment. She and that hot husband of hers have flown with us a couple of times. They're really nice. Well, good for you, Nanny

Flynn," the stewardess said and chuckled. Then she became all business. "Better get your safety belt fastened. We're going to be taking off shortly, and so you don't worry, the flight is expected to be smooth as silk the whole way."

The stewardess didn't lie. After a small whiskey, Maureen put her seat back and slept almost the entire way. A steward wakened her in time to have a bit of a snack, and she visited the lavatory for a quick wash and to brush and straighten her hair before they landed. As she exited the plane, the red-haired stewardess was waiting for her.

"Good luck!" she said with a smile and a friendly wave.

"Thanks," Maureen said.

They checked her bags and her papers at Customs before finally waving her through. And there was Michael Devlin waiting for her, as he had promised.

"Welcome to the States, Maureen Flynn," he greeted her.

"Thank you, sir," she replied a bit shyly.

He put her baggage on a cart and led her through the terminal to the short-term parking lot, where he unloaded her possessions into a Chrysler Caravan. "I work in the city three days a week and telecommute from home the other two days," he explained. He helped her into the car. "It's about an hour-and-a-half to two-hour drive," he said. "Take a look at the skyline as we skirt the city." Then he got behind the wheel.

Maureen had never seen such big roads as the ones leading from the airport. The traffic was fast and furious. They traversed a large bridge and continued onto another large highway. Maureen couldn't stop looking. The city looked magical with its tall towers. It almost sparkled on what was a beautiful late-spring day. And then suddenly the metropolis was gone, and the highway was edged in trees. Some of them were already flowering. Tall, symmetrical, fluffy white trees.

She couldn't stop looking. It was so different from Ireland. It was as if she had been put down on another planet. Her employer spoke little, but she hadn't expected a lot of conversation. He was an Irishman, and it had been her experience that men didn't really do a lot of talking unless they had a strong opinion to express. The great highway became a smaller parkway. After a while Michael Devlin swung the car off it, and they traveled down a country road into a charming village.

"Welcome to Egret Pointe," he said. "We're almost home."

"It's lovely," Maureen said. "Can I walk to the village with the children?"

"We live in the village," he said, turning from Main Street onto Colonial Avenue, and then onto Founders Path. "It's the house at the end," Michael Devlin said. "The style is called American Empire."

"It's a big house, it is," Maureen said. "I come from a farmhouse in Monaghan."

He pulled into the driveway and gave one honk. "Ah," he said, "here's my missus and the two older ones."

Emily welcomed the nanny warmly. Sean and Emlyn hung back shyly, but stooping down, Maureen quickly coaxed them from their mother's side. "How do you do, Master Sean and Miss Emlyn?" she said.

"Mama says you're our nanny," Sean spoke up. "What's a nanny?"

"Well," Maureen said, "it can be a goat, but I'm not a goat, am I?"

The two children giggled.

"Another kind of nanny is the lady who takes care of you so your mama can write her wonderful stories," Maureen continued. "I'm that kind of nanny, and I've come all the way from Ireland to look after you, your sister, and your twin brothers. I hope we're going to be friends. I have lots of brothers back in Ireland, so I know a lot about little boys and what they like."

"Do you like trucks?" Sean wanted to know.

"Yes, I do," Maureen said, and she stood up.

Sean grabbed her hand. "Come on, then, Nanny, and let me show you my trucks. I have lots of trucks."

"A moment, Sean Michael," his father said. "Nanny Maureen has had a very long trip to come to us. I think we should show her to her room first and let her unpack. Plenty of time for your trucks."

"Yes, Dad," the little boy said obediently.

Maureen was impressed. She had heard that American children were a bit overindulged and spoiled, yet the child had immediately obeyed his father.

"I'm so glad you're here," Emily said. "Now I can get back to work!"

Maureen settled into the Devlin household, and over the next few days, she established a nursery routine. The children now had their dinner in the middle of the day, which allowed their parents some time alone at night. Essie, the Devlin housekeeper, was very helpful and full of useful information. Maureen soon met Rina Seligmann, who was the wife of the town's doctor and Emily's friend and pseudo-maternal figure. She began to learn the history of Egret Pointe. She would put Emlyn and the twins down for their nap and take Sean to nursery school three afternoons a week. She had decided on her half day.

"Unless you need me, I'll be taking Saturday afternoons off along with my Sundays," she told Emily. "But if you have a Saturday event, I can change that."

Emily had agreed it was a perfect solution.

Maureen hadn't availed herself of the Channel since she had arrived. Her trip had been tiring, and getting established in a new routine had left her wanting nothing more than a good night's sleep. On her second half Saturday off, she had gone to five o'clock mass at St. Anne's. On her first Sunday, when she had gone with the Devlins, Father Porter had informed Maureen that he had received an e-mail from her brother Seamus.

"Father Flynn asked me to keep an eye on you," the priest said.

"Seamus worries too much, but I suspect it was our mum who put him up to it," Maureen replied with a smile.

Father Porter chuckled, nodding in agreement. "You're settling in, then?"

"I am," Maureen answered him. "They're a fine family, and the children are just little dears. I suspect I'm very fortunate to have found such good employers."

"You are. You are," the priest agreed.

This Saturday, as she hurried from St. Anne's, Maureen could think of nothing but the visit she was going to make to the Channel tonight. She had found the remote for it tucked discreetly into the drawer of her bedside table, its A and B buttons almost beckoning her with their newness. Maureen had only one fantasy. Maybe she would eventually program a second, but tonight she needed to be ravaged by her Celtic warrior.

It seemed like forever since she had known his company, and the Channel itself had been a revelation to her. Her friend Brigid had told her all about it. Brigid came from Dublin. Almost everyone at Ballyglen Nanny College had had a subscription to it for their personal televisions. If you didn't bring a telly to school, you had no access to the Channel. Despite her less than generous financial circumstances, Maureen had managed to find the money to purchase a small set from a girl who was leaving Ballyglen.

She hadn't really believed what Brigid had said about the Channel, but she did think it would be nice to have a telly to watch when she had the time. She had gotten a student discount from the cable company, even though she had taken their most basic package, adding only one premium offering, the Channel. The first night she had tried the Channel, it had both scared the wits out of her and hooked her.

Maureen had treated herself to supper at the Egret Pointe Luncheonette before returning home to bathe and get into her bed. Taking the remote in her hand, she pointed it at the television across the room. She drew a deep breath and pressed the A button. Immediately she was in a field of white oxeye daisies. It was high summer, and a warm breeze blew across the land. Nearby was her small village of Ennis. A village of the elderly, women, and a few children.

It had never been a large settlement. The men who had fathered the few children were usually passing strangers, for the village men had either been lost at sea or had gone to fight and never come back. Still, they managed, and each Beltane sent the village elders to the Great Gathering with several young women to barter off into marriage. There were always eager chieftains ready to bargain generously for a bride from Ennis for themselves or their sons. The lasses from Ennis were known to be exceptionally skilled in bedsport and extremely fertile.

As Maureen sat in the warm sun among the daisies she thought she heard a scream, and at first she put it down to the screeching raven hovering above her. But then the raven swooped down to perch upon her shoulder. Startled, she made to shoo it away, but she stopped when the raven spoke to her. The bird was magic, and magic was to be respected.

Run! the bird's creaky voice hissed in her ear. *Warriors have invaded your village. They mean to enslave your people!* Then the bird flew off.

Maureen jumped up, and as she did, she heard the screaming from the village.

She saw several of her friends running into the meadow pursued by tall Celtic warriors. One by one the girls were caught and brought to the ground. Shocked, she watched, unable to move, as the men pulled their manparts from their leather leggings and fell upon the captive maidens. She heard their shrieks of outrage, which gradually turned to moans of distinct pleasure.

"Here's one little bird not yet caught," a deep male voice next to her said.

Maureen jumped, startled, then turned to run, but it was too late. A large hand reached out, grasping the neck of her gown to prevent her flight. She squirmed, trying to free herself. "Let me go! Let me go!"

His laughter rumbled like thunder across the meadow. "Oh, no, little bird," he said. "You are my possession now and belong to me." He turned her about so he might look more closely at her, smiling because he obviously liked what he saw.

"I am not little!" Maureen told him, still struggling to escape that iron grip. "I am the tallest girl in the village." And at six feet in height, she was.

"You're little to me," the warrior replied. As he was six feet six inches tall, she did appear little to him. "Now stop wiggling, lass. You're caught and you'll stay caught. My men and I have come to Ennis with a purpose, and we'll not relinquish it."

"What purpose?" Maureen stopped writhing. She was curious, and the man didn't seem to have murderous intentions.

"We're warriors, but it is time for us to find a home, defend it, and sire children so our names and our blood may be perpetuated," he replied as, pulling her close, he fondled her big breasts. "Ahh, you have fine tits," he said and sighed. But catching himself, he said, "Ennis is known for its dearth of men but for the elderly. We've come for wives, and a permanent place to lay our heads."

He was very handsome, Maureen thought, looking up into his face. Blue eyes that rivaled the sky itself, and long black hair pulled back into a horse tail. "Do you have a name?" she asked him tartly. She was no longer afraid. His explanation of why he and his companions had come was reasonable, and frankly, she was tired of waiting to be chosen to go to the Great Gathering at Beltane. It was unlikely she ever would be taken because of her great height, but the warrior didn't seem to mind that she was tall.

"I am called Toryn of the Thousand Pleasures," he responded. Then, kicking her legs from beneath her, he brought her to the ground.

Maureen gasped as the wind was knocked out of her, rendering her helpless. She realized she was about to suffer the same fate as her friends and be claimed by this stranger. Her eyes grew wide as he drew his manpart out and massaged it to its full potential. She supposed she should at least attempt to escape him one more time, but she was mesmerized by the sight of his penis as he swelled and lengthened. Too late! He fell to his knees, holding the great beast.

"Are you a virgin?" he asked.

"Why?" Maureen wanted to know.

"It makes a difference in how I will take you this first time," Toryn of the Thousand Pleasures said. "I am not a barbarian to ravage you unthinking."

"I've never known a man," Maureen told him, "but our maidenheads are removed by the village healer when we reach our twelfth year so our husbands may enjoy us from the beginning. You're huge! You'll split me in half with that big manpart of yours."

"Nay, little bird," he assured her. "Now that I know you can't flee me, I'll play a bit with you, and you'll enjoy what follows." He pushed her gown up to her waist. "We'll sleep naked together in our bed, but since you'll have to walk with me back to the village, I won't rip your gown from you." Sitting back on his heels, he reached out to cup her mons. Then he pressed down on it with his palm.

A dart of pleasure raced through Maureen, lighting up her eyes.

"Ahh," he said, smiling, "you liked that."

"I did," Maureen admitted, unable to help herself. She reached up and slid her hands past his leather vest, caressing his smooth bronzed chest.

"I liked that," he told her. Then he ran a finger down the pouting slit dividing her nether lips. He was a little surprised but also pleased to find she was slightly moist. She had a fine full bush of reddish brown curls. Her nether lips were very plump. Toryn pushed himself back; then, leaning forward, he used his two thumbs to part those succulent lips. His eyes widened with approval. Her lover's bud was large, in keeping with her size. As he touched it with the very tip of his tongue, he saw it quiver.

"Wh-what are you doing?" Maureen's voice shook just a little.

"Giving you the first of a thousand pleasures," he answered her. Then his mouth closed over her clit, and he sucked hard on it several times. Her squeal told him that she was not unhappy with his actions. Indeed, she seemed to press herself against his lips. Releasing the sensitive little morsel of tasty flesh, his thumbs still holding her open, he licked around the sweet pinkish walls of her cunt. In very short order her juices were flowing copiously. *"Now,"* he said as he raised himself up, then fit the head of his manpart into the entry to her body.

She felt it there and trembled. "Now what?" she wanted to know.

He pushed himself slowly, slowly, slowly into her body, allowing her time to adjust to the mass now probing her. "Now you are to be fucked, little bird," Toryn of the Thousand Pleasures told her.

Oh, the gods! She felt his manpart filling her tightly, stretching the walls of her cunt, yet not hurting her at all. Indeed, it felt good to be filled. It was as if she had been waiting all her life for this. He began to piston her, slowly at first, then with a quicker rhythm that made her head spin.

"I want to go deeper," he groaned into her ear.

Maureen knew what was expected, for the old wise-woman who had removed her virgin shield had taught each girl what was expected of her. She wrapped her legs about her warrior. *Ahh, the gods! It was sweet. Almost unbearably sweet.*

Faster and faster and faster, but it was still not enough for Toryn of the Thousand Pleasures, which surprised him. This girl was unique, unlike any other he had ever fucked. *"Deeper! Deeper! I must go deeper!"* And when she unlocked her legs from about his torso, he raised them up, resting them on his shoulders as he fucked her harder and deeper, harder and deeper, harder and deeper.

Her head was spinning. Her need for his passion escalated with each stroke of his mighty penis. *The gods! The gods!* "Don't stop!" she pleaded with him, eyes closed.

"I can't," he groaned as he continued the rhythm.

The sun beat down on them. She could smell the grasses upon which they lay. The oxeye daisies were blowing in the light breeze about them, wafting that peculiar daisy scent. And then something incredible happened. Maureen felt as if she were being lifted up and up and up. She was flying, and then she found herself hurtling down into a dark abyss of warm and overwhelming sweetness. *The gods! The gods!* It was all too wonderful. Maureen felt exhilarated, yet she wanted to weep. His cry brought her back to their reality.

With a groan of shameless satisfaction, Toryn of the Thousand Pleasures rolled off of the girl who had been beneath him. "The gods!" he exclaimed. "Thanks be to the gods, for they have brought me the perfect woman! And you gained pleasure from our coupling." It was a statement, not a question.

"I did!" Maureen told him honestly as she drew her gown down and sat up.

He tucked his manpart away beneath the leather of his leggings as he arose from the meadow floor. He reached out and pulled her up. "Come along now, little bird," he said to her. "I believe that my men and I have introduced ourselves properly now to our new wives. 'Tis time to return to the village and reassure the elders that all is well."

"Do you have an old wife?" she wanted to know.

Toryn of the Thousand Pleasures laughed. "Nay, little bird. You are the first."

In the village only the head elder protested Toryn's band of warriors taking over the village. "The women of Ennis are greatly valued," he said.

"And how much of that value goes into your purse?" Toryn wanted to know.

The head elder blustered, offended, but he did not answer the query.

"There are sixteen of us," Toryn of the Thousand Pleasures replied in measured tones. "It is unnatural to live as you do. A village needs strong young men to help it survive, headman."

"We have managed well so far," came the reply.

"Until today, when we came and took your women for our wives," Toryn of the Thousand Pleasures countered. "You are fortunate in us, headman. We want homes and wives. We could have burned your village to the ground, slaughtered the elders and children, and carried your young women off. Instead we have taken sixteen of them for wives and will become part of this community. And you yet have a group of pretty lasses for the next Great Gathering."

"He's right!" the village healer woman said. "Do you think you could defend us, old man, in times of strife? Ha! Nay, you could not. I welcome Toryn of the Thousand Pleasures and his men to Ennis."

Ping. Ping. Ping. The Channel is now closed.

Maureen yawned, turned over in her bed, and went to sleep. Her fantasy village of Ennis had become more home for her than the little town in which she had been raised. She felt safe there. That was the best thing about the Channel, other than the delicious sex. Sometimes Toryn of the Thousand Pleasures and his men arrived for the first time. On other days, they had been there for months, and she and Toryn had unbridled sex in her small single-room hut with its straw roof.

As the weeks went by, Maureen settled into the Devlin household. She liked her employers very much, and the children were delightful. Her friend Brigid, however, was not having as easy a time of it. The old nanny in Lord O'Brian's household resented the younger, more efficient woman. The children, poisoned by their old nursemaid, were rude and dismissive of her. Lady O'Brian, in an effort to maintain some kind of order and peace, was forever assigning her unpleasant tasks. Brigid wrote she wasn't certain she would remain even until Christmas. Maureen felt guilty briefly, but shook it off. Brigid could have taken a position out of Ireland and done quite well for herself.

With the holidays coming, Maureen felt a moment of homesickness. It faded as quickly as it had come as the village of Egret Pointe was decorated and the shop windows bloomed with a singular theme, which this year was a 1776 Christmas. It was very new to Maureen, yet very comforting at the same time. Along Main Street the black iron lampposts with their clear glass shades were twined with greenery, apples, and nuts. A large red bow was tied at the top of each post beneath the glass.

Maureen took both Sean and Emlyn to the library for story hour. It was there she met the elderly Nanny Violet, who worked for the Marshalls, whose youngest son was not fully grown. Nanny Violet was not coming to story hour, however. She had come for a book to read. Nanny Violet had introduced Maureen to Nanny Jane, a young Englishwoman of Maureen's own generation.

"Who do you look after?" Maureen asked Jane.

"The holy terror who is Miss Kathy's little one," Jane said with a chuckle. "Just walking, and I can hardly keep up with her. It will be lovely to have a friend my own age here. Do you go to church?"

"St. Anne's," Maureen replied.

"St. Luke's," Jane responded, naming the town's Episcopal church. "When do you have off?"

"Half Saturday and all Sunday," Maureen said.

"Oh, good," Jane said and smiled. "Me too. Maybe we can go to the films together."

The friendship was born.

One morning as it grew near to Christmas, Essie, the Devlins' housekeeper, asked Maureen if she would run to the butcher counter at the local grocery store for her. "You could drop Sean off at nursery school," Essie said, "and then go for me. Emlyn and the twins will be napping then. I know you use that time to get things done for the children that you can't do when they're about, but it would be a great help to me, dear."

"No biggie," Maureen said. "Should I get some money from the missus?"

"No," Essie said. "We have a house account and pay monthly. I just need you to pick it up. It's a big order."

"Santa's going to bring me a dump truck that really can dump," Sean Michael informed Maureen as she drove him to nursery school.

"He'll only be bringing that truck if you are a good boy," Maureen reminded her little charge, looking at him in her rearview mirror. When they arrived at the school, Maureen unbuckled Sean Michael and brought him inside to his teacher, Mrs. Gundersen. "Santa's bringing him a dump truck," she said, grinning at the teacher.

"So I've heard every day since December first," Mrs. Gundersen replied with a smile and a chuckle. "Do they have it yet?"

Maureen nodded, and then with a wave, she was off to the butcher counter at the grocery store to pick up the meat order for Essie. There was no one at the counter when she arrived, but there was a bell with a little card that read *Ring Me for Service*. Maureen smacked her palm down on the bell twice. She waited but no one came. She smacked the bell again, this time more loudly.

Suddenly the door behind the counter swung open. "Keep your drawers on now," she heard a distinctly Irish voice say as a man came out into view.

"That's hardly a proper way to greet a customer," Maureen said sharply.

"Glory be!" the man said with a chuckle. "It's a wee Irish lassie." He was very tall, with blue eyes and black hair that was cropped short and neat.

"I've come for Mrs. Devlin's order," Maureen said in frosty tones. "Is it ready?"

"For you, darlin', yes! Mrs. Devlin's prime cut of beef, loin of pork, and five pounds of chopped chuck are ready. Where's Essie, and where do you come from? There's a bit of the north in your voice."

"You've a lot of questions for a butcher boy," Maureen replied pertly. "Monaghan, if it's any of your business, and it isn't."

"I'm a Donegal man myself. Toryn O'Donel is me name," he told her

"*My* name," she corrected him. "Stop trying to sound like something people make us out to be. You're Irish, not an actor from the Abbey like Barry Fitzgerald or Victor McLaughlin. You're an educated man if you grew up in Donegal. Where did you get a name like Toryn? It's hardly a saint's name." Toryn! His name was Toryn? The coincidence sent a shiver down her spine.

"And a good thing too," he said with a laugh, "since I'm no saint. It's an old family name. The family claims we have an ancestor who was called Toryn of the Thousand Pleasures." He handed her a large shopping bag over the counter. "On account, right?"

Maureen grew briefly dizzy with his words. "Yes," she said, pulling herself together. "On Mrs. Devlin's account."

"Hey, are you all right? You've suddenly gone pale as milk," Toryn O'Donel said. Then he came around the counter and took the bag from her. "Let me help you out to the car with this, lass. It's heavy. I don't even know your name, but you know mine." He took the shopping bag in one hand and her arm with the other, then led her back through the market and out into the parking lot.

Maureen had to admit the steadying hand was welcome. Certainly there couldn't have really been a man known as Toryn of the Thousand Pleasures. She had made him up out of whole cloth. Toryn of the Thousand Pleasures was a figment of her imagination. The cold air helped clear the dizziness away. "I'm Maureen Flynn," she introduced herself. "You don't really descend from someone called Toryn of the Thousand Pleasures, do you?"

"So it's said in Donegal," he replied. "Was it the thousand pleasures that made you faint, Miss Maureen Flynn? Certainly a proper nanny wouldn't have any knowledge of such things. *Or do you?*" Toryn O'Donel grinned down at her. He had to top her by a few inches, she suddenly realized.

Maureen pressed the key remote. "You can put the bag in the backseat," she said.

"Yes, madam," he replied. "I don't suppose you'd like to go to a movie sometime. Do you like the cinema?"

"With the likes of you?" Maureen sounded indignant. "I don't keep company with strangers, Mr. O'Donel. Thank you for your help." She got into the car and drove off, but she couldn't help peeking in her rearview mirror. Lord, he was handsome!

Essie thanked the young woman for picking up the roasts. She inspected the delivery, nodding with a smile. "That new young butcher they have really knows how to cut meat," she said in an approving voice. "Look at the prime rib. Just the right amount of fat on it to roast beautifully. What's in the case is trimmed too fine to satisfy both the food police and the weight-conscious."

The following Saturday evening, Maureen went to the five o'clock mass. Afterward, as she was leaving the church, she felt a hand on her elbow. She turned and found herself facing Toryn O'Donel. "I'll be thanking you to take your big paw off of me, Mr. O'Donel," she said sharply.

"I thought you might change your mind and take in a movie with me if I introduced you to someone who could attest to my character," he said, his blue eyes twinkling. "Ah, Father Porter, there you are. Will you please tell this stubborn lass that I'm a respectable fellow and won't eat her up if she goes to the films with me?"

The priest chuckled. "Why, Toryn, don't tell me Miss Flynn has put you off."

"He says you'll attest to his good character," Maureen said, smiling.

"Well," Father Porter said, "he's my nephew, so I'm apt to be prejudice."

"You're not Irish!" Maureen exclaimed.

"No, I'm a Yankee-doodle dandy," the priest responded, "but my oldest sister married an O'Donel and has lived in Ireland for almost forty years. Toryn's a good fellow, and if he misbehaves, you'll be sure to tell me. I think you're safe for a movie."

"I haven't said I would go," Maureen replied.

"But you haven't said you wouldn't," Toryn said. "Will you?"

"Well, I was planning to meet my friend Jane for supper," Maureen said. "I'd hate to disappoint her. She's a nanny like me and alone in this country."

"Is she the little blonde who looks after the Blairs' little girl?" he asked.

Maureen nodded.

"If I could get my friend Gary from the Produce Department to join us, do you think this Jane would come?" Toryn inquired.

"Well," Maureen considered, "it is a bit late to ask, isn't it? Perhaps another time, Mr. O'Donel. Good night. Good night, Father." And Maureen hurried off.

"Well, now," the priest said, smiling, "I believe that's called a put-down, nephew. She's a fine girl, however, and if she'll finally agree to go out with you, remember she's a lady and treat her as such. She's not one of those light skirts peopling the Salty Pig."

"Now, Uncle, what would you know of the Salty Pig?" Toryn teased his uncle. "A good priest such as yourself."

Father Porter smiled. "I'm called on to minister to all

souls, not just the ones who come to mass on Sundays and saints days, Toryn. I should tell you that I'm responsible for Miss Flynn since I've gotten into e-mail correspondence with her brother Father Seamus Flynn. I hope, however, that won't deter you."

"It won't," the younger man replied. "I intend on marrying Maureen Flynn eventually, Uncle. I knew she was the one the moment she came to the butcher counter to pick up the Devlins' order the other day. But, for pity's sake, don't say anything to my mother yet. She'll be planning a wedding and naming the children for us." He didn't want to encourage his mother until it was a done deal.

Father Porter laughed heartily. "Indeed, she will. You're her youngest, and she wasn't happy when you up and came to the States. But she's like all mothers. She wants you happy and settled with a good woman. Now, since you're not taking Miss Flynn to the pictures, will you come and share supper with your uncle?"

"I will!" Toryn O'Donel responded, his eyes lingering on Maureen's retreating figure as she went to the car and got in.

Maureen felt his eyes on her back. It had been a long time since she had had time for a boyfriend. Of course, he wasn't her boyfriend. He was a fresh-as-wet-paint Irishman, but he was so handsome. A lot like her fantasy. Maureen swore softly to herself as she drove to meet Jane for supper at the luncheonette. How the hell could that be? She had never set eyes on the butcher boy until the other day.

Jane was waiting for her in a booth. "Are you relieved of your sins?" she teased.

Maureen slid into the booth. "Do you ever go to the IGA?" she asked.

"Sure. Mrs. Blair has Mrs. Bills cleaning that big new house of theirs, but I do the marketing for her with the little one," Jane said.

"What do you think of the butcher?" Maureen asked.

"Karl? He's nice for an old guy. Why do you ask? Oh! My! God! It isn't Karl. It's that hot new butcher! He's Irish, isn't he? Do you like him?"

"I neither like nor dislike him," Maureen said. "He's very fresh, I'm thinking."

"He's hot," Jane said in her clipped English accent. "And he's nice. He's always giving a slice of bologna to the little kids. Did he come on to you? Oh, you are so lucky! I would love to have a nice boyfriend."

"Did you know his uncle is the priest at St. Anne's?" Maureen said. "I suppose that makes him respectable after a fashion. He asked me to the pictures after mass."

"And you said no?" Jane's jaw dropped with surprise.

"Of course I did. We were meeting for supper. I wasn't going to leave you high and dry. He did offer to get his friend Gary and make it a foursome."

"Gary from Produce? Well, it wouldn't have been so bad, I suppose," Jane allowed. "I've noticed Gary eyeing me. He seems harmless."

"I told the butcher boy maybe another time. I don't want him thinking we're easy and can be picked up with no notice," Maureen said. "Besides, I have other plans after we eat." She smiled mysteriously.

"You girls know what you want?" The waitress was by their side.

They ordered.

"What plans?" Jane asked when the girl had gone.

Maureen leaned forward. "Do you know about the Channel?" she asked Jane.

Jane's blue eyes grew wide. She nodded, and then said, "Don't tell me you have the Channel? Oh, you are so lucky!"

"I asked Mrs. Devlin for it before I agreed to come over," Maureen said. "I only use it Saturday nights since I have Sundays off, but it's wonderful to have it."

"I don't think Mrs. Blair ever heard of the Channel," Jane said. "I wouldn't have dared to ask for it. Besides, I never even met the Blairs before I came to work for them. They hired me through the agency Mrs. Blair's sister-in-law, Mrs. St. John, used to work for when she was a young girl. You are sooo lucky."

Their food came, and the two girls ate while chattering about the households in which they worked. They made plans to go into the city and see the decorations before the holiday season was over. And afterward they parted to return home, Jane to watch reruns of *True Blood* and Maureen to access her fantasy of the Celtic warrior called Toryn and the first-century AD village of Ennis. Toryn of the Thousand Pleasures was suddenly becoming more real now that she had met his twenty-first-century descendant.

Snuggled in her comfortable bed with its soft and pretty pink flannel sheets topped by a warm down comforter, Maureen pressed the A button on her remote and awakened naked amid a bed of furs, his warm lips pressing against her lips. She sighed contentedly as his big hand caressed her full round breasts. Then her heart beat faster as that same hand swept down to her mons, two fingers pushing past her nether lips and into her vagina. He began to frig her, the long, thick fingers slow at first, and then moving with increasing speed until she sobbed a small release and begged him, *"More!"*

He smiled into her face and withdrew the two fingers, then pushed them into her mouth. She sucked on them, her eyes closing with pleasure as she imagined another digit in her mouth. As if he read her thoughts, he positioned himself over her chest, withdrew his fingers, and replaced them with his cock. He had discovered that Maureen had the most skillful mouth and tongue when it came to pleasuring a manpart. Now it was his eyes that closed.

Reaching up, she fastened her two hands about the twin cheeks of his ass and began to knead the flesh, her fingers pressing deeply into his muscles. Toryn of the Thousand Pleasures felt his head spin with the pure deliciousness of it. Her mouth urged his cock onward, her hands stroking and massaging his flesh. Then she surprised him by thrusting a single finger into his fundament. He groaned loudly and, unable to prevent himself, spilled his seed into her mouth. Maureen swallowed it eagerly.

"Sorceress," he whispered in her ear, even as he realized he was still as hard as a rock. "Release me and get on your hands and knees," he commanded her.

Obeying him, she waited, breathless, to be impaled upon his great cock. He did not disappoint her, one hand resting on the back of her neck to keep her position submissive, the other guiding his manpart into her. She gasped as she always did at his entry. He simply filled her, and the walls of her vagina tightened and released as he began to fuck her. The pleasure rose up to consume her until she was certain she was dying, but she never did. Instead it burst over her in a shower of magical stars that always left her to wallow in her satisfaction until she was forced to release her hold on it.

And he came again with a roar like a beast, his juices spurting hard into her as she cried out. "The gods, little one! How is it you can unman me so easily?" he groaned as he fell away from her, pulling her back against him as he did so, a hand moving to clasp one of her breasts.

Maureen laughed weakly. "If I had known that fucking was so wonderful, I would have started doing it years ago," she told him.

"It is only perfect because it is between us," he told her. "We are life mates, and always will be. We will grow old, and die one day, little one, but we will return eventually to human form, and I will find you again though it take a thousand or more years to do so. You are mine!"

His words startled Maureen. "Fantasy end!" she said, and she was back once more in the lovely room that was hers in this house. Outside her window she could see the moon glistening on the snow. *I will find you again though it take a thousand or more years to do so. You are mine!* His words echoed in her brain. Had there really been a Toryn of the Thousand Pleasures who once lived in an ancient Ireland of Druids and gods? And was Toryn O'Donel his descendant, or even that Toryn reborn? She didn't know, and it certainly wasn't something she wanted to discuss with anyone. At least not right now. Maureen sighed, and fell into a restless sleep.

Christmas came. Her first holiday away from home. She had always gone home for Christmas. She called her mother, and to her surprise, Mrs. Flynn was not her usual dour self.

"Your brother tells me that the priest there is keeping an eye on you," she said.

"Father Porter," Maureen replied. "He's a very nice fellow, Mum. You can tell my sister that I do attend mass every Sunday."

"I will," Mrs. Flynn replied. "Frankly, she's a wee bit too holy for my taste, Maureen, but she seems to have a calling. I hear your priest has a nephew."

Oh, Lord! "Yes, Mum."

"And he's a butcher. It's an honest trade. You could do worse," her mother said.

"Mum! I've not even gone out with him yet."

"Has he asked you?" came the pointed query, and Maureen knew her mother knew the answer to the question, so she couldn't lie.

"Yes, but it was very last-minute, and I had promised to meet my girlfriend for supper, Mum. I've told you about Jane, who's a nanny here too. We both get off half Saturday and all of Sunday."

"Is she a good Catholic girl?" Mrs. Flynn wanted to know.

"She's an Anglican, and goes to St. Luke's every Sunday morning," Maureen said.

"Well, I suppose even if she is English she's all right if she goes to church. I'll ask your brother to inquire of Father Porter."

"Are you having a good Christmas, Mum?" Maureen wanted to bring this conversation to a close as quickly as possible now.

"Oh, yes. Your brothers are all here, and what do you think? Michael's gone and found himself a girl to marry."

"That's wonderful, Mum. Give him my congratulations. Do you know her?"

"Oh, yes. She's a good local girl. Flora Bailey," Mrs. Flynn responded.

"Of course. I knew her in school," Maureen said. "Well, that's surely a fine Christmas gift for you, Mum, isn't it? Did you get the packages I sent?"

"You shouldn't spend your money like that, Maureen," her mother scolded. Then she relented a bit. "Everyone was delighted with your choices."

"I'm glad you all had such a good Christmas. I'll have to ring off now, Mum. It's almost two o'clock here, and we're having Christmas dinner. I'll write you all about it."

"Yes, do," her mother said. "I read your letters to the family."

"Merry Christmas again, Mum," Maureen said.

"Go out with that young man, Maureen. You can't be a nanny forever, living in someone else's home instead of your own," her mother advised. "Merry Christmas, my daughter, and God bless you."

"You too, Mum," Maureen said and rang off.

. . .

Toryn O'Donel called her the day after Christmas.

"How did you get my number?" Maureen demanded to know.

"Father Porter, who got it from your brother," he said, laughing. "They're quite a club, the priests are. Will you go out with me on New Year's Eve?"

"I can't. Mrs. Devlin and her husband are going to a party. I have to be in the house to babysit the children," Maureen said with genuine regret.

"Do you think they would allow me to come over and keep you company?" he asked her. "What if I ask my uncle to speak with them and vouch for me as a respectable citizen who'll not kidnap their wee ones or ravage their nanny?"

She laughed. She couldn't help it. "All right," she heard herself saying. New Year's Eve dates never came to anything anyway. And it wasn't likely her employers were going to agree, priest or no.

But Emily Devlin did agree, much to Maureen's surprise. "Father Porter spoke to Mick, and Essie says he's a lovely young man. How can I say no? I write romance, for goodness' sakes. Of course your young man may come and keep you company on New Year's Eve, Maureen."

"He's not my young man, Mrs. Devlin," Maureen said.

"But he wants to be," Emily Devlin replied, laughing.

Maureen saw Toryn O'Donel at the IGA the next day when she stopped in to pick up some lamb chops. "My missus says you can come," she told him. "But remember, the children come first."

"I like children," he said, smiling at her as he handed her the brown paper package of lamb chops. Their hands touched.

Maureen blushed, to her embarrassment, and her legs felt suddenly like jelly. Still, she managed to say, "Then I'll see you New Year's Eve. Don't come before nine."

The Devlins were just leaving as Toryn O'Donel arrived on New Year's Eve. Maureen introduced him to her employers.

"You're a Donegal man, Father Porter tells me," Mick Devlin said, looking the young man up and down.

"I am, sir," Toryn replied politely.

Mick Devlin nodded. "Have a good evening, then," he said as he escorted his wife out to their car.

"Gracious," Emily said to her husband as they pulled out of their drive. "He is one big handsome man, isn't he?"

"We're going to lose our nanny," Mick said grimly.

"Oh, darling, don't be silly," Emily told him. "This is their first date."

"He's got a look in his eye that Irishmen only get when they decide it's time to marry, angel face. I know that look. I had it when I met you."

"Pinfeathers, Devlin," his wife said. "You might have gotten it later on, but in the beginning, I just wanted to learn what real sex was all about, and you were more than ready to teach me. Besides, if they get married somewhere down the line, they wouldn't go back to Ireland. They came to the States because the opportunities are better. He's got a good job. The gossip, Essie tells me, is that when Karl retires the Irishman will be head butcher. And Maureen has been trained as a nanny. She won't leave us."

"I want to convert the carriage house into living quarters," Mick said.

"Why, you clever man," Emily said, approving her husband's suggestion. "If we can offer them living quarters when they marry, we'll certainly keep our nanny."

"Until they want to have children of their own," Mick replied.

"Children?" Maureen said. She and Toryn were settled in the den before a roaring fire. The children were all in bed, and the twins were sleeping through the night now. "Yes, I'd like children one day, but not as many as my mum."

"How many did she have?" he asked her.

"Thirteen, all living. We've got a priest, a nun, one girl married, and a couple of farmers among the adults. The younger ones seem more interested in getting more education. Besides, there's not enough land to support them all," Maureen said.

"There're six in my family," Toryn told her. He put an arm about her, drawing her close. "Only one girl, poor thing, and she's the eldest."

"I don't envy her," Maureen replied. His arm about her shoulders felt very comforting, and she couldn't help snuggling a little against him.

"So how many do you want?" he asked her.

"Two or three should do it for me," Maureen told him.

"That's fine with me," Toryn told her. "I'm glad we're in agreement about that."

"There's no agreement between us," Maureen said, pulling away from him.

"There's going to be," he responded, drawing her back

closer to his side. "You're the girl I'm going to marry, Maureen Flynn. I knew it the first time I laid eyes on you. I even told my uncle you were the one."

"Did you indeed?" Maureen said. "You're a bold man, you are, Toryn O'Donel!"

"I am that," he agreed. Then, turning her slightly and tilting her face up to his, he gave her a long, slow kiss.

Maureen could have sworn her toes were curling. To her complete surprise, she melted into his embrace, slipping her arms about him and letting his kiss sweep her away. One big hand slipped beneath her sweater to unfasten her bra and cup a breast. The kiss deepened, and his tongue slid into her mouth to stroke her tongue as his thumb rubbed the nipple of the breast he was cupping. She should stop him. Yes, he was much too forward for a respectable girl, and she was a respectable girl. But, dear Lord, his kiss, his caresses felt so damned good. She was going to stop him. Just another moment or two and she would make him desist from this shameless behavior.

His head was spinning. The touch of her lips set off those odd flashbacks he sometimes got. He could see them in a bed of furs making very passionate love to each other. He knew he should not be so bold with her. No one, his priestly uncle and Mr. Devlin included, had to tell him that Maureen Flynn was a proper girl. But the fragrance that seemed to surround her, the softness of her skin, her sweet response seemed to be playing havoc with him. He was finding it absolutely impossible to cease his behavior, but finally, and with the greatest effort he had ever made, he broke off the kiss.

Maureen's lips were swollen. Her green eyes gazing up

at him were befuddled. "Wha-what just happened here?" she managed to say.

"God, you felt it too, didn't you?" he answered her.

She nodded, realizing as she did that his big hand was still on her breast.

"Do you want me to go? I'll go if you say it," he told her.

Here was her escape, but instead she heard herself saying, "No. I don't want you to go, Toryn O'Donel. Unless you want to go," she added.

"I don't want to go," he replied. "I want to kiss you again, Maureen Flynn." And he did, taking her lips in a furious kiss that seemed to awaken a fierce passion in them both. They devoured each other with their mouths, and then his hand was leaving her breast, slipping beneath her wool skirt, and sliding slowly, slowly up her leg. Reaching her thighs, he let his fingers gently stroke the soft interior flesh, his kisses moving across her face as he did.

Maureen had had sex once or twice in her life. It had been hurried and certainly nothing like this. She quivered as his finger brushed the curls of her mons, then ran along her slit. She could feel the moisture already beginning to rise. He found her mouth again and gave her a delicious, deep kiss, their tongues exploring each other as his finger slipped between her nether lips to begin stroking her clit. *The gods! The gods!* The voiceless words formed in her mind, and she moaned softly as the finger played with her. Maureen felt herself squirming against his hand, actually encouraging him, and she couldn't help it. She shivered with a tiny orgasm.

Damn, she is passionate, Toryn thought, *and we are*

*going to make beautiful babies. I want to fuck her so
badly, but I can't tonight. She wants it now, but tomorrow
she'll be furious with herself, and especially with me, but
she needs release.* He pushed a single finger into her vagina
and began to frig her.

Maureen moaned with undisguised pleasure. *"More!"*
she pleaded with him, and cried with pleasure as the one
finger became two, which moved faster and faster, harder
and deeper, until she released a sobbing climax, the walls
of her vagina spasming around his hand as she rode it.
And when it was over, she turned to hide her face in his
sweater.

"No," he said. "Don't turn away from me, little one."

Maureen stiffened at those two words on his lips. Her
fantasy Celtic warrior, Toryn of the Thousand Pleasures,
called her that.

"I don't want you ashamed of what just happened between us. I told you we're going to marry. Hard as it may
be to believe, little one, I love you. You've haunted my
dreams for years, and when we met a few weeks back, I
couldn't believe my luck to have found you, little one." He
caressed her hair.

"Crazy as it sounds, I've dreamed of you too," Maureen admitted to him. She could keep silent, push him
away, and continue to live in a fantasy world every Saturday night. Or she could have the flesh-and-blood reality of
her fantasy and a happily ever after just like in one of Mrs.
Devlin's novels. She sat up, touching his face. "You were
lovely to pleasure me, Toryn O'Donel, but what of yourself?" Reaching out, she touched the hard ridge in his
slacks, stroking it gently.

His warm hand covered her hand. "I'll live. Hey, look

at the clock on the mantel. It's almost midnight, Maureen Flynn. Let's turn on the telly and watch all those crazy people down in Times Square."

"Mrs. Devlin left us a little split of champagne in the fridge," she said. "I'll get it, and we'll toast in the New Year in a proper fashion."

Several minutes later they counted down the seconds with everyone else, shared a quick kiss, and raised their glasses to celebrate the New Year.

"It's a new beginning for us both," Toryn O'Donel said to her.

Maureen nodded. "I know," she agreed.

On Valentine's Day he gave her a small engagement ring, which she accepted. They planned their wedding for March 17, which was a Saturday. Their lust for each other was just too great. Maureen feared she would be pregnant if they didn't marry quickly. They had decided to refrain from the final act of sex until they were married. Neither was a virgin, but they didn't discuss the past. It was their future together that they were interested in.

"I knew we were going to lose our nanny," Mick Devlin said when Emily told him of the engagement.

"We're not losing Maureen," his wife told him, laughing.

"Have you seen how that butcher boy looks at her? She'll be pregnant on her wedding night—I guarantee it."

"No, she won't," Emily said.

"They're both good Catholics of the old school, for God's sake," Mick grumbled.

"They're not in Ireland anymore, and Maureen has

seen Dr. Sam. They both want children, but they also want to wait a bit and put some money aside. When will the carriage house be finished for them?"

"Beginning of March," Mick answered her. "All you women have everything nicely in hand, angel face, don't you?"

"Yep," Emily answered him. "And not only that, I've done about a third of the new book. You can tell J.P. when you two have your weekly sparring session at the editorial meeting that I'm right on schedule."

"I'll tell her whatever you want as long as we don't lose our nanny. Are they honeymooning, and for how long?"

"You are such a selfish pig, Devlin," she accused. "And yes, they'll be off for a week at Disney World in Florida. Maureen and I already have her temporary replacement lined up. Annie Marshall is letting us have Nanny Violet for a few days. She won't be sleeping over, but she'll be here during the day."

"I am not a selfish pig, angel face. I've just grown used to having my wife back," Mick Devlin said. "I'll bet the twins decide to walk when Maureen's away, and with four toddlers, there'll be merry hell to pay. Nanny Violet will have her work cut out for her."

Father Seamus Flynn was flying from Ireland to celebrate the wedding mass with Father Porter for his sister and Toryn. Neither Mrs. Flynn nor Mrs. O'Donel had ever flown, and neither was of a mind to, even for the wedding of their children. Toryn's closest brother, Francis, lived and worked in the city.

He would come to stand up for his younger brother, and Maureen's friend Jane would be her attendant. The two girls had had a wonderful time shopping for wedding outfits. Maureen had finally settled on a winter white silk suit with a narrow skirt, and a fitted jacket with a peplum. She found a wide headband with a wisp of veiling. Jane, who was a pale blonde, chose a pretty turquoise dress.

The renovation of the old carriage house behind the Devlins' big house was completed. The downstairs still housed Mick and Emily's precious Austin Healeys, along with a new small, efficient furnace. But the upstairs had new wood floors, wiring, and plumbing. It had been divided into two bedrooms, one large, one small; a living room with a fireplace and a small eating area; a galley kitchen; and a bathroom. Maureen was stunned by her employer's generosity, for Emily had insisted that she and her nanny shop for furniture, and then all the ladies Maureen had come to know in Egret Pointe gave her a traditional bridal shower in the Devlins' spacious living room.

Afterward, looking at all of her gifts, Maureen couldn't help but cry. She had received bedding, towels, washcloths, pots, glasses, and dishes. Nanny Violet came with a fine large brown English teapot and a set of cups and saucers. "I can't believe everyone's generosity," she said to Emily.

"Americans, like the Irish, are very generous people," Emily said as she helped Maureen put everything away in the carriage house apartment.

The seventeenth of March dawned sunny and mild, as it sometimes did.

"Luck of the Irish," Mick Devlin said.

The wedding was set for two thirty at St. Anne's, with cake and champagne punch afterward at the Devlins'. Sean Michael was to be the ring bearer, and little Emlyn the flower girl. Emily thought her son looked adorable in his short navy pants and Eton jacket. Emlyn preened in front of her mother's closet mirror, admiring her floaty pink dress. "I pretty," she declared, and her father heartily agreed.

It was a simple ceremony with a brief mass. The IGA had closed for two hours so all its employees could see the handsome assistant butcher wed to the pretty nanny. The cashiers all sat together, sniffling happily. Karl, the head butcher, had brought his wife. Emlyn Devlin played her part beautifully, almost skipping down the aisle, tossing rose petals as she came. She was followed by Sean Michael, who was serious and intent upon not dropping the silk cushion, which held the two simple wedding rings. Jane, with a small multicolored bouquet, preceded the bride. Mick Devlin brought Maureen down the aisle to where Toryn and his brother stood awaiting her. He put her hand into that of her groom and gave her a kiss on the cheek before joining Emily. The vows were spoken. The mass celebrated. The cake cut. A toast drunk to the happy couple. The Mulcahy chauffeur took the bridal couple to the airport.

"Well," Mick Devlin said, "there goes our nanny."

"She'll be back." Emily laughed and secretly hoped that Maureen's wedding night would be as wonderful as hers and Mick's had been.

Maureen, of course, knew nothing of the island where

her employers had spent ten naked days making love after their wedding. What she did know was that Toryn O'Donel, her *husband*—the word sounded so strange and yet familiar—was a worthy descendant of his ancestor, Toryn of the Thousand Pleasures. Honeymoon sex was supposed to be explosive, and it certainly was. Fortunately, they had been upgraded to a cottage when they checked in, which meant they didn't disturb their neighbors.

There was a wonderful round sunken bath in their suite. They couldn't resist. Oddly, Maureen didn't feel any shyness about taking her clothes off before him. His blue eyes followed her every move, even as he was removing his own travel garments.

She had a lovely body, he thought. Long legs, high, full round breasts, a great butt.

Maureen was counting his assets as he looked at her. Wide chest and shoulders. Narrow waist. Tight butt, and a seriously long penis that touched a cord of memory in her.

Holding hands, they stepped down into the warm tub. The water came to his waist. Wrapping his arms about Maureen, Toryn gave her a long, sweet kiss. Feeling her breasts against his smooth chest, her belly and thighs against him, his cock began to stir.

Feeling it, Maureen boldly reached down and gave him a little squeeze. Toryn cupped her mons in his big palm, whispering in her ear as he did so exactly what he was going to do to her. Maureen giggled and told him what she would do to him. They kissed again as he backed her up against the wall of the tub. She continued to play with his cock.

"My, what a fine spirited laddie you have here, husband," she told him. The column of flesh in her hand had thickened and lengthened, and it was very hard now.

"The better to fuck you with, wife," he told her. "Put those sexy long legs of yours about me, little one. I very much need to be inside you now."

She eagerly complied, and felt him guiding his penis to the entry of her vagina. "Yes!" she encouraged him, and then he began to push himself inside her. The sensation of him filling her, stretching the walls of her cunt until she thought they could not be stretched any more, was mind-blowing, especially when he began to thrust back and forth, back and forth, back and forth. With virtually no foreplay, he was bringing her to a climax. His hands cupped her bottom now as his thrusts grew deeper and harder.

"Don't stop!" she gasped as the first wave hit her.

"I can't," he groaned. "I don't want to! I want to be like this with you always. I've waited forever for us."

This wasn't her fantasy. This was her new reality, and Maureen decided that it was better than anything she had ever experienced. They remained in the tub fucking and fucking until finally, after she had experienced several small climaxes, they came together in an explosion of passion that left them both breathless. And when they had finally recovered, they adjourned to the big bed and took up again where they had left off. They seemed unable to get enough of each other.

After three days of sex and room service, Maureen suggested that since they were at Disney World, they might want to see some of it. He reluctantly agreed. Four hours later they were back in their honeymoon cottage, naked and making love again.

"We'll come see Disney World again another time," Toryn said.

"We could have stayed in Egret Pointe at the inn rather than come all the way down to Florida," Maureen said.

Toryn laughed. "It's warmer here."

"We have the AC on," she reminded him.

"Funny," he said. "I'm not cold. Are you?" He pulled her down onto the bed on her back. "I'm horny," he told her, grinning.

"You are always horny," Maureen said. "I'm beginning to wonder what manner of man I've married."

"One who's hot for your body," he said, pushing into her in a single motion. "And you're hot for me too, or you wouldn't be climaxing every time I fuck you, Maureen O'Donel. Admit you want me." He began moving on her, and they were both quickly overwhelmed by the passion they seemed to generate in each other. It lasted most of the night, and when they were finally exhausted, they realized that they had missed dinner.

"We can't keep this up when we go home," Maureen told him. "I have four children to take care of, and you've got your job too. Maybe we should limit the sex to certain nights of the week."

"Nope," he said. "We're both young, and we'll manage."

"I hope you're right," Maureen answered him.

"If we go to bed early," he said, "we can fuck each other's ears off and then go to sleep. If we get six to eight hours we'll be all right."

Maureen laughed. "Okay," she said. "I'm game." And then she wondered if her mother and father had been this way with each other, their actions leading to thirteen children. She had always thought of them as a sex-once-a-week couple. And after her father had died ten years ago, she wondered how her mother had managed without sex. She wasn't the kind of woman to have a BOB.

They returned home to Egret Pointe to the carriage house behind the Devlins' big Empire-style house. Both were due back at their jobs early in the morning, Toryn to the IGA at seven thirty and Maureen to the Devlins' at eight. On that first day back, after the children had greeted her enthusiastically, she had seen to their breakfast and dressed them. They had played, and she had helped Essie with some errands, taking the quartet out with her. After lunch she had taken Sean Michael to nursery school. Essie had seen the other three put down for their naps, although Emlyn was beginning to consider that she didn't need a nap.

Returning to the quiet house, Maureen went into the den and dialed the Devlins' satellite provider. "I'd like to cancel the Channel," she said, giving them the account number. "Yes, the last bill has been paid. Thank you." She put the telephone back in its charger. She felt a small sadness, but then, she didn't need the fantasy of Toryn of the Thousand Pleasures anymore. She had his descendant, Toryn O'Donel, and to her delight the reality had turned out to be even better than the fantasy.

J.P. AND
THE REGENCY RAKE

J. P. Woods was one of the most powerful women in the book business. As CEO of Stratford Publishing, she was a woman to be both feared and courted. Little was known about her personal life other than that she came from a town called Bug Light on the far north coast of Maine and that she had graduated from a prestigious New England women's college with honors. She had begun her career in Boston, staying with a small publishing house for three years, and then come to New York, working first for Penguin in their NAL division, and finally settling at Stratford Publishing, where she swiftly scampered her way up the ladder of success.

At one point there was a rumor that she was Martin Stratford's illegitimate daughter, fathered when he was in college. Martin, now chairman emeritus of Stratford's board, found that rumor very funny. The other rumor—that J. P. Woods was or had been his mistress—he didn't find amusing at all. It suggested that he was a fool. It implied that J.P. wasn't worthy of the position to which he had appointed her. And it was even further from the truth than the first rumor. But Martin Stratford was the only person in the publishing world to know the truth of J. P. Woods's background. He knew she had worked damned hard to get where she was today, and he knew that she deserved everything she had accomplished, given her beginnings.

Jane Patricia Woods had been born the oldest child of a Maine fisherman and his wife. She had four younger siblings: two brothers and two sisters. When she was fifteen, her father had been lost at sea. Life hadn't been easy before he died, but after he died, it was horrific. Fortunately, they owned the small house in which they lived. It had belonged to her paternal grandparents. They were long dead, as were her mother's people but for an older sister. Her mother worked in the local general store. They applied for and got food stamps and heating aid. And on Saturday night her mother went to the only bar in town, where she would pick up a man, bring him home, have sex with him, collect a few dollars, and then send the guy on his way. Along with her minimum-wage job, it kept the lights on and allowed for a few extras, like shoes and school supplies.

Everyone in Bug Light knew what her mother did on Saturday nights, but the truth was, she wasn't the only widow in town supplementing a poverty-level income by going to the bar and picking up a man. More important, she went to the bar only that one night a week, and was in church with her kids on Sunday mornings. She didn't flirt with anyone else's man, and she didn't allow any man accompanying her home to remain in her house longer than it took him to fuck her. As far as Bug Light was concerned, Dorcas Woods was a reasonably respectable woman. And they all knew that if she had had a better choice, she would have taken it.

But one night the man her mother brought home didn't leave as he should have. Unable to perform, he had knocked Dorcas unconscious, then beaten her to a pulp. Then he'd crept down the hall to the bedroom where J.P. and her little sisters slept. J.P. had awakened to a hand over her mouth, a faceless man atop her. She tried to buck him off, but he was too firmly seated. She was terrified and angry at the same time. Then he spoke.

"Your whore mama didn't do what she should, girly, so you're going to do it for her. You a virgin?"

J.P. nodded, her eyes wide.

"I ain't had a virgin in a long time, girly, but I'm going to enjoy popping your cherry for you. Maybe next time your cold-ass mama will do her job better, 'cause if she doesn't, I'm coming back. You got sisters, don't you?"

J.P. nodded.

"They're younger, right?"

Her head bobbed.

"Good, 'cause I'll give them a poke too. Hey, maybe I'll do it tonight." He laughed. The sound was like that of a donkey braying. And all the while he was speaking, he was massaging his flaccid penis, trying to bring it to a point where he could use it. He wasn't having a great deal of success, however. "Damn! You're like your mama, girl. I ain't never had no trouble with my dick before. You're going to have to suck it, girly." He slid up on her, his hand moving from her mouth so quickly she had no time to scream. He pinched her nostrils shut with one hand, pushing his penis into her mouth when she gasped for air. "Bite me and I'll kill you, girly. Now, start sucking!"

J.P. thought she was going to die then and there. She could feel the bile rising up in her throat. She was going to vomit, and then she heard a loud thwack and her attacker fell forward on her with a deep groan. As he did, his penis pulled out of her mouth, to her great relief, and she threw up all over herself.

"You okay, sis?" It was her fourteen-year-old brother, Joe, and he was holding his baseball bat. "Pete," he called to his thirteen-year-old sibling, "help me get this son of a bitch off Janie. Did he hurt you, sis? You okay?" he repeated.

She burst into tears as they pulled the man away. She was covered in vomit, but filled with relief to have escaped the worst, although having a dick in her mouth was hardly the best.

"Ah, crap, Janie, don't bawl like that." He wanted to hug her, but considering the mess on her thought better of it.

"Get him out of here," J.P. said to her brother. "And see if Mom's all right. He obviously wasn't happy with her and came in here. How did you know something was wrong, Joe?"

"Marybeth came and woke us up. She heard the guy when he was talking to you," Joe said. "I didn't think to check on Mom. I just got my bat and came to rescue you."

"My hero," J.P. told her brother. "Really. Can you see his face? Who is he?"

"Maintenance guy down at the school," her younger brother said. "He's always looking at the girls in my class, and he licks his lips a lot."

"Marybeth, you go find Mom. You boys take him out of here," she instructed.

"We ought to call the sheriff," Joe said.

"Look, he didn't rape me, and I don't want it known all over town that he tried to," J.P. told her brother. "They tolerate what Mom does Saturday nights, but someone is sure to say she let the guy into our room to get more money. You know how people are. Then we'll have to deal with Social Services. They'll separate us, and we'll end up God knows where or, worse, a group home."

"Yeah, you're right," Joe agreed. "But you're sure you're okay, sis?"

"I will be when I've taken a shower," she told him. "Codfish cakes really stink when you toss 'em up, don't they?"

Her brothers laughed. This was the Janie they knew: sensible and sharp of tongue. Following her instructions, they dragged the body of the man from her room. She heard it *bumpbumpbumping* as they descended the stairs. The creep's face was going to be a mess, and he deserved it. She went into their little bathroom, stripped off her nightshirt, rinsed it out, swished some Listerine around in her mouth, and then took a quick shower. Quick because the water wasn't very hot, and it was a winter's night. Wrapped in a towel, she hurried back to the room she shared with her sisters. Marybeth was sitting on the bed, comforting eight-year-old Julie.

J.P. quickly pulled on her other nightshirt. Marybeth

looked pale. "You okay, sweetpea?" J.P. asked the eleven-year-old.

"He beat up Mom," Marybeth said. "I think she might be dead."

Julie began to cry.

"Hush up, peapod," J.P. said. "I'll go and look."

But Dorcas Woods wasn't dead. She was badly beaten, however, and finally conscious again. "Call your aunt Faith," she told her eldest. J.P. nodded and did as she was told. Faith Leighton was their only living kin. She was a spinster.

Aunt Faith came and, seeing her younger sister's condition, said, "Do you think you have a concussion?"

"No, just a lot of bruising, maybe a rib or two out of place, and I think my right wrist is broken," Dorcas said. "I'm lucky."

"Yeah, you look it," Aunt Faith told her. "Well, let's get you patched up."

In the morning, it was their aunt who escorted them to church. "Poor Dorcas fell on the ice last night. She bruised herself up pretty bad and broke a wrist," Faith informed the pastor in a voice for all to hear.

"Bad night all around," Pastor Clarke replied. "They found Ed Gary, the school's maintenance man, on the beach this morning, half dead from the cold. Both of his legs was broke, and his two arms as well. His face was so black-and-blue they hardly recognized him. They think he was drunk and fell off the bluff."

"Ought to get rid of that man," Faith Leighton said sharply. "I understand he's always leering at the girls in school, especially the younger ones. How long before he's drunk and something happens?" she finished meaning-fully. "You're on the school board, Pastor. You should do something."

A murmur of assent was heard from those standing around them.

The pastor raised an eyebrow. "I hadn't heard that, Miss Leighton. But you're absolutely right. Can't have a fellow like that around our kids. The board is meeting this Tuesday night. I'll bring it up."

"If you don't, I will," the owner of the general store remarked. "I'm on the board too." Then he turned to Faith Leighton. "I expect Missus Woods will need a few days to heal," he said. "Tell her to take the week, and I'll not dock her pay. Hard enough for that woman without having to lose a week's wages when she's sick."

"I'll come in after school, Mr. Brown," J.P. said. "And I'll work all day Saturday for you, sir."

"Mighty obliging of you, Jane. You're a good girl," the storekeeper said.

There were no more Saturday nights for her mother after that. J.P. and her two brothers got jobs after school, which was not easy in a small town in northern Maine. If there were some who suspected that Ed Gary's injuries and Dorcas Woods's injuries were connected, they said noth-ing. And Ed Gary was gone once the hospital released him.

The incident, however, had driven home a hard lesson to J.P. She didn't want to be anyone's victim again, and she didn't want to spend the rest of her life in Bug Light.

A straight-A student and valedictorian of her high school class, she had been accepted at an excellent wom-en's college. She wanted to go, but the aid package just wasn't enough, and so she made a deal with the college. She would attend the local community college for two years, keep a straight-A average, and then transfer to them. In return, they would give her a full scholarship, including room and board, for her last two years.

She had worked filleting fish down on the Bug Light town dock winter and summer, even as she worked to keep her scholarship those first two years. She didn't know which was worse: summers, when the stink of the fish was overpowering in the heat, or winters, when her hands almost froze in the icy cold. She had helped her mother with the household expenses while putting aside half of what she earned for the day she left Bug Light. And then it came.

She quit working a week before her departure, showering several times a day because she thought she would never get the smell of fish off of her skin and out of her hair. The men down on the docks, who had all known her dad, had scrabbled together a hundred dollars for her as a going-away gift. J. P. Woods cried for one of the last times in her life at their kindness. But the man she recognized as the head of Bug Light's small fishing fleet put a beefy arm about her, saying, "You've more than earned our respect, Jane Patricia. Your dad would be proud of you. You ain't going to come back here, I suspect, but don't forget Bug Light and where you come from."

She never had. Hard work could get you anywhere in life if you persisted at it. Luck was something you made. But J. P. Woods's biography only mentioned her hometown of Bug Light, Maine; her college; her work history; and the few awards she had received. She never spoke of her family, and if asked, she would only say that they were small-town people. Few asked, however, and most assumed she came from a privileged background because of her alma mater and her beautiful manners.

Martin Stratford had done some investigating on his own when he began to notice J. P. Woods. "Where did she come from?" he asked his longtime secretary, Alice.

"NAL," Alice said.

"No. *Where did she come from?*" he repeated.

"How much do you want to know?" Alice asked.

"Everything," Martin Stratford said.

Several days later Alice had put a folder on his desk. Martin Stratford learned that the up-and-coming young female executive in his company was the daughter of a fisherman and a sales clerk in a general store in a little Northern coastal town in Maine with the absurd name of Bug Light. He read how she had worked her butt off to get into a good school and then negotiated with her college so she could go. He nodded and smiled to himself as he read. This was a woman who knew how to work hard and how to take advantage of opportunities, and she had no qualms about beating out an opponent. This was the person he wanted to run his company when he decided to retire. Not that he would ever really retire completely. But one day he was going to want to start to do a few of those things on his bucket list; and when he did them, he wanted to know his publishing house was running smoothly. So he had begun to groom J. P. Woods to take his place. And eventually she had.

J. P. Woods was both respected and feared in her position as head of Stratford. Once she had gained a certain level within the company, she chose a gay male assistant.

One of his duties was to pick young men working their way up the corporate ladder to sexually service his boss. If J.P. were a man, she would have been accused of sexual harassment, but no young guy wanted to admit he had been coerced into having sex with a woman. It was embarrassing.

But J.P. had met her match with Michael Devlin when he had come from Random House in London to be Stratford's editor in chief. Mick had a reputation as a lady-killer, but he wasn't about to sleep with her—a fact he made very clear. Not being able to control this man frightened J.P. She knew that Martin Stratford was going to retire shortly, and she was wondering if he was having second thoughts about her taking over his publishing house. Had he brought Mick Devlin in to undercut her? Martin could be a bastard when he wanted to be. But Devlin had assured her that all he wanted to do was edit. Martin had given her his chair at Christmas, and damned if Devlin hadn't gone and married Stratford's prize romance author, Emilie Shann.

J.P. had always had mixed feelings about Emilie Shann. She was beautiful, talented, and successful. Martin adored her, but J.P. had hated the sappy romantic drivel she had been writing. She had hinted broadly to Emilie's agent, Aaron Fischer, that unless Emilie could write sexier, which was what the market was now demanding, she wouldn't have a future with Stratford. And damn if the little prissy miss hadn't gone and done just that. She had written one helluva sexy blockbuster. J.P. liked Emilie a little better for rising to her challenge. And when J.P. had taken her aside and asked her if she knew about a woman-only network called the Channel, Emilie had said yes, it was addictive but wonderful. She suggested J.P. try it. And she had.

God, how she wished she could get someone to write about the Channel. What a book that would be, especially if other women then tried it themselves. But J.P. was smart enough to know that if the secret of the Channel came out, it would destroy it. She was having far too much fun to do that. She had created a persona within the Channel that suited her perfectly.

As the widowed Duchess of Manley she was both outrageously beautiful and rich. She led a life considered shockingly scandalous by the *ton,* but was nevertheless accepted because of her wealth. Everyone thought that eventually some fortunate man was going to pin down the naughty duchess and find his way into her heart. But the Duchess of Manley had no heart. She was as cold as ice.

She had hated the arranged marriage into which she had been forced, and she privately rejoiced when her abusive husband broke his neck going over a water jump. Lady Jane had been the duke's second wife. As he already had an heir and a spare, her wifely duties were to oblige her husband in any and every way he demanded. The duke, a sensual man, had taught her more than any respectable woman should know about sex. While he preferred having a wife to keeping a mistress, he wanted that wife to behave in their bedroom as a mistress would and in public like the Duchess of Manley should.

Lady Jane had not followed the proper etiquette for mourning, coming out of black three months after her husband's demise. All of London was shocked. Her stepson protested, but she ignored him. He was a weak fool.

The *ton* was shocked further when she appeared at the first ball of the new season clad in a scarlet gown. The gentlemen, however, were delighted—to the outrage of several mamas with nubile daughters to marry off. How could their virginal darlings compete with the magnificent duchess? And she did prefer younger men to older ones.

"They have more stamina in bed," she was reported to have said. "One prefers a two-year-old stallion to one who is four."

The beautiful dowager duchess soon grew bored, though, and sought an outlet to relieve that ennui. Lady Jane found it when a friend complained that she was never going to find a rich wife for her brother if he didn't learn how to behave properly with the young ladies. Lady Jane heard herself saying, "Would you like me to train him? Young men, like young stallions, frequently need schooling."

Her friend had giggled, but then, seeing that the dowager duchess was serious, said, "Would you charge for such training, Jane?"

"Of course," the lady answered. "That for which you pay nothing is worth nothing, Augusta. The fee will depend on the difficulty involved. I will lure your brother home with me at the next ball and keep him a few days. Tell anyone who asks after him while I have him that he has gone down to the country on estate business for your widowed mother."

And so it had begun. Soon certain ladies of the *ton* were sending their brothers, their young male relations, even their husbands to the Dowager Duchess of Manley to be schooled in proper behavior toward women of all stations. J. P. Woods thought if someone like Emilie Shann knew of her fantasy, she would be very surprised by it. The fantasy relaxed J.P. after her long, hard days at work, but because she was disciplined, she visited the Channel only three times a week.

Tonight she had come home after a particularly trying day of dealing with this new hell of electronic rights. Everything in publishing was changing so quickly, it was more than difficult to keep up with it. And the pirates were at work already downloading titles from books contracted before 1994 that were being negotiated for now. Stratford's rights people were working as quickly as they could. Agents were screaming, authors were being demanding. She wanted her old publishing world back, but J. P. Woods was no fool. She knew that wasn't going to happen.

The car service dropped her off in front of her building on upper Fifth. The doorman leaped to open the door and greet her. He held a large umbrella over her head as she got out, even though the building had an awning. It had been raining an icy February rain all day. *Better than snow,* she thought as she hurried to the elevator.

"Good evening, Ms. Woods," the elevator man said. "Looks like it was a rough day." He closed the door and pressed the button marked 6.

"It was, Pablo," she admitted.

"My wife's waiting for that next Emilie Shann book," Pablo said.

"It's coming," J.P. promised as the elevator door opened on the sixth floor.

"Good night, Ms. Woods," the elevator man said.

"Good night, Pablo," she replied.

There were only three apartments on her floor. J.P. pushed her key into the door marked 6A, opened it, and went in, closing and locking the door behind her. The apartment was quiet and neat. It was Friday, and the maid had been in today. After hanging up her coat in the foyer closet, she went into the kitchen and opened the refrigerator, pulling out some salad greens, a white Zinfandel dressing, butter, and some cheese. She fixed the salad, dressed it, and put it on a tray next to an empty plate and a glass of Pugliese Bella Maria wine. She needed carbs tonight. Slicing two pieces of white bread from a loaf her sister had sent her, J.P. set up a grilled cheese sandwich.

Then she left the kitchen and went into her bedroom to undress and bathe. The hot water from the a half dozen showerheads felt wonderful on her neck and shoulders. She stood under them for several long minutes before turning the water off and getting out to dry herself off. She tossed on a full-length flannel-lined tee completely out of character with her power-dressing persona. The New England girl still left in her wanted to be cozy on a cold night, central heat or no. Then she went into the kitchen and grilled her sandwich in butter until it was crispy brown and the cheddar was oozing out of it.

J.P.'s apartment had a small dining room, which, like the living room, looked out over the park below. She took her meal into the dining room, and sat eating in the dark silence while enjoying the twinkling skyline across the park. She wasn't a woman who was afraid of being alone. Indeed, she relished it, and having no one in her private life to answer to. Jane Patricia Woods was self-sufficient, both in her real life and in her fantasy life. As soon as she washed her dishes, she was going to take up that fantasy. She was still tense from the week she had just endured.

Finally she climbed into her bed. Pressing a button on her night table signaled the doors of the entertainment center opposite her bed to slide open. J.P. settled back. Tonight she would be schooling Lord Reginald Bowie, whose bride, Lady Penelope, was tired of being blamed for their lack of an heir, when the truth was that dear Reggie, while a notable womanizer, found it difficult to get it up for his wife. J.P. pressed the A button on her remote and was immediately in a bedroom in the duchess's London town house.

"How do you want 'im, m'lady?" Flint, one of the two footmen holding the half-conscious man between them, asked her.

"Strip him completely," Lady Jane said.

"Wha . . . Where . . . am I?" the man asked groggily.

"Your wife has sent you to me for training, Lord Reginald. Your behavior is really not to be borne, I'm afraid."

"Penny?" he mumbled. "Doesn't do her duty."

"How can she when you don't do yours?" Lady Jane said. "Oh, yes, I know all about your ability to fuck any little dancer or shop assistant to a fare-thee-well, but you cannot, it seems, manage to fuck your wife. And if you do not, my dear Reggie, then there will be no heir for your title. No, no! We cannot have that, and so you must be trained to do your duty, dear boy. Lady Penelope is counting on me, and I will not fail her."

While she spoke, the two brawny footmen, Bertie and Flint, quickly stripped Lord Reginald Bowie naked. At a signal from their mistress, they half dragged the man to a stand. Lady Jane picked up the riding crop that lay on a tabletop. She slid it beneath his penis, then lifted up the limp bit of flesh and shook her head. "You will have to do better than that, Reggie," she told him. "This is really quite a pitiful display." Then she removed the crop, laid it aside, and said to the footmen, "Prepare him."

They dragged the nobleman across the room and slung him facedown over a bar covered in silk that was fitted upon two sturdy wooden legs. His head hung down. They spread the lordling's legs and fastened them with manacles to the floor, then fastened his wrists to the frame of the device. The manacles were lined in lamb's wool to prevent chafing. It was not her intent to damage her pupils.

Lord Reginald was suddenly quite clearheaded. "What are you doing to me?" he demanded of her. "How dare you imprison me? I shall go to the authorities and have you jailed for this outrage! I don't care if you are a dowager duchess. Your late husband would be appalled by the aberrant behavior you are exhibiting."

Lady Jane laughed. "No, my lord, he would not. You see, dear Frederick taught me everything I know. And you will not report me to anyone. Like the others before you, and those yet to come, you will not want to make public what is done by me in this house to those sent to me for training in the proper decorum of how to perfectly pleasure a woman." She undid the sash of her scarlet silk robe and laid it aside. She was garbed in white muslin drawers and a tightly laced black corset that barely contained her full breasts. The corset was decorated with dainty white rosettes that matched those on the black garters she wore to hold up her white silk stockings.

"Now, Reggie, let us see how quickly we may bring your cock to a good stiff stand." She automatically reached out her hand to receive the wide leather tawse that Bertie handed her. Then she smacked Lord Reginald's bare bottom several times. He yelped with surprise. Lady Jane looked to her footmen. "Well?" she said.

"Not yet, m'lady," Flint said. "I think this one will take a fair amount of punishment. Remember Baron Boston?"

Lady Jane nodded. "Yes, he was difficult at first, but then he came on quite nicely and turned out to be one of my best pupils." She plied the tawse across Reggie's plump buttocks, smacking him first this way and then that. When he began to whimper, she whacked him harder. "Don't be such a child, Reggie. Surely you've been birched, and this is far easier." After a few long minutes, it became obvious that her pupil was not going to respond to the tawse. Lady Jane laid the tawse aside and picked up her riding crop and began punishing him with it.

He howled and swore dreadfully at her, but she continued wielding the crop, and Flint began to nod in the affirmative. "He's coming on now, m'lady. A few more blows should do it for you." And after she had delivered them, the footman reached out and grasped Lord Bowie's distended cock. "Good and hard, m'lady," he told her.

"He must come on sooner than that," Lady Jane said, annoyed. "Poor Penelope should only have to whip him a few blows to get him ready." She reached into a basket on the nearby table and drew out a small object. As she dipped it into a dish of olive oil, she spread the cheeks of Lord Bowie's bottom with the thumb and forefinger of her other hand.

"Wha-wha-what are you doing?" he whimpered.

"I'm inserting a small dildo into your fundament to make certain you remain rigid. It's no bigger than my thumb, Reggie, and surely you had a cock in your ass when you were at school. I was told all the boys do at one time or another." She slowly and carefully inserted the dildo. The object was to give him pleasure, not pain. "I will leave you now. Lady Worthington's ball is tonight, and I must make an appearance. I understand that notorious rake the Earl of Pelton will be there. He left for India the year before I had my first season and hasn't been back since. All the mamas are even more afraid of him than they are of me." She laughed mischievously. "Flint, adjust his head so he is more comfortable. I will take up where I left off when I return."

"Yes, m'lady," came the dutiful reply. "Shall we twist the dildo at all?"

"Perhaps just twice to keep him primed," Lady Jane said, and hurried off to get dressed for Lady Worthington's ball. She was anxious to see if the Earl of Pelton would actually show up. The rumor was he had gone to India to avoid the consequences of dallying with a wealthy young Englishwoman in her first season. Others, however, said that Pelton was simply an adventurer at heart. He had a younger brother married to the daughter of a marquess, and the two of them had already produced three sons and a daughter. The earldom was quite safe without his taking a wife. Lady Jane was actually quite curious to learn which story came closer to the truth. Smithers, her maid, was waiting for her as she entered her bedchamber.

"The Earl of Pelton is to be at the ball," Lady Jane

said. "I will want to attract his attention without seeming too obvious."

"The emerald green silk chemise dress then, m'lady. I had actually gotten out the black silk, but if you're looking to be noticed by the gentleman, then the green," Smithers said. "Most of the gentlemen are used to you wearing black. The green with your red hair will be stunning, m'lady."

"And get out my emerald set," Lady Jane said. "All the women will be wearing pearls, and the maidens dainty lockets. The emeralds will attract him if nothing else will," she said and laughed.

Smithers dressed her mistress quickly, arranging her long red hair in a chignon, which was distinctly unfashionable in this day of short coifs and curls. She fastened the Manley emeralds about Jane's neck, while her mistress affixed the matching earrings into her ears. "The young duchess will have a fit when she sees those emeralds," Smithers said and chuckled.

"She is much too young at twenty to carry off emeralds like these," Lady Jane noted sharply. "As dowager it was my choice to choose first those gems I wanted from the Manley jewels."

"You're much too young to be a dowager duchess," Smithers said.

"I know," Jane replied with a smile, "but being the Dowager Duchess of Manley offers me far more freedom than I had as its duchess, or would have as another man's wife. Men are good for little else than being bed partners, and I have my pick of those."

Her carriage was waiting in front of the town house.

She arrived at Lady Worthington's ball just fashionably late enough so she did not have to stand in a long line to be announced. Escorted up the broad staircase by one of her hostess's well-trained servants, she was brought to the entry of the ballroom. The majordomo did not need to ask or be told.

"Lady Jane Fellowes, Dowager Duchess of Manley," he called out in his deep stentorian voice.

Jane descended the marble steps into the ballroom to be greeted by her host and hostess.

"My God, Jane, you look quite spectacular tonight," Lord Worthington said, kissing her hand and wishing he were younger. The woman really had the most magnificent breasts, and they were practically falling from her fashionable bodice. He forced his eyes to her face to meet her amused stare.

"You will frighten every mama here tonight trolling for a husband for her daughter," Lady Worthington said with a quick laugh. "The gentlemen are already beginning to swarm in your direction. It is really quite unfair of you." Then she lowered her voice. "Charles Pell is back from India. Did you ever meet him?"

"No," Jane said. "But I will admit to being fascinated by the gossip surrounding him. Will you introduce me? I imagine the mamas are worried by his presence too."

"Not at all," Lady Worthington informed her. "Some of them are bold enough or foolish enough to think their little virgin will attract his honorable intentions."

"Gracious!" Jane said. "I hope he doesn't have any of those."

Both Worthingtons laughed at this clever remark, and

then Lord Worthington said, "I will introduce you, my dear. Walk with me so I may be envied by every fellow in the ballroom. With all due respect to my wife, you are the most beautiful woman here tonight." He took her hand and placed it in his crooked arm. Then they began to traverse the distance across the ballroom, for the dancing had now stopped briefly.

Jane looked at her objective as they walked. He was tall. Six feet plus an inch or two, with a body that looked hard without the benefit of a corset. Dark hair cut fashionably short, but without ringlets or sideburns. His garb was quite traditional, but stylish, with buttoned knee breeches and a dark evening coat. Because his back was to her, she couldn't see his face.

Reaching the spot where Lord Pell stood chatting with several other gentlemen, Lord Worthington brought them into the small circle. "Charles, I have brought the Dowager Duchess of Manley to meet you. She is, like all the ladies here tonight, quite intrigued by your reputation."

"As I am of hers," Charles, Lord Pell, answered, taking up Jane's hand to kiss it.

She laughed. It was a very bold statement, and the other gentlemen in the circle had paled at the Earl of Pelton's remark. "Perhaps one day we shall trade stories, my lord," she said, smiling. "Worthington, you may now take me back to your good lady, as I have satisfied my curiosity." Then she turned away from him to return to where her hostess now stood.

"An excellent put-down, my dear," her companion said. "His words were uncalled for, and I must apologize for it."

"Please do not. The apology will come from him in time, I assure you," Jane said.

Then she went on to enjoy the ball, dancing every dance with a different partner, and refereeing a dispute between two young bucks who wanted to escort her to the buffet, settling it by having one bring her champagne and the other a plate of food.

Finally she had had enough, and her carriage was called to be brought around. A Worthington footman helped her into her vehicle and shut the door. It was then that she became aware that fact she was not alone. "Have you come to tender me an apology, my lord?" she asked as the carriage began to draw away from the Worthington town house. "You were quite rude, you know."

He laughed in the darkness. "I owe you no apology for speaking a truth everyone knows," he said.

"And what truth is that?" she inquired.

"That the Dowager Duchess of Manley is a bold and independent woman who takes and discards lovers with the same rapidity and skill as a fishmonger sorting through a basket of winkles," he replied. "And then, of course, there is a rather wicked bit of gossip spoken of in such hushed whispers that I can scarce believe it true. Do you really take certain gentlemen and train them to be better and more considerate lovers?"

"Come home with me and learn the truth of it. My current pupil is awaiting my return. His wife sent him to me, as the wives of many of my clients do," Jane answered.

He reached out and pulled her into his arms. His mouth came down on hers as one hand plunged into her low-cut bodice to fondle a breast.

Jane kissed him back, for while his actions had taken her by surprise, his kiss was exciting and delicious. As for the hand on her breasts, it was well skilled. Finally she drew away from him. "There will be time for this afterward if you decide to remain," she told him breathlessly.

"Will you *train* me, madam?" he inquired of her.

"I do not believe you will need any training at all, my lord," she told him.

Ping! Ping! Ping! The Channel is now closing. And it did with its usual efficiency, just as the fantasy was becoming quite interesting. J.P. wished, as she often did, and suspected other women did, that the Channel could be accessed twenty-four-seven. But she knew if that were to come to pass, the secret would most likely get out, and the Channel would disappear from their lives.

She spent her Saturday, another dull rainy day, indoors. She read a manuscript that one of her younger editors was very enthusiastic about: a paranormal romance, which she was surprised to find actually engaged her interest. The editor had told her it was the first book in what could be a long series if it was successful. Paranormal and urban fantasy were hot right now, and Stratford was in business to turn a profit. She decided to give the young editor an opportunity.

She took a Post-it note and wrote on it: *One book with an option to check out the next book. If it works out, we can sign her to multiple books later.* Then she signed her name and returned the manuscript to her briefcase. Michael Devlin, her editor in chief, had already seen this manuscript and approved it based on her decision. It was a new author, after all, even if the genre was hot. She was more comfortable with Devlin now than she had ever been. To her surprise, he had been totally honest with her when he said he didn't want her job—he just wanted to edit. And while he would argue with her privately, once she had taken Martin Stratford's place, he never challenged her publically.

The sky was darkening over the park again. Lights were coming on in the buildings on the other side of it. J.P. stood, briefly looking out and wondering if someone over on Central Park West was doing the same thing. She had hardly eaten all day. Only yogurt, a pear, and a piece of dark chocolate. Now she broiled herself a small fillet of beef and fixed herself a salad with fresh spinach, red onion, and orange slices. She hadn't gotten into the Channel until almost ten o'clock last night. Tonight she wanted to be ready to enter it at eight p.m. sharp.

She wasn't quite certain where in her imagination Charles Pell, the Earl of Pelton, had sprung from, because she didn't usually create powerful men with whom she would interact. She wanted lovers of her choosing, who felt honored that the Dowager Duchess of Manley had selected them. Lovers who could be easily discarded. From that terrible night when she was sixteen and Ed Gary had tried and failed to rape her, she had avoided men who oozed sexual power. Not that her attacker had. He had been a drunken bully. But J. P. Woods had always suspected that that variety of bully lay deep in all males of the species. Better safe than sorry. Better to be the one in control. So from where had this fascinating and obviously dangerous man sprung?

She ate her supper while watching the news in her

small den. Nothing vital. No terrorist attacks anywhere in the world today. No war casualties to report. The former Bachelorette had caught her fiancé, who was purportedly the man of her dreams, banging her best friend, who then announced she was pregnant by the guy, and the engagement was off. *What a moron,* J.P. thought. Who finds love in six weeks, let alone in a lifetime? But hope always sprang eternal, didn't it?

She showered, got into her bed naked, opened the doors of the entertainment center, and, at the stroke of eight, pressed the A button on her Channel remote. She and the earl were walking up the stairs of her house. "I usually change into something more comfortable when I work," she told him. "And I have never invited a spectator to observe my methods, so you might perhaps want to wear a masque so you are not recognized. It might make it more difficult for my pupil."

"Who do you have as your prisoner tonight?" he asked her.

"Reggie Bowie," she told him.

"My God! He's a notorious womanizer," Charles Pell exclaimed.

"Shopgirls, servants, dancers," Jane told him. "But he is unable to get it up for his poor wife, and Penelope is being blamed by his family for the lack of an heir. Before she goes to the extreme of being impregnated by a lover, she wanted to see if I could do anything with him. It is a typical case, I assure you, my lord. He is a man who enjoys the feeling of power that he gets with a woman of lower station. He cannot, however, bring himself to the same state with his wife, who is a very pretty and delightful young woman."

"But what can you do?" the earl asked her.

"You will see," she told him as she entered her bed-chamber, the earl behind her. "Smithers, this is the Earl of Pelton. He will be joining me this evening. Help me undress so I may get back to my pupil." She stepped behind a painted screen, and when she emerged, she was in her black satin corset with the white rosettes, and white stockings held up by black-and-white garters. She wore no drawers now, since they would interfere with her mission. "Come along now, my lord," Lady Jane said briskly, and she handed him a black masque that would cover the area around his eyes and nose.

He put it on, then followed her up a flight of stairs to enter another bedchamber, where two footmen were waiting.

"How has he done, Flint?" Lady Jane asked her servant.

"Back to his old self, my lady. The first time we moved the dildo he came," Flint said in disgusted tones. "No control at all, I'm afraid. Then he fell asleep."

"Lower his head, then, and we shall begin anew," Lady Jane said. "My friend wishes to watch my work." She did not introduce Charles Pell.

The earl looked about him. The room contained a large canopied bed. There was also a table with several baskets on it, and the rather odd contraption to which the lady's victim was fastened. He watched as his hostess ordered the dildo removed from the man's asshole. "What is the tawse for?" he inquired.

"For smacking his bottom until his cock rises, but he needs my riding crop for that. Most of my pupils take to the tawse, but some do not, and so I use either the crop or a dog whip. He needed the stronger urging of the crop. Wake him, Flint. The drunken sot must be awake for this."

"When his cock is at a stand, what will you do with him then?" the earl asked.

"I'll want to see how he wields his weapon, and I will make corrections to his technique so that when he goes back home in a few days, he'll give Lady Penelope some real pleasure."

"Will she have to whip him?" the earl wondered, curious.

"Oh, yes. Men like this are rarely able to perform without a little bit of encouragement. He'll behave as always with his lower-class mistresses, but to satisfy his wife, and get an heir on her, he will require punishment."

"Fascinating," the earl remarked. "I have heard of men like that, women too, for whom pain must precede pleasure."

"Bertie, go and fetch Miss Montague. We will need her services shortly." Jane turned back to the earl. "Montague is my companion," she explained.

"And she is willing to help you in these endeavors?" He was surprised not just by the two footmen, but by a lady's companion who would partake in such undertakings.

Miss Montague arrived. She was an elegant young woman with proud and definitely aristocratic features. She had skin like a gardenia and mahogany-colored hair. "Who is it this time, my lady?" she asked, putting aside her Circassian wrapper, beneath which she wore a white silk corset trimmed with pink ribbons. Her white stockings were held up by garters of pink rosettes. She looked every inch the innocent lady.

"Lord Reginald Bowie, Monty," Jane answered. "Flint, is he awake?"

"Yes, m'lady."

"Reggie dear, we will continue what we began earlier," Lady Jane said. "The Worthington ball was quite nice, by the way. I saw Lady Penelope dancing with that Austrian baron—I believe his name is Von Falken. He spent most of the evening paying a great deal of attention to her."

"Dirty bugger trying to seduce a man's wife," her prisoner muttered. "Let me go! I need to challenge the fellow to a duel. Must protect the family honor."

Lady Jane sighed. "Reggie dear, you will not be released until you have been trained to my specifications, and we have only just begun." She smacked his bottom with three swift blows of her riding crop.

He yelped, surprised. "Bitch!"

Lady Jane began now to wield the crop in a steady cadence. "Count for me, Flint. I need to see how many whacks it will take to bring his cock up." She turned to the earl. "Once we have determined that, we can work on making him come on quicker. A half dozen smacks to his arse should be more than enough."

"He's good now, my lady," Flint called out. "It took fourteen blows."

Lady Jane ran her hand over Lord Bowie's scarlet bottom soothingly. "Now, then, Reggie, you are going to fuck this nice young lady, and we will see how well you do."

Bertie undid the manacles, and the two footmen raised the man up, allowing him to regain his balance. Lady Jane took the lordling by his very stiff penis and led him over to the bed, where Miss Montague now lay facedown, her bottom elevated and ready.

Lord Bowie's eyes bugged, and then he licked his lips. "Who is she?" His cock twitched in Jane's hand.

"It doesn't matter," the dowager duchess responded. "Now, fuck her, Reggie."

Grabbing the girl's hips, he pushed eagerly into her wet vagina, thrust two or three times, and came with a groan.

"Oh, dear," Lady Jane said, shaking her head. "That is not at all the way to fuck a woman, Reggie. Did you gain pleasure?"

"Aye, I did," came the answer.

"But your partner did not, and you will find that you will gain even more pleasure when you give pleasure." Jane turned to the earl. "My lord, would you like to show him exactly how it should be done?"

"With pleasure, madam," the Earl of Pelton said. He walked over to Miss Montague and ran his hand up and down her beautiful back several times, caressing her buttocks with one hand as he unbuttoned the fly on his satin breeches to pull out a fine-looking cock. Then, holding her steady, he entered her slowly, eliciting a small moan of pleasure from the girl. "What a lovely tight cunt you have, my dear," he complimented her.

"Thank you," the young woman replied politely.

The earl began to move on her, first with slow, deep strokes of his penis, and then he began to increase the tempo of the movement. Miss Montague murmured a sound of decided pleasure and wiggled her bottom into him.

"Observe, Reggie, how the gentleman has taken the time to gentle her first before beginning to fuck her. He is not in any hurry, and listen to her little cries of appreciation. He begins slowly, gradually increasing the friction of his cock in her cunt."

"Oh! Oh! Oh!" Miss Montague exclaimed. "I am coming! Oh! Oh! Oh!"

The earl stiffened and gave a mighty groan as he released his juices.

"Now you see how they have both enjoyed the interlude. That is the way it ought to be when a man and his wife couple. But you! You have not fucked your wife since your wedding night a year ago. You have let her take the blame for your lack of an heir. You have really behaved in a dastardly fashion, but when I am through, you will fuck your wife with great regularity until you have that heir your family requires. Now it is late. Put him to bed, Flint. Monty will attend to him for an hour or two."

She swept from the chamber, the earl behind her as she returned downstairs to her own chambers. "Smithers, go to bed," she instructed her maid, who curtsied and hurried off. Lady Jane turned to the earl. "Are you staying?" she asked him.

"How could I refuse such a gracious invitation?" he asked, amused.

"Unfasten my corset for me, then," she instructed him. He came behind her and began unlacing the elegant little garment. When he had finished, he let the corset drop to the floor and, reaching around, gathered her breasts into his hands.

"These are quite the finest tits I believe I have ever seen, madam," he told her. He cradled them in his palms as if weighing them. Then, bending over her, he first kissed her shoulder, and then nipped at her ear. "You are going to be fucked, madam, as you never before have. I am a master at the arts of Venus, and know how to prolong pleasure. You have never had a lover like me, Jane. You will not so easily discard me. You will be mine until I decide you will not," he told her.

"I cannot be owned. The late duke thought he was buying a new toy when he married me. It was my second season, and I was only seventeen. Like everyone else, I thought it was an honor to be married to a man like Manley. But I was wrong. He had heirs. He only wanted an ornament, a plaything. Everything I do to train these thoughtless men who think only of their own pleasure I learned from my husband, whose interest was in himself only. Fortunately I was wise enough to comply with his every wish, and eventually he learned I had an intelligent mind. I despised him. I probably even hated him. But I was the wife he demanded. He left me a very wealthy woman for those nine years I spent as his possession. Of course, part of the reason he did so was to annoy his weakling heir." Lady Jane laughed. "I have helped myself to the best of the jewels, and no one dares say nay to me. However, I do not go to Manley Hall. I am happy in my London house, and I have a cottage by the sea near Bath. But do not think to own or control me, my lord."

"It is your fantasy, madam," he surprised her by saying. "I am only here because you want me here. Like everything else around you, I am a figment of your imagination. I suspect, however, the reason you brought me into your life is that you are ready to share your passion with a strong man, not one of these London dandies whom you have had as your previous lovers. You said yourself that

pleasure can be gained only by both parties not just taking, but giving." His thumbs began to circle her nipples. "I
can be gone anytime you choose to banish me, Jane." His
lips found the crook of her neck and pressed a deep kiss
into it.

It was her fantasy. Jane could banish him when and if
she wanted to do so. But not just yet. She leaned back
against him briefly and felt the hard ridge in his breeches
pressing against her arse. She had seen that lovely cock of
his earlier, and Monty should not be the only one to enjoy
it. Jane had never seen her companion respond to a man's
cock with such enthusiasm. Nor had she ever seen Monty's face light up as it had when he was fucking her and
when she came. "Take off your clothes," she said.

Releasing her, he laughed. "Wouldn't you like to do
it?" he asked her teasingly.

She was going to refuse, but then she decided otherwise. Undressing him could prove to be a great deal of fun.
"I think I would," she answered him, turning about to face
him. She undid his fine linen shirt, which she noted was
embroidered with his crest, and removed it. He had no
plainer shirt beneath it, as was the custom. Her hands
smoothed over his bare chest, which was devoid of hair.
The skin was firm and taut. Bending her head, she licked
first one of his nipples and then the other. She unbuttoned
his satin breeches and pushed them down. "You have no
drawers on," she exclaimed, half shocked.

"No, I don't," he replied. "I find drawers spoil the line
of the garment."

"And the lack thereof makes it far simpler for a man
gone seducing," Jane said.

"Ah, madam, you have found me out." He chuckled as he stepped from the cream-colored satin breeches.

He was magnificent in his nudity. Strong broad shoulders and chest. A narrow waist and hips, a tight firm arse, long legs, and a fine penis that she intended to put to good use several times before the Channel closed tonight. Looking up into his startlingly bright blue eyes, she ran her hands over his body. The flesh beneath her hands was smooth, and it was firm. He was a man who cared about his appearance, like all of these London dandies. Yet he was not one of them. She stepped close enough to him so that the tips of her nipples just touched his chest.

He smiled down into her face. "You are pleased with what you see, madam?"

"How can I not be?" Lady Jane responded.

His arm went about her waist, pulling her closer. He tipped her face up. Then his lips met hers in a deep and passionate kiss that seemed to go on and on and on. Jane felt every bit of antagonism she had ever felt for men drain instantly away. The kiss was magic, as was the man now holding her in his arms. How had this happened?

He broke the kiss off, caressing her face with gentle fingers. "The need to control began that terrible night when you were but a girl. Never had you felt more helpless and frightened than when that man straddled you, attempting rape. You vowed then you would never be weak, be in a position to be controlled ever again."

"How . . . ?" she began, startled by his words, but he gently pressed two fingers to her lips, smiling.

"I am your creation, my love," he reminded her. "You have no secrets from me, Jane. But by building such a

strong fortress about yourself, you have also denied yourself what most women want. Love. Marriage. Children."

"I have my career," she responded. "I am exactly where
I've always wanted to be."

"But you are lonely," Charles Pell said. "And you rein-
force your need to be powerful by *training* these foolish
men whom their foolish wives send to you. You have taken
lovers, but only those whom you could bend to your will.
You have never really shared yourself with any man, fantasy or real, for fear of losing control. But with me, that
will change. You are finally ready to be loved, Jane. And I
will love you, but not as a supplicant at your whim. As an
equal partner in the relationship that we will begin to form
this night." He smoothed his hand down her unfashion-
ably long hair. "Do not look so surprised, my love. I am
your creation. If you were not ready, I should not be here."

"I am not sure," Jane said softly.

"Aye, you are," he informed her. "The rule of the
Channel protects you, my love. At any time you find yourself fearful, you may end the fantasy. But you will not."
Then he picked her up in his arms and walked to her bed,
where he gently laid her down, joining her. "Tonight," he
said, "you will let me take the lead, and you will trust me,
Jane."

"For now," she replied.

The words hadn't even died on her lips when he began
to caress her practically naked body. The stockings and
garters still encasing her shapely legs added to their shared
excitement. His touch was gentle, almost tender. She practically purred with the simple pleasure his hands were offering her, stretching her length that he might not miss an

inch of her soft skin. And just when Jane thought he could get no better, he began to kiss and lick her flesh. She sighed with pleasure at his actions.

"You are delicious," he told her, stopping a moment to smile into her face.

"You do not feel the need to hurry?" she said, noting his swollen cock.

"No, I do not. The delights we will share joined will be even better for waiting."

Then he continued to explore her slowly with hands and lips and tongue. He did not confine his erotic actions to just her chest and belly. Whispering for her to turn over, he explored the line of her spine, a finger tracing the bone from her neck to just above her arse. His hands fondled the rounded hills of her buttocks, pulling them apart, a finger pressing against her fundament, but going no further.

"Ohh!" Jane gasped as a short burst of pure desire flamed up in her cunt.

Gently he nudged her onto her back again, and cupped her mons with a big hand. He could feel the heat, the moisture, and faint throbbing. He squeezed, and another little cry escaped her. Her legs fell open to him, and taking the invitation, he went down on her, spreading her labia open, finding her clitoris with his tongue, tasting her, feeling his cock grow tighter, savoring the essence of her on his tongue and lips.

None of her lovers had ever made love to her as the Earl of Pelton was now making love to her. They had but one goal in mind, and that was to fuck her. And the truth was that she had entertained the same goal. All she had ever wanted was a cock in her cunt, a quick orgasm, and a farewell kiss. And she had led the dance herself, deciding whom she would take to her bed to satisfy her libidinous nature quickly, and then be gone. She had wanted lovers who would play stud to her mare in heat. Nothing more.

Yet suddenly this fantasy of hers had taken an entirely different turn. For the first time in her life she was experiencing being made love to, and it wasn't frightening, and she didn't feel helpless. She felt—she searched for the right word—she felt "cherished." His tongue was truly wicked as it foraged in her flesh. Jane cried out with a small clitoral orgasm, begging him, "No more, my lord. I want you inside of me. I need you!"

He complied, kissing her with his lips and tongue so that she tasted herself, which added to the level of her excitement. Then, mounting her, he pushed slowly, slowly, slowly into her. She was almost ready to scream with her desire, but remembering how he had brought Monty on so nicely, she refrained from complaining. Fully sheathed, he said to her, "Look at me, Jane," and she did. "Do you feel the throbbing?"

She nodded and contracted her vaginal muscles about him.

"Ahh, wicked one, do not tease me, else I am not able to give you all the passion that you deserve," he cautioned her. Then he began to move upon her, the cadence of his rhythm increasing until the world began to spin about them.

"Ah God! Ah God!" Jane cried out. "It is so good, Charles. So good! Do not stop. I beg of you. Ah, yes! I am dying! I come! I come!" And she did as she had never done before. Her vagina spasmed and spasmed and spasmed. She saw stars, and yet she felt totally in control of herself.

"My love! My love!" he cried just a moment behind her, his juices pouring into her in almost violent spurts of his passion.

Ping. Ping. Ping. The Channel is now closed.

"Good night, my love," Jane heard him whisper as she came to herself in her bed.

"Damn!" she said. "Damn, and damn again!" She had just experienced the best sex she had ever had with an incredible man, and the Channel closed on her? She wanted more! She wanted him back! And she wasn't going to be able to get him back for several days. She couldn't play in the Channel every night, not with the week she had ahead of her.

Her schedule was just too tight with the quarterly sales meeting and finalizing the autumn list and Martin Stratford's semiannual family board meeting, where she had to answer the questions his uninterested daughters asked only because they were concerned with how much money they could get from their father's publishing house shares if Martin took the company public, which he wasn't going to do, or if some big conglomerate wanted to add Stratford Publishing to the list of their company. There weren't many family-owned publishing houses left these days. J. P. Woods wasn't a happy camper right now. But she did have a few more hours of shut-eye coming, and she had better take it if she was going to be on top of her game.

Monday morning the halls of Stratford came alive with frantic whispers passed from office to office, desk to desk. J. P. Woods was on a tear.

Her longtime assistant, Gloria, plunked the paranormal manuscript on the young editor's desk. "Approved, but don't go gushing your thanks, kid. Madam Publisher isn't happy today for whatever reason. I'll tell her you're thrilled. When she calms down, you can do it personally."

"Gotcha," the editor said, but she couldn't keep the excitement from her voice.

"What's bitten her?" Mick Devlin, the editor in chief of Stratford, asked Gloria. "She was fine on Friday. She get stood up or something over the weekend?"

"Far as I know, she stayed home," Gloria said. "Don't say I said it, but maybe she's going through the change. Women have a tendency to get in serious moods when that happens. You wouldn't know that yet with your lovely young wife."

"Four kids, deadlines, and an occasional bout of PMS is bad enough," Mick responded with a grin. "You mean it's going to get worse one day?"

"Just about the time those twins of yours are teenagers," Gloria replied with an answering grin.

Every dark, wet, and icy winter's day dragged that week. J. P. Woods had never known such a long, slow week. By Thursday she was desperate to return to her fantasy, but Friday was the board meeting. Then her sister Marybeth called to say their mother had fallen on the ice and broken her hip.

"Can you come up?" she asked. "She shouldn't be alone when she comes home from the hospital, and I just can't be running over there all the time. Julie won't help out at all now that she has that job down in Boston."

"Find someone Mom would like to live in," J.P. said.

"I know your family keeps you hopping, but Julie and I can't just pick up and run to Maine. She just got her job, and it's the one she's been gunning for over the last few years."

"But you're head of a company," Marybeth complained. "Why can't you come home and help out, Janie?"

"Precisely because I am head of a company," J.P. answered. "Listen, sis, I saw that Mom has a decent house, and all of you have extras because of me. Now, you stayed in Bug Light, Marybeth. Find a good woman who likes to play poker. Someone who will look after Mom, cook, and keep the house for her. I'll try to get up sometime in the spring. But I can't come now."

"It must be wonderful to be so important," her sister sniped.

"It is," J.P. said sharply. She didn't have to feel guilty.

"If the boys had stayed home . . . ," Marybeth began.

"For what?" J.P. wanted to know. "Dad's boat went down with him. If it was difficult earning a living as a commercial fisherman twenty years ago, think of how tough it is now. Bug Light is practically all old people at this point. The military is the best place for the boys, and they've both attained the rank of chief petty officer. In twenty-five years, they can retire with good pensions. It's a helluva lot better than they could have done staying home. Now, find someone to stay with Mom. I'll pay for it."

"But, Janie," her middle sister whined.

"I've got a meeting, Marybeth. Doc Parsons still taking care of Mom?"

"His son," came the answer.

"I'll call him. Tell Mom I send my love."

And J. P. Woods hung up. Just what she needed. Another complication in her life. And when the hell had it all become so difficult? After consulting her address book, she phoned her mother's doctor and was put through immediately. "How serious is it, Seth?" she asked the young doctor.

"Going to put a pin in her hip," he said. "She's in reasonably good health, Janie. You coming home?"

"Can't right now, but in the spring. I've asked Marybeth to find someone to come live in with Mom."

"I've got a good woman for the job," Seth Parsons said. "Marybeth isn't too good when it comes to judging character."

"I'll pay a hundred dollars more a week than the going rate in Bug Light, Seth. I'll take your advice and let you handle it. Call my sister. She'll be relieved."

"You sound tense, Janie," the doctor observed. "You keeping healthy?"

"I'm fine, Seth," she told him. *Fine except that I want to be with a man who's a total fantasy, and I can't be with him until Friday night, and then only for eight hours at a time. Fine except life sucks.* "Thanks for your help. Call me if Mom needs anything, okay?" She rang off. She didn't want to talk anymore, especially with people who called her Janie and reminded her of a time and place she would rather forget.

And then it was Friday. While the day dragged, J. P. Woods's mood lightened. Just a few more hours and she would be with Charles Pell again. Would they pick up where they had left off? Would he fuck her again until she was begging for mercy, and loving every minute that his cock was flashing back and forth in her cunt? She didn't care. She just needed to be with this man, who had so tenderly brought her alive and aware of true passion. She wanted to be in his arms, and this time, she would touch and lick and kiss his strong body, as he had done to her the other night. But she couldn't take another week like the one that had just passed. She had to be with him more than just a few hours.

She rushed home, almost too excited to eat the light supper she had prepared for herself this morning, but she heated it up, gobbled it down, and bathed. Then, at exactly eight o'clock, she climbed into her bed and pressed the A button on her Channel remote. She didn't even have time to blink before she found herself alone in her bed in her London town house. Where was he? Where was Charles Pell, the Earl of Pelton? Had he left her? "Smithers!" she called to her maid, and the woman came.

"Did the earl say he was coming tonight?" she asked.

"After midnight, my lady. He was delivering Lord Reggie back to his wife. A right good job you did with that one. Miss Montague says the difference between the first time Lord R. fucked her and last evening was like night and day."

"Thank you," Lady Jane said. "Do we have champagne on ice, Smithers? If not, see that it is done, please. The earl and I will celebrate our success with Lord Reggie."

"Right away, my lady," Smithers said, and bustled out of the bedchamber.

They had schooled Lord Reginald Bowie together, she

and Charles! The knowledge excited her. Yes, they had. Graphic and sexual recollections of how they had done it suddenly flooded her memory. It was amazing that he was so like she was. They were a perfectly matched pair. "I will never let him go," Lady Jane murmured to herself as she waited for her lover.

Smithers returned with the two footmen, Flint and Bertie. One carried a footed silver champagne bucket, the other a large bottle of the bubbly. Smithers had two crystal glasses in her hand. Directed by Smithers, they set everything up as it should be, and then Flint opened the bottle containing the golden liquid, pouring her some.

"You've both done very well," Lady Jane said, praising the two footmen as she sipped her champagne. "You may all have the rest of this evening off," she dismissed them, and the three servants backed from the bedchamber.

It was not long before the door opened again and Charles Pell stepped into the room. "Good evening, my love," he said. He walked across the Aubusson carpet, poured himself a glass of champagne, and raised it to her. "We are celebrating the return of a chastened and more sensitive Lord Reggie to his wife, I presume."

"We are," she replied. "And perhaps we may also celebrate the passion you and I will soon share." Jane looked at him coquettishly over the rim of her glass.

"Indeed, my love," he agreed. Then he said, "Jane, my darling, I have had the most wonderful idea. Surely there are young ladies in as desperate need of training as there are gentlemen. Would it not be as much fun to school a stubborn woman as it is to school a difficult gentleman?" His sipped the sparkling liquid in his glass.

"Charles!" she cried. "What an absolutely marvelous idea! I agree. We shall expand our little enterprise to include certain ladies. I shall be jealous, of course, when you fuck them, you know."

"And I shall be jealous when they lick and suck your juicy cunt for me," he told her. "But, my love, we shall have such great fun, won't we? I would advise, however, that we move down to my country seat near Barrow in Suffolk once the season is over. We will give grand house parties together, which will allow us to discreetly get the word out regarding our little enterprise."

"People will gossip that I am your mistress," Lady Jane said.

"Will you mind?" he asked her.

She smiled at him. "No. Not as long as you continue to love me."

"I will always love you, Jane," he told her sincerely, and the look in his blues eyes told her he spoke the truth. Then he stood up, set his champagne aside, and quickly disrobed so that he might join her in the bed.

Jane held out her arms to him in welcome. She had waited a lifetime for a man like this. Yet, until she had met Charles Pell, she had never believed that such a man actually existed. Naked flesh touched naked flesh, and within moments the world was exploding about them. She wanted nothing more than this world, this life, this man, and she would have what she wanted. She deserved it, damn it.

"Mr. Nicholas!" His secretary's voice cut through the silence in the office. The sound was a bit tinny coming through the old-fashioned intercom. He supposed he should really have it upgraded. Everything else in his offices was up-to-date.

"Yes, what is it?" he answered.

"We have a problem with the Channel, Mr. Nicholas."

"A problem? What kind of a problem?" Mr. Nicholas demanded to know.

"We have a client who refuses to leave, sir," the secretary said.

"What time zone, and who is it?" he asked.

"United States, Eastern Standard Time zone, and it's J. P. Woods, the publisher," was the reply he received.

Hellfire and brimstone, Mr. Nicholas thought. What had brought on this bit of foolish emotionalism on J. P. Woods's part? She was a cold, practical woman, and he actually had high hopes for her eventually. Well, he had best see to it himself. "I'll take care of it," he said. "It's a Regency fantasy, isn't it?"

"Yes, sir."

Mr. Nicholas picked up a rather complicated remote, programmed it, and then pushed an A button. There, up on the enormous flat-screen television, a scene of an elegantly appointed bedchamber appeared. J. P. Woods was sitting up in that bed, clutching the hand of her lover. Mr. Nicholas pushed the A button a second time so that he might be in the room with them. "My dear Ms. Woods," he said by way of greeting, "this is not acceptable. Not acceptable at all. You need to be gone from the Channel now."

"Who are you?" J. P. Woods, aka Lady Jane, demanded. "And how dare you materialize in my private quarters? This is my fantasy. I did not ask you into it."

"I am Mr. Nicholas, CEO of the Channel Corp. This pleasure dome is available from eight p.m. in the evening until four a.m. in the early morning. No client of the Channel may remain beyond those eight hours, Ms. Woods."

"It's my fantasy, sir, and I am not relinquishing it for the next sixteen hours before I may come back again," J.P. said.

"Ms. Woods, you are a powerful, respected, and even feared woman in your reality," Mr. Nicholas said.

"And in my fantasy, I am a wealthy, sought-after woman of some mystery," she told him. "I like it better."

"You like being fucked," he said bluntly. "Here in your fantasy you may be as wanton, as perverted as you wish, and none of your contacts in the real world knows your secret. If they knew, you would appear weak, even helpless, and you do not want that, Ms. Woods. You wish to put forth an aura of strength, and you do."

"You don't understand," J. P. Woods cried.

"Then make me understand," Mr. Nicholas said.

"Since that horrible night when my mother's john tried to rape me, threatened my sisters and my whole family, I haven't been able to really trust men. I am always watching, wondering what it is they will want of me and how they will somehow try to force me to their will. Because of that, I have never been able to fall in love. How could I? I couldn't show any signs of weakness. I couldn't allow myself to be taken advantage of and ruin my reputation in publishing. My business is like a small town. Everyone knows everyone. Everyone is always looking for an advantage over someone else."

"But," Mr. Nicholas said, "you have gained all you

have by virtue of your hard work and your determination not to be taken advantage of, my dear Jane. Why on earth would you give all of it up for a simple fantasy?"

"I have found the perfect man," she answered him.

"Of course you have. You created him. He is your fantasy," Mr. Nicholas replied. "All humans create fantasies to help them get through their lives."

"He loves me," she responded. "He seeks nothing from me other than my love."

"And he will be here for you when you return to the Channel tonight, my dear."

"I am not going," J. P. Woods said quietly. "And even you cannot make me give up my fantasy to return to the world of my reality."

How does she know that? Mr. Nicholas wondered angrily. But it was true. If someone held tightly to a fantasy of true love, it was impossible to detach them from it. He sighed irritably. "Ms. Woods, I cannot allow you to remain here. I need you where you are as head of Stratford Publishing. You have a certain value to me in that place. I am, however, in a position to make a deal with you in exchange for your returning to your reality."

"What kind of a deal?" J.P. asked, intrigued in spite of herself. "And just who are you?"

Mr. Nicholas looked directly at J.P., his black eyes engaging her eyes in a hard gaze. "Is it really necessary for me to say it, my dear?" he asked her pointedly. "In this persona, however, I am the CEO of the Channel Corp."

An icy shiver raced down J.P.'s spine as a new and rather frightening reality assailed her. "N-no. It isn't necessary for you to elaborate further," she replied. "I understand." Then, regaining her equilibrium, she inquired, "What kind of a deal, sir?"

He smiled at her. "I will put Charles Pell into your reality, Ms. Woods. He will come to you from London as an author you very much want to sign. And while he will exist in your reality, I will also allow him to continue to exist in your Channel fantasy. He will need no period of readjustment, for he will remember you quite well. Indeed, you may take up exactly from where you left off tonight."

"It is a very generous offer, Mr. Nicholas," J.P. said slowly. "Too generous, I fear."

"Why so?" Mr. Nicholas asked her, smiling again. He admired her astuteness.

"What else do you want of me?" J.P. asked him.

"If I do this for you, my dear, you will belong to me from the moment of our agreement," he told her frankly.

"But I could remain here in the Channel," J.P. responded quietly.

"You could if you forced the issue," he agreed. "But that should anger me. You don't want to cross me, my dear. I know you well. You are a woman who needs to be in charge of her life and everything around it. Stay here and your Charles might become rather engaged by one of those young women he has suggested that you train together. I could see that you grew old rather than remaining the nubile and delicious creature that you are here in the Channel until you repulse him, for he will always remain young."

"I will grow old in my reality," J.P. reminded Mr. Nicholas.

"But very slowly, my dear," he promised her. "You will

be one of those women who ages gracefully because of your rather excellent bone structure. The same will happen to your Charles. I can guarantee that your libidos will never age. You will always want each other."

"I can't become one of those women who allows love and sex to control her," J.P. said. "I should lose my authority if people thought I was weak. That is why my passions are released only within the Channel. I am thought to be cold and heartless. It is better that way."

Mr. Nicholas laughed heartily. "You shall remain as hard as iron, and cold as ice publicly," he promised her. "Such is your nature, my dear, and it will never change. Charles will appear smitten by you. People will talk, but they will not laugh. He will be profitable for Stratford. Your influence in the publishing world will be increased by the belief that you discovered him. Every book he writes for you will be a bestseller. And all you must do to gain this, my dear Ms. Woods, is to leave the Channel now."

"I could leave, and you might forget your promises to me," J.P. said.

"I might," he agreed, "but I will not. I never forget either a promise or a fault. As I have said, Ms. Woods, you are important to me."

"When will I see Charles again?" she asked.

"You have an appointment for lunch with him and his agent, Aaron Fischer, today," Mr. Nicholas told her.

J.P. considered everything Mr. Nicholas had said. If she refused to leave the Channel, he could make her life hell. Then she laughed softly at her thought. But if he kept his promise . . . if he kept it . . . she would be happy, and her career would flourish. Talk about having your fudge cake and eating it too. She turned to her lover, who had remained silent through all of her conversation with Mr. Nicholas. "Charles?"

"Do it!" he said without a moment's hesitation.

J.P. looked at Mr. Nicholas. She held out her hand to him. "I agree," she said as they shook.

Mr. Nicholas nodded. "You will not regret your decision, my dear," he said.

"I hope not," J.P. replied.

Ping. Ping. Ping. The Channel is now closed.

Monday morning dawned sunny with just the hint of possible spring in the late February air. J.P. arose, showered, and dressed, pulling a tweedy winter white-and-beige silk-and-cashmere skirt up over a sexy cream silk garter belt and stockings. The push-up silk bra matched and was so flawlessly made that not a seam showed when she had donned the cream cashmere turtleneck sweater. She slid her feet into a pair of beige four-inch pumps. Standing before her mirror, she pinned a large gold monogrammed pin onto the sweater and clipped a pair of gold lion's-head earrings onto her lobes. The lions had ruby eyes.

"You're looking perky this morning," her assistant, Gloria, said as J.P. came into her office. She took her boss's soft wool wrap coat and hung it in the closet.

"I'm having lunch with Aaron Fischer and that new English author today," J.P. said. "I have a really good feeling about it. What's his name?"

"Charles Pell. He's some sort of lord, I hear. Do you want me to Google him?"

"Might be a good idea," J.P. agreed. "You know I always like to know what to expect with a new writer. What's the name of the book?"

"*The Regency Gentleman's Guide to Twenty-First-Century City Living,*" Gloria said. "You're forgetful today."

"I thought I was coming down with something," J.P. lied. "I slept most of the weekend. I'm still a bit groggy. Get me a caramel latte and I'll wake up." She hurried into her private office. Just a few more hours. She and Charles would be together again forever, or whatever it was that passed as forever in this day and age. She could hardly wait, but she had to stop acting like a kid with her first boyfriend. Suddenly she was nervous. Maybe this hadn't been such a good idea. No! Yes, it was!

At eleven forty-five Gloria 's voice came over the intercom. "Aaron Fischer for you, J.P."

Oh, my God! Why was Aaron calling? Their lunch date was at twelve thirty. She picked up the phone. "Aaron, good morning."

She was greeted by a deep cough, and then Aaron's hoarse voice said, "J.P., I'm sorry. I've come down with bronchitis. All this damned crap about flu shots and pneumonia shots, but can anyone do anything for bronchitis? No. Rest, the doctor says. Chicken soup, my sister says. I can't make lunch, but Charles can. I've made a reservation at his hotel, the Park Leicester. That okay with you?" He coughed again.

"Perfect," J.P. almost purred. Lunch be damned. She was going to show Charles just what a nooner was. She grinned. Then, remembering the agent on the line, she said,

"You do sound dreadful, Aaron. Please take care of yourself, and get well very soon, Aaron," J.P. told him sincerely. Then she hung up.

"Gloria," she called through the open door between their offices, "have the company car ready to take me over to the Park Leicester Hotel at twelve ten."

"Will do," Gloria responded.

"I think I'll go home after my luncheon," J.P. said to her assistant. "Mick works from home on Mondays, and I'm still feeling a bit under the weather. Are there any impending emergencies?"

"All's quiet on the literary front," Gloria replied. "You get some rest, J.P. Stratford couldn't do without you. You're our rock."

J.P. smiled to herself at Gloria's words. She was hardly a warm-and-fuzzy boss. She knew she was feared, but she was also respected. And they just might have had to do without her if she had remained in the Channel. She didn't know why it had happened, and she wasn't even certain of when, but she suddenly realized she needed someone. Husband? Mate? Lover? Friend? It didn't really matter which. It was just so damned hard to be strong all the time. Being strong for yourself was one thing. But having to be strong for everyone around you was too damned difficult.

Her sister Marybeth, despite having a good husband with a decent job and two nice kids who gave her no trouble, couldn't pull herself together enough to get a responsible caregiver for their mother, keep J.P. informed, and send her the bills. No. Marybeth dumped everything on J.P., and with no respect for her older sister or her position, she expected J.P. her to drop everything and come running up to Bug Light, Maine, to make everything all right again. Well, screw that!

Their younger sister, Julie, who was down in Boston with her dream job—and probably, knowing Julie, several boyfriends—couldn't take the time to drive up home to see their mother or to phone J.P. with an up-to-date report. And their two brothers—mom's broken hip wasn't going to get them emergency leave from the military. Besides, they were on the other side of the world.

Why did everything have to fall into her lap? Wasn't looking after Stratford now that Martin was easing his way into retirement enough? Not that Martin would ever really let go until he was dead and buried.

I'm tired, J.P. Woods thought. *Not that I'll ever show it. The weak get eaten alive.* She looked up as a couple of pages were laid before her.

"I Googled Charles Pell," Gloria said. "The car is downstairs waiting."

"I'll be there in a minute," J.P. told her assistant, and scanned the two pages. Basic stuff. Charles Pell had been born in 1962.

She was younger by half a year. Eighth Earl of Pelton, his younger brother and his nephews his heirs. Never married. The usual English public schools; degrees from both Oxford and Cambridge. Man about town. Still considered eligible. Old title, but little visible wealth. Brother was a professor at Oxford. J.P. got up from her desk, took her coat from the closet, and put it on. She cinched the belt, picked up her purse, and left her office. "See you tomorrow, " she told Gloria.

Her heart was beating rapidly as the car pulled up to the Park Leicester Hotel. The doorman opened the door to help her out, and there he was, smiling at her. J. P. Woods had to restrain herself from running into his arms. This was, after all, suppose to be the very first time they had ever met.

"Ms. Woods," he said, "how delightful to meet you. I am Charles Pell." Then, taking her arm, he led her into the hotel lobby and toward a bank of elevators. "I thought rather than eating in the restaurant, we'd have lunch in my suite. It's lovely, by the way. Do you treat all your authors so well?" Without waiting for a reply, he drew her into the elevator.

It was automated. He pushed the CLOSE button first, and then the floor button. The doors snapped shut, and the elevator shot up as Charles Pell pulled J.P. into his arms and began to kiss her hungrily. "I can't wait to fuck you," he groaned into her ear. Then he let her loose as the elevator came to a smooth stop. The doors opened. They stepped out. An elegant matron who had been waiting smiled a frosty impersonal smile at them as she stepped into the transport.

Charles led J.P. down the carpeted, papered, chande-liered corridor, finally stopping at a door at the far end of the hallway. He swiped the key card and practically pushed her into the foyer of the suite as the door closed behind them. Her coat and purse were quickly on the floor. Her skirt, sweater, and bra swiftly followed. She yanked his jacket from him, almost tore the buttons from his shirt, and unzipped his fly. His eyes swept over her, appreciating the garter belt and stockings.

"Why, you naughty slut," he said and chuckled, noting the absence of panties. He backed her up against the foyer wall, his hands sliding beneath her buttocks to lift her up. "You are all ready to fuck, aren't you, my Lady Jane? Well, we may not have the trappings of your Regency town house, darling, and I am indeed going to give you a good fucking right now, but afterward prepare for a most thorough spanking. You are obviously in this reality a very bad girl." Then he thrust deep and hard into her.

She gasped with delight as his penis penetrated her, her legs wrapped tightly about him, her arms about him, their mouths mashing together in a hot kiss.

Afterward he followed through with his threat, spanking her until her buttocks were pink and her cunt was tingling. Then he took her to bed, and they spent the next few hours fucking. J.P. was amazed. A fantasy lover who couldn't be tired was one thing. But a real live man who couldn't be tired. It was absolute bliss, although she was shortly going to have to go home and get some serious rest or she would be a mess at the weekly editorial meeting in the morning.

"You're behaving as if we had been separated for weeks instead of just a few hours," she finally said. "And I'm starved to boot." Then she smiled a rare smile. "You're here! You're really here! I don't know how Mr. Nicholas did it, and I don't care. You're here!"

"You have a final opportunity, dearest Jane, to change your mind," he told her. "You do understand that you've sold your soul for me. Do you really love me that much?" His big hand stroked her face as their eyes met.

"I love you even more now than I did last night,

Charles," J.P. said softly. "Now we can have a life together in my reality."

"We can have double the pleasure since the Channel is still available to you, darling," he said. "We are going to have such fun now that you have renovated Pell Hall. We shall school recalcitrant wives and naughty young misses who tease without giving back in return. We shall take a pupil a month. Six gentlemen, six females, in alternating months."

"I don't know if I need or want such entertainment now that you are here with me in my own reality," J.P. said. "In this reality you are about to become a bestselling author. There are talk shows on television, podcasts, and radio for you to do. I'll have to explain all of that to you so you understand. We'll have to open a Twitter account, a Facebook page, and a MySpace page. You'll need to learn all about computers to do that. There is much more to selling books these days than just printing them and putting them into the stores, Charles."

"I will leave all of that in your capable hands, my darling, but I must have some amusement for myself," he told her.

"You have me," J.P. murmured, fondling his genitalia as her lustful nature began to rise up again.

"But I need more, Jane," he told her candidly. "I crave excitement."

"This is a dangerous century, Charles," she warned him. "There are diseases that didn't exist in your time. The pox can be cured now, but there are worse diseases that cannot and cause death."

"I will find us a female lover who is clean that we may

share," he said. "Then I shall be satisfied. You do love me, Jane, don't you?"

He smiled his devastating smile at her, and hard once again, he put her on her back. "Think what fun we will have with a pretty young creature to play with, darling." Then he fucked her until she was barely conscious and actually sore.

Be careful what you wish for. She suddenly remembered the old saying. But she did love him.

A year later she did not. Even Mr. Nicholas, with all of his power—Mr. Nicholas who had promised her so much—was unable to keep Charles Pell under control. "You lied to me," she accused him, having managed to get an audience with him. Mr. Nicholas shrugged, fatalistically reminding her that Charles was her creation. Taking him from his Regency world and placing him two hundred years into the future was obviously responsible for the change. He was a creature made to absorb the world around him, and the twenty-first century was a world of excess. "Even my opposite cannot control humanity successfully," Mr. Nicholas said.

With his initial success the Charles Pell who existed in the twenty-first century had swiftly gained the reputation of a serious playboy. Publicly he had exquisite manners, endearing himself to hostesses on the highest rung of society. He was charming and solicitous to his publisher, J. P. Woods, a difficult woman, it was said. Once he had attained the rank of a literary lion, J.P. had had a very difficult time keeping him under control. Charles Pell was quickly becoming tabloid fodder, and he was as great a burden as the rest of her family was. She was exhausted keeping up with him. He was not the man she had fallen in love with in the Channel.

The sex was becoming boring and even a little dangerous. Charles was constantly looking for new excitement. Discovering that even young women in this new century were not innocents, he began to bring other men into their bedroom at the Park Leicester, where he had taken up permanent residence. There was a vacuous young blonde about twenty who was both outrageously handsome and tireless, a light-skinned black man, and an arrogant Hispanic who spanked her before putting her on her knees to service him. The final straw for J.P. was a young Asian boy of seventeen whom Charles actually bought from a Snakehead he had met in Chinatown. The boy was to service them both. He spoke no English, but readily understood was what required of him. But J.P. drew the line at sex and drugs. It just wasn't her thing. Charles became very nasty when she wouldn't do coke with him.

J.P. was beginning to fear for her reputation as her lover's behavior became more dangerous. Worse, he was late with his next book, *The Regency Gentleman's Guide to Twenty-First-Century Country Living*. J.P. wasn't even certain that he had begun it or that there was a manuscript. He refused to allow her access to his work, saying it wasn't ready yet for her critique. After two due dates had passed, J.P. appealed to Aaron Fischer, only to learn that Charles had fired him. When she questioned him about it, Charles told her he didn't need an agent since he had her.

It was at that point that J. P. Woods realized that she

wanted this Charles Pell out of her life, but because he was her creation, she was, Mr. Nicholas said, responsible for him. *Great! Another fucking burden for me to carry,* she thought irritably. *Why couldn't I have been content with things the way they were? For the first time in my life, I let my heart rule my head, and look what a mess I've made of things. I want to go back to the way it was. Is that even possible?*

And then one morning, some months later, Gloria came into her boss's office. She was ashen. "It's his lordship," she said.

"Oh, crap, what's he done now?" J.P. asked, immediately irritated. She hadn't seen Charles in over a week now.

"He's dead!" Gloria said, and then she sat down.

"*What?* How? When? Are you absolutely certain?"

"The police are outside. They want to speak with you. I'll tell you what they told me. He and some flavor-of-the-month starlet were doing . . . coke, for God's sake! Afterward, while they were having rather loud sex, according to the guests on the fifteenth floor, someone got into the suite and shot them. The police say it was a hit. The girl had been living until recently with some gangster type who threatened to kill her if she left him." Gloria paused. "She did, and the police think he did. I'm sorry, J.P. I know he was your protégé." The way she said it, J.P. realized Gloria thought he was something more but wouldn't voice that thought.

J.P. was stunned. Charles. Her Charles, whom the twenty-first century had turned from a tender caring man into the worst son of a bitch alive, was dead. Good riddance!

"Yes," she said. "It's a tragedy, Gloria. He has family in England. I'll notify them, and we'll ship his body home. At company expense, of course. The recent royalties due him will more than pay for a very fancy wake at Frank Campbell's. Despite his recent behavior, Stratford Publishing doesn't want to appear ungrateful or unfeeling," J.P. said calmly. "You make the arrangements when we can claim his body. Get someone from PR to write a nice juicy obit. I'll want to see it first, of course. I'll call his brother in England as soon as we are certain of the facts in this matter."

Gloria nodded. "Will do, J.P.," she said, rising from the chair and hurrying out.

J. P. Woods smiled to herself. She still had the Charles Pell who did love and adore her in the Channel. She hadn't visited him in months, but he wouldn't notice the passage of time. She reached for her phone and dialed Mick Devlin's extension. "Mick," she said when he answered, "Charles Pell has gone and gotten himself murdered. Come into my office, and I'll tell you everything. We've got a funeral to attend."

TIFFY AND
THE SULTAN

"It's not a real fantasy if the guy looks like your husband," Carla Johnson said to her friend Tiffany Pietro d'Angelo.

"Why not?" Tiffy said. "I love Joe. Always have. Always will."

"The Channel isn't about love," Carla replied. "It's about wild and crazy guilt-free sex with no complications, girl! You've got this new Arabian Nights tale all worked out, and the hero is going to look like Joe? Ewwww? What's the matter with you?"

"Well, if not Joe, then who? I don't want it to be someone I know. I'd die of embarrassment when I ran into them next," Tiffy declared. She was a very pretty petite woman with a fluff of champagne blond hair.

"Pick an actor you like," Carla suggested.

"Maybe I'll just think tall, dark, and dangerous and see what pops up," Tiffy said.

"That would work nicely," Carla said. "I always like surprises. Especially the dark and dangerous kind."

"It's been forever since I've been to the Channel," Tiffy said. "Even with the kids gone, there just doesn't seem to be any time right now. The office has been so busy. Did Joe tell me that you're going with them to that lawyers' conference next week?"

"Yep," Carla said. "I haven't been to the big city in ages. I'm in the mood to do some serious shopping, and we've got tickets for a couple of shows. Why don't you come, Tiffy? It would be a terrific outing for us all. You and Joe should make more time for yourselves. Taking that long cruise last winter with Rick was an eye-opener. You won't live forever, sweetie. You should enjoy life while you can."

"I can't, but I wish I could. It sounds like fun," Tiffy said. "But I'm the only one other than Joe who understands the complexities of the Van Duzer estate trust. They're leaving for Europe next week and won't be back for a couple months. They always want to go over everything and update stuff before they travel. Joe has to be in the city for that conference. He's on two committees and chairs one. So that leaves me. I don't mind. It will give me time to try out my new Arabian Nights fantasy. I'm really in the mood for it too." She sighed. "It seemed easier when the kids were young and at home. We always seemed to have time for everything, even with bake sales and chauffeuring them to dances and sports. And our summers at Camp Cozy—I really miss those times."

"Water under the bridge," Carla said sanguinely. "I'm not one to look back a whole lot. I'm always too curious about what lies around the next corner." She chuckled. "So I'll go to the city and spend Rick's money on some clothes for our vacation next winter, and you'll stay home, deal with the Van Duzers, and play in the Channel."

"You guys are going away again?" Tiffy was surprised.

"Yep! We're taking a cruise to South America. We'll be going to Machu Pichu, and we'll be in Rio for Carnival," Carla said. "And we get to spend a weekend in Patagonia."

"Wow!" Tiffy exclaimed. "I guess you two really like cruising."

Carla grinned mischievously. "All year long it's either hurried sex now and again or no sex," she confided. "But get Rick away from Egret Pointe and the law offices, and he turns into an animal. Every day, Tiffy! And sometimes more than once. If I had known that a grown-up vacation would turn him on so much, I would have planned them years ago. But now that I know, we're going every chance we get."

"I am so envious," Tiffy said with a sigh.

"Maybe you and Joe should take a real vacation," Carla suggested.

"Yeah, one day," Tiffy replied, but it didn't sound like she had much hope. "Joe loves what he does. He wants to do it all the time. He's just like his cousin Ray."

"Well, if you can't get him to take you away someplace romantic, then I guess you're just going to have to keep visiting the Channel like I used to do," Carla replied.

Tiffany Pietro d'Angelo nodded. "I'll feel better after I've lived out this new fantasy," she assured her best friend.

The next few days were busy ones. Tiffany personally packed Joe's luggage, matching the ties, the shirts, and the suits for him. She saw that he had enough socks and that the two pairs of shoes he carried were polished to a glossy shine. She put in a pair of pajamas, Joe's comfortable flannel robe, and his worn leather slippers. His toiletry bag had everything he would need and a few things he might need. She tucked silly notes in his pockets, where he would find them and smile.

She pulled all the paperwork for the Van Duzer trust so she could reread it and be ready when the elderly couple came in next week. Tiffy knew they weren't going to change a thing in their carefully worked-out trust. They never did. But each time they went off traveling, they would insist on coming in beforehand and going over everything again. They were sweet people, and in a small town like Egret Pointe, law offices like Johnson and Pietro d'Angelo were apt to be more patient and accommodating than large city firms would have been.

The firm had called a limo service from the city to come out and take Carla and the two men into town. "It's a legitimate business expense," Rick Johnson said. "And it's no more expensive than garaging the car for a couple days."

Tiffy fussed with Joe's tie a final time as he prepared to get into the waiting limousine. "I've put in Tums and Pepto just in case," she said. "Don't overeat or eat the hot stuff. It always sets you off."

"I'll be fine," he assured her. "You're sure you'll be okay with the Van Duzers?"

Tiffany nodded. "They're coming on Wednesday afternoon, and you know they won't do anything. After I've dealt with them, I might take the rest of the week off. You know, Joe, we haven't gone off together in a long time. Perhaps I'll plan a getaway for us." She looked hopefully at him. "Maybe Bermuda? You could play golf," Tiffy tempted him. "I know how busy the office is, but what about Christmas week?"

"The kids," he began.

"Have jobs and lives of their own," Tiffany said, her voice suddenly edgy. "They can do without us for one damn Christmas. I want to go away with my husband. *Alone.* Without the distractions of their problems or your office."

Joe Pietro d'Angelo looked surprised. "Well, gee, Tiff, if that's what you want, then make it so. But let's do something more exciting than Bermuda. I hear Barbados is pretty nice. Find us something really first-class on the ocean with help. If we're going to go, let's do it right," Joe told her. Then he gave her a kiss and climbed into the car.

Carla, who had heard the exchange, gave her friend a thumbs-up before the door shut, and the limo took off. Tiffy walked over to her own car, which she had taken out of the garage earlier. She climbed in and drove into the village, parking in the office's lot, which was behind the building. It was a reasonably quiet day. There were no appointments because both lawyers were gone. It was an excellent time to catch up on paperwork.

The following day the Van Duzers came in at eleven o'clock sharp for their appointment. Mr. Van Duzer, a tall, distinguished gentleman with snow-white hair, was dressed in a dark suit, a white shirt, and a striped tie. His wife wore a wool suit and a fur coat. Her jewelry—three rings and a strand of pearls—was the real thing. As expected, they went over everything with Tiffy but made no changes to their family trust.

"I'm sorry we missed Joe," Mr. Van Duzer said pointedly.

"He's chairman of one of the committees at this conference," Tiffy said, "and their presentation was first thing this morning after the welcome breakfast. However, we went over everything before he left, Mr. Van Duzer. His advice was not to make any changes, as you have so wisely decided."

"Such a lovely man, your husband," Mrs. Van Duzer said in her sweet, high-pitched voice. "Do tell him we'll call from London if we need to make any changes."

"Of course I will, and you have a wonderful visit with your daughter and her family," Tiffy responded as she escorted them out of her husband's private office. They wouldn't call. They always said the same thing, she thought, smiling. She turned to the two secretaries. "I'm going home, ladies. I won't be in the rest of the week since we don't have anything to do. Feel free to take Friday off. Joe and Rick's orders."

"Thanks, Mrs. Pietro d'Angelo," the two women chorused.

Tiffy's cell began to ring as she left the office. Looking, she saw it was her husband. "I'm just leaving," she told him by way of greeting. "The Van Duzers have been cosseted and catered to, and they are now gone off to catch a plane," she told him. "How are you?"

"We're doing okay. Conference is really interesting."

"I gave the girls Friday off. Said you and Rick said to do it. There's nothing to do, and I'll check the voice mail," Tiffy told him.

"Good idea," he agreed. "What are you going to do? If you want, you could come into town now, and we'll spend the weekend."

"Too late. My hair needs touching up, and I've got to research our winter trip," Tiffany told him. "You'll be home Friday night, sweetie. We'll do dinner at the inn on Saturday, okay?" *And I'll be a happier camper for having visited the Channel,* she thought with a small secret smile.

"Okay. Enjoy the rest of your day and tomorrow," he said.

Tiffy drove home, put the car in the garage, and fixed herself a chicken sandwich and a salad, which she ate with a glass of Winter White wine from the Pindar Vineyards out on Long Island. A glance at the clock told her she had several hours until the Channel opened up for the night. She took a leisurely bath, then lay down for a nap. When she awoke, it was dark. Checking the lighted dial on her bedside clock, she saw it was almost eight. She rolled over and reached up beneath her night table, where she secreted her Channel remote. The remote worked on all the televisions in the house, but tonight she didn't have to hide in the den or her craft room in the finished basement.

She glanced again at the clock, which, clicked from seven fifty-nine to eight o'clock. Tiffy pointed the remote at the television in the small painted entertainment center across the room, and clicked the B button. Instantly she was in the harem of her father's palace. The warm air was perfumed faintly with the scent of the damask roses in the gardens beyond the gold-veined, cream-colored marble pillars. She gazed from amid the multicolored silken pillows where she lay, taking in the scene surrounding her.

Her persona in this fantasy was that of Princess Hestia, the sultan's daughter, who was known as the Star of Cinnabar.

In the center of the large chamber where she now lay was a fountain tiled in several shades of blue. In the fountain's center was a small spray, its rainbow droplets catching the sun as they sprinkled into the air. Gold and silver fish swam lazily in the water. Her own mother was dead, but her father's other three wives, his two current favorites, and his half dozen concubines peopled the room, along with female servants and several eunuchs. Somewhere a musician played a stringed instrument as Hestia's own personal slave woman slowly brushed the princess's long pale golden hair.

Her deep violet blue eyes were sharp—she watched everything about her. The gossiping wives. The two favorites preening and beautifying themselves in an effort to outdo each other. The younger concubines giggling as they sat telling each other stories. Hestia was seventeen and a widow. Her father, the sultan, indulged her as he did no one else among his women. She was the only daughter of his second wife, who had died giving birth to another child when Hestia was ten.

After her mother's death, her father had kept the child of his heart close. He might have given her in marriage to a powerful lord, but instead, to keep her near him, he had married her off to the eldest son of his vizier. Hestia had been content with his decision. She was her young husband's first wife, and his family was honored to have her among them. But then tragedy had struck. Her husband was killed in a fall from his horse when they had been married less than a year. Once it was determined that Hestia was not with child, she was returned to her father's house. Happy to have his favorite child returned to him, the Sultan of Cinnabar was in no hurry to marry her off again.

Her knowledge of sexual practices complete, the princess had a bit more freedom than the other women had. She had bribed one of the younger eunuchs to go to the marketplace and purchase a fine dildo for her. She had given him exact instructions, and he had not failed her. Now, because he'd kept her secret, she allowed the eunuch the privilege of using the dildo on his mistress for her pleasure whenever she felt the need. For a time it had sufficed, but of late Hestia had felt the need for more than a dildo.

The head eunuch, Abu Abu, came into the harem. At once all the women were alert, but he passed them by and went to where the princess lay having her hair brushed. A short plump man of mixed race, his skin was pale brown and his eyes the black of midnight. Hestia had known him her entire life. He bowed low. "Princess, your esteemed father requests that you come with me. He would speak with you on a matter most serious." Abu Abu held out his fat hand to her.

Hestia smiled and took it, letting him pull her up. "If Papa wishes my presence," she said in her melodious voice, "I will certainly come, for I am a dutiful daughter." Then she followed the head eunuch from the harem to her father's library, where not only the sultan but her half brother, Prince Omar, awaited her. Crossing her arms over her chest, she bowed to her father and then to her brother. Omar was the heir. They had never liked each other, but as heir he was entitled to her respect. Hestia knew how important it was to be polite to him. Her very life could depend on him one day.

"You are to be married, my daughter," the sultan began.

Hestia remained silent, waiting for more information. Her heart was pounding with a mixture of excitement and fear.

"It will be a political alliance, my daughter," the sultan continued. "You will become the first wife of the new Sultan of Sherazad, and the sultan's sister will be married to your brother, Omar. You and your brother will meet the sultan and his sister, Princess Shalimar, at the Forest of Palms oasis, which is located at the border between our two kingdoms. Speak now, daughter, and tell me your thoughts."

"Will the sultan be satisfied that his sister is a second wife, Papa?" Hestia wanted to know. "Especially as I will be the sultan's first wife?"

"Omar has divorced Amira. Princess Shalimar will be his first wife. When that has happened, he will remarry Amira, who is content to be second in his life," the sultan answered his daughter.

Hestia turned to her half brother. "How can you do this to Amira?" she asked him. "Amira has always loved you, and you would relegate her to second place for this princess, whom you have never laid eyes upon?"

"An alliance with Sherazad is important to Cinnabar," Prince Omar answered his sister. "The sultan's sister cannot be placed second in my household. Amira understands that. Why do you not? This time, sister, you will have a strong man for a husband. A man who will tame your unseemly independent spirit, not some besotted boy who was honored by your presence in his bed and who could not get you with child. It is your son by the sultan and my son by the sultan's sister who will one day rule these two kingdoms and keep peace between our two countries."

"You make it sound as if I am a piece upon a chess board to be played to the best advantage," Hestia said to her brother angrily.

"That is exactly what you are!" he crowed. "I am astounded you understand that."

"Papa! I don't want to leave you!" Hestia played her strongest card first.

"And I do not want to lose you," her father said, "but this match is too important for me to ignore. Your brother is right in this matter, Hestia, my dearest. You must wed with this sultan, and his sister with your brother. I wish it as Sultan of Cinnabar, and my wishes cannot be denied, daughter." He turned to his head eunuch. "Abu Abu, take the princess back to the harem. Have the women prepare her for her journey, which will begin in three days' time."

"Papa, *please*!" Hestia begged, but the sultan turned his face from her, and her half brother looked smugly at her.

Oh, Tiffy thought. *This is really going to be a fun fantasy. Make it ten days from now.*

She found herself in a litter being carried down a desert road. It was hot. Not a breeze stirred. Her litter was set atop a white camel. The beast's sure-footed motion was a rolling gait. Hestia was not happy. They had been on this desert road for well over a week now, but she had been assured that by sunset they would reach the Forest of Palms oasis. She reached for the water skin she had been supplied with this morning and sipped the brackish liquid. Then she lay back and dozed, for the heat had made her head ache.

The complaining of the camels and the sensation of her beast lowering itself to its knees awoke her. She awaited her eunuch to help her from the litter. Gazing through the diaphanous curtains, Hestia could see the oasis was a large one. The large section of palms growing on one side of it gave it its name: Forest of Palms. A magnificently large pavilion and several slightly smaller pavilions were already set up. From the top of the largest tent hung the green banner of Sherazad, with its circle of silver stars. From atop a slightly smaller pavilion hung the flag of Cinnabar, red with a gold crescent moon.

Her eunuch came to help her from the litter, leading her to the smaller of the two large tents. Her half brother was already there. She had barely spoken to him in the past two weeks. "Well, royal brother," she said, "what now?"

"Have your slaves bathe you, and prepare to meet your new husband, as I will shortly meet my new bride," Prince Omar told her. "The sultan has just arrived. It will be at least an hour before he sends for us."

The hour passed and then two. Hestia was bathed and ready, dressed in a turquoise kaftan embroidered with gold threads and small crystals. There were matching silk slippers on her feet. Tiffany was fascinated by the track this new fantasy of hers was taking. She was enjoying letting it play out, and she had determined that the sultan would not look like her husband. Carla was right. Being naughty was what the Channel was really all about, wasn't it?

"Princess, your royal brother says that the sultan is asking for your presence," her slave woman said in a soft voice.

"Tell my brother that I have traveled for ten days to arrive at this meeting place. If the sultan still wishes to have me as his wife, he will come and fetch me," Hestia said. "I am not some peasant woman to be sent for."

The slave woman looked terrified at her mistress's words, but she obeyed the directive and delivered the message to Prince Omar, crying out as he slapped her face in response. "Ask my sister if the heat has driven her mad. She is to come at once!"

Having heard her slave woman's cry of pain, Hestia stepped from her curtained chamber. "I am a princess of Cinnabar," she said to her brother. "The sultan should come to greet me, as you will go to greet him and his sister. How dare he demand my presence? Sherazad may be strong, but Cinnabar is an older and more respected kingdom. It is proper for you to greet Princess Shalimar in her brother's tent, but I am not some slave girl to be sent for by this sultan. And you, brother, lose face for Cinnabar, for our father, for yourself by allowing it. You and the sultan must greet each other on an equal footing. You must not appear the supplicant."

Prince Omar considered his half sister's wise words. Then he nodded. "The sultan shall come to you, Hestia. I thank you for thinking of Cinnabar first, as you have always done. I shall tell our father of your loyalty. Now, pull your veil across your features, and when I have done what must be done, the sultan will come to you."

The prince left her. Hestia waited patiently, lying amid a pile of pillows. Her slave woman watched at the entry of the tent for the approach of the sultan. Suddenly she hissed, "He comes, Princess!" Then she scuttled into a dim corner. Hestia arose to greet her new husband, for the contracts exchanged between Cinnabar and Sherazad before her departure from her father's palace had already made their marriage a fact.

He strode into the pavilion in a swirl of white robes. Upon his head was a white turban, the length of silk falling from it concealing his face from her. He was a tall man.

Hestia stood, crossed her arms over her breasts, and bowed from the waist in a gesture of respect. The air between them almost crackled.

"So," the deep voice said, "you would have me come to you, Princess."

"It is proper that you do so, my lord sultan," Hestia replied. "I am your bride, the Star of Cinnabar, not some woman of the streets."

"You are my wife now, Princess of Cinnabar. This is the one and only time that I shall indulge such bold behavior," he warned her. The dark eyes above his face covering locked onto her violet blue eyes. Then, reaching up, he unveiled her. For a long moment he stood staring at her beautiful face. Then he nodded. "It is an acceptable bargain I have made," the sultan said, "although my sister is fairer than you." Then he took her hand. "Come! The wedding feast is to begin shortly."

She was astounded by his words and by the fact that she had yet to see his face. *Oh, please, don't let it be Joe this time,* Tiffany silently prayed. She couldn't imagine her sweet practical husband ever being this insolent. But the Sultan of Sherazad's audacious manner led her to believe that he was going to fuck like a stallion. Hardly able to wait, she felt a tingle of excitement in her clitoris.

In the sultan's great pavilion, she met Princess Shalimar, and Tiffany had to admit to herself that the sultan's sister was an extraordinary beauty. Her skin was like a gardenia in color. Her long hair was the blue-black of a raven's wing. Her eyes were like fine sapphires. Her features were delicate. A slim nose, thick dark eyelashes, a generous mouth, high cheekbones in a heart-shaped face. Prince Omar was already entranced with his exquisite new wife.

Seeing her brother reenter the pavilion, Shalimar laughed aloud. "Oh, Ahmed, do unveil your handsome face so your bride may see it. He can be so wicked sometimes," she remarked. Then she kissed Hestia upon her cheeks. "I hope you will be as happy in Sherazad as I intend being in Cinnabar."

"I hope so too," Hestia replied, but her eyes were on the face of the sultan, which was now uncovered. He was every bit as handsome as his sister was beautiful. Black hair, and the dark eyes she could now see were deepest blue. Strong but elegant features that included a long, narrow nose, a sensuous mouth, and a squared chin with a cleft in it.

"I assume you find me pleasing," the sultan said drily.

"I assume you find me pleasing," Hestia countered.

Shalimar laughed again. "Oh, Ahmed," she said, "you have been given a wife who will, I suspect, never bore you."

The feast was quite generous, considering where they were and how long it had taken them to even get there. There were roasted lamb and roasted chickens. There were saffron rice, hot flat bread, minted yogurt, fresh fruits, crisp honey cakes, and sweet wines. And when the meal was finished, slaves brought around basins of fragrant water and linen towels to wash the excesses of the meal away from hands and face. The sultan had brought a troupe of acrobats to entertain them. But then the sun began to set.

Prince Omar arose, drawing his bride to her feet as well. "I thank you for your hospitality, my lord sultan," he said, "but the time has now come for me to take my bride to my tent so our marriage may be consummated. My father looks forward to his grandchildren, and the assurance that his grandson will follow me onto Cinnabar's throne. We will bid you our farewells in the morning before we go." Then Prince Omar led Princess Shalimar from the sultan's tent and across the compound to his own.

The slaves had cleared away all evidence of the meal. The acrobats were gone. The oil lamps had been trimmed and were now burning low. Outside the pavilion, the encampment had grown quiet with the night. The sultan's voice cut the silence.

"You have been married before, I was given to understand," he said.

"Yes, to the son of my father's vizier. My father did not wish to lose his only daughter," Hestia explained. "My husband died when his horse stumbled in a race and threw him. Ali's neck was broken. He died instantly, the physician said." Tiffany felt a bit guilty, for the unfortunate Ali had had Joe's face.

"Did you love him?" the sultan wanted to know.

"Yes," she said, "but the truth is, we had grown up together. We were friends."

The sultan nodded. "He took your virginity," he said. It was more a statement than a question.

Hestia nodded. "Yes."

"Good! Initiating virgins is a boring project at best. All the hysteria and weeping. I do not have a large harem, and I have abstained from my women ever since this treaty between your father and me was initiated. I intend to spend the next few days here at the oasis with you. Understand that you will be on your back much of that time. You are more beautiful than I anticipated, and I am eager to fuck you. And there is the matter of an heir for Sherazad."

"Of course, my lord," Hestia murmured.

He led her through a curtained hallway in the tent to a separate chamber. "Do you need your woman?" he asked.

Hestia shook her head as she stepped into the curtained space. Looking about, she gasped, amazed. There was a small pool with a low rock waterfall in one corner. "How . . . ?" She looked to the sultan.

"We know this oasis well," he replied. "I had the pavilion set up in such a manner that the pool with its falls was enclosed. I am pleased that you like it."

"I do!" Hestia told him. Taking her gaze from the water, she saw that the chamber contained a large mattress covered in black silk that had been set upon a platform, some low tables, and a number of silk pillows in jeweled shades of ruby, emerald, amethyst, sapphire, and aquamarine. *Ohh,* Tiffy thought, *this place is just made for seduction.* The princess turned to face her new husband. "Shall I disrobe for you, my lord sultan?"

He nodded. "And when you have, you will undress me, Hestia."

"As my lord wishes," she replied obediently. The kaftan had a keyhole neckline, and below it was a row of cleverly hidden buttons. She undid the buttons, stepping from the garment when they were all undone and laying it aside. Next she quickly undid the narrow braids on either side of her head, putting aside the bejeweled chains that had been plaited into them. Then, shaking her head slightly, she shook her long golden hair free.

His deep blue eyes followed her every move, admiring both the perfection of her body and the beauty of her long hair.

Now she turned to undress the sultan. First she removed the turban from his dark head, smiling as she ran her fingers through his thick, wavy hair. Next came the white shirt, which opened to reveal a smooth bronzed chest. She ran her hands over his skin, pushing the shirt over his broad shoulders and from him. She undid his bejeweled sash and, kneeling, drew down his full pantaloons, lifting his feet in turn from the legs of the garment to find herself facing his swelling cock.

His hands rested upon her shoulders. "Do you know what to do?" he asked her.

"Yes, my lord sultan."

"Then do it, Hestia. Slowly, using your tongue skillfully. When I command you to cease, you will do so immediately, arise, and go to the bed, where you will lie upon your belly with your bottom raised for my pleasure. Do you understand me?"

"Yes, my lord sultan." God! He had a wonderful cock. It was long, and it was thickening before her eyes. Hestia took it between her thumb and forefinger and circled her tongue around the edge of its tip two or three times. Then she took just the tip into her mouth, sucking hard on it, hearing his sharp intake of breath. Slowly, slowly, she engulfed him bit by delicious bit until she had almost absorbed his entire length. She might have taken him all into her mouth, but it would have made it difficult to suck. She began to work her mouth and tongue over, around, and about the fleshy peg between her lips. She felt the fingers of one hand kneading deeply into her scalp.

Hestia heard his quickened breathing, and even a groan of satisfaction, but then his deep voice commanded her, "Stop!" She did so reluctantly. Then, rising to her feet, she went to the bed and lay upon her belly, drawing her knees up beneath her. She was wet, and she was eager for him now. He came up behind her, a big hand reaching beneath her to cup her mons. To her own surprise, she moaned eagerly.

He laughed, then pushed a finger between her nether lips and found her clitoris. "Is it always this big?" he asked her, not really expecting an answer. "What an eager little bitch you are, Hestia. I think we will very much enjoy each other tonight." He tweaked the flesh, and she screamed softly as a bolt of pleasure slammed into her. "Do you want to be fucked, Princess of Cinnabar?" he teased her wickedly.

"Oh, yes, my lord sultan!" she admitted to him. "I want to be skewered by that great cock of yours. It has been forever since I have enjoyed a man. Not since Ali died."

Her admission pleased him. "I will fuck you as he never did, Princess of Cinnabar," he told her, "and you will scream for the entire camp to hear with your admittance of the pleasure that I, and I alone, can give you."

"Then cease your talk, my lord sultan, and prove to me your words!" Hestia challenged her new husband. She felt him position himself. Then, without any further foreplay, he drove himself deep into her eager body. She cried out at his fierce entry and the sudden realization that his hand was on her neck, holding her in a submissive position as he thrust deeper and deeper, harder and harder into her.

Wow, Tiffy thought. *This guy really knows how to work it. He wasn't bragging. Geez, Carla was right. It's better when it's not Joe.*

"Submit to me, Hestia," the sultan growled in her ear. "Submit to your master!"

"Not yet!" she gasped. "Not yet!"

"You are too greedy," he accused her.

"Can you not hold your seed in check any longer, my lord sultan?" she taunted.

"I will pour myself into you a half dozen times before the dawn comes, Princess of Cinnabar," he promised her, and his cadence quickened until she was gasping with the pleasure that was threatening to consume her.

"Scream for me, Princess of Cinnabar," he said. "I can already feel the walls of your sheath beginning to quiver with excitement. Scream for me!"

She climaxed as she never had before. Waves of pleasure rippled over her, making her dizzy. She felt his cock stiffen and then burst with his lust for her, and Hestia screamed with the delight that they were giving and had given each other. Perhaps not as loud as he would have wanted her to scream, but loud enough for the guards outside the entry to the pavilion to hear and to grin at the vocal evidence of their master's prowess.

Ping! Ping! Ping! The Channel is now closing.

"Crap!" Tiffany swore softly as she found herself in her own bed again. "That's the shortest eight hours I've ever known." *Well,* she thought, *I did have to set the backstory for this fantasy.* Then she realized she was lying on her belly, which was something a woman rarely did at her age. She rolled over. She felt a little guilty that her fantasy lover hadn't had Joe's face. And he sure hadn't had Joe's middle-aged body. Still, all in all, it had been a highly successful evening in the Channel. She could hardly wait for tomorrow night to come. Her clitoris twitched with the lascivious thoughts she was entertaining. But tonight's adventure had to have been the most intense she had ever had in the Channel. And she had liked it. Oh, yeah! She had liked it very much.

Her sultan was a very bad boy, but she had enjoyed his macho tactics. His hand on her nape as he fucked her had been strangely exciting. Tiffy shivered. She had never known the Channel to be quite so thrilling. And all because she hadn't imagined Joe's face as the face of her lover. For the first time since she had begun visiting the Channel all those years ago, she felt as if she had done something bad. But she knew she was going to do it again and again. Her sultan was fascinating, and she hadn't learned enough about him yet to be bored. She seriously doubted that his skillful dick would ever bore her. After she managed to calm her thoughts, Tiffy fell asleep.

Carla called Thursday afternoon. "I'm on my cell in Bergdorf's loo," she said. "How was it without the guy having Joe's face? Tell me you changed the face."

"I did," Tiffy admitted.

"And?"

"Dy-no-mite!" Tiffy giggled.

"Details, damn it!" Carla demanded.

"It was the first time I've done this fantasy. I put it on the B button, but I had to play out the backstory last night. Still, I managed to get one great fuck in before the Channel closed. He had me on my belly with his hand on my neck holding me down. God, if Joe did that, I'd be so embarrassed, but being the seventeen-year-old princess of Cinnabar with a sultan for a bridegroom, I somehow managed to soldier on," Tiffy said.

"He did that to a virgin?"

"Princess Hestia, the Star of Cinnabar, isn't a virgin. She's a widow," Tiffy explained. "And not having had a man since Ali died, she was hot to trot with the sultan."

"You want more of it?" Carla asked.

"You betcha," Tiffy replied. "This guy and I have only just started to have fun. I'll be back in the Channel in just four more hours."

"I'll be sitting in a theater," Carla said, sounding just slightly envious. "Would you believe Rick got tickets to *Mary Poppins*?"

"Have fun," Tiffy said and chuckled. "I suspect I'll be having more fun. Do you miss the Channel, Carla?"

"Not anymore," Carla said candidly. "Not since Rick and I began to have a life together again. But I'll still enjoy hearing your adventures, just like you always enjoyed hearing about Captain Raven. Well, I just wanted to make certain it worked out for you. I'll see you Saturday, Tiffy. Have fun tonight."

"I will!" Tiffy promised, and when eight o'clock came she pressed the B button and found herself in her husband's harem. She looked about her and saw she was alone. Upon their return from the Forest of Palms oasis, the sultan had given the half dozen young women in his harem as gifts to men he wished to keep loyal. He came into the harem to join her.

"For now, my Star of Cinnabar, you are all the woman I need," he assured her.

"I like knowing that you will only make love to me," Hestia said quietly.

"In time I will want more variety again," he replied. "I sometimes enjoy making love to several women at a time."

"As long as it's my cunt that encloses your cock, my lord sultan," Hestia said.

He had laughed at her remark. "Perhaps I shall have you restrained and watch while two or three maidens make love to you in my place."

She wrinkled her nose, but then said, "If it would please you, my lord sultan."

"You please me very much," he replied with a smile, reaching out to caress her heart-shaped face. "How fortunate I am that your first husband died. Had he not, I should have had to attack Cinnabar and kill him in order to have you for myself."

"You would have done that for me?" Hestia answered him, surprised. "I thought the only reason for our marriage was political, my lord."

"Nay," he told her. "The tales of your beauty are spoken far and wide. I am not the only one who sought your hand, my Star of Cinnabar. The caliph in Baghdad also wanted you, as did the Great Khan in Samarkand."

"They are more powerful lords," Hestia said thoughtfully. "Why, then, did my father choose you?"

"Because our two armies joined together are capable of defending either of our kingdoms should they be attacked. Your father loves you very much, wife, and here in Sherazad you are closer to him than you would have been in either Samarkand or Baghdad. But enough of such talk between us. I need more of your passion, Hestia."

They were now lying naked upon a black silk mattress. Reaching out, he cupped one of her breasts. It was perfectly round and firm in his palm. His thumb rubbed about her nipple slowly, and he watched it stiffen beneath his touch. He leaning forward and his tongue encircled the nipple slowly several times before he took it into his mouth to suckle upon her, grazing the tender flesh lightly with his teeth.

She moaned softly, feeling a corresponding tug in her nether regions. When he had finished with one breast, he moved to the other, increasing her desire. His other big hand moved to enclose her mons, and unable to help herself, she pressed into his palm. She was beginning to burn with her lust for him. He felt her, the heat and damp of her, and now leaned forward to take her lips with his. Their tongues immediately found each other and entwined in a sensuous frolic as he pressed a finger past her labia to tweak her clit with increasing vigor, causing her to gasp into his mouth.

He would not release her lips from his kiss, even as he pushed two fingers into her vagina. The fingers moved slowly, sensuously within her, and she rode them, moaning until she experienced a small climax. He spoke no words of love or devotion to her, his deep blue eyes holding her gaze as he withdrew his hand from her and sucked her juices from his fingers. Tiffy's princess persona felt weak with her burgeoning need for his cock.

He did not disappoint, mounting her, their eyes still locked, and pushing into her with great restraint until he was fully sheathed. She made to lock her legs about his torso, but he grasped her by her calves and instead drew her limbs over his shoulders. Then, leaving constraint behind, he began to fuck her vigorously, pushing harder and deeper with each thrust. He seemed to sense when she was near her climax, drawing back to deny her so he might enjoy the tight wet heat of her cunt a bit longer.

Hestia screamed at him when he withheld the pleasure she sought of him. Her nails raked down his long, hard back in protest, but he merely laughed at her. Tiffy protested at this behavior, for this was *her* fantasy. Shouldn't it all be just as she wanted it? But then it occurred to her that he was giving her pleasure such as she had never before known. Her body rose to meet his downward thrusts, and suddenly she was spinning out of control. She saw gold and silver stars and moons behind her closed eyelids.

"That's it, my Star of Cinnabar," he groaned hotly into her ear. "Let me fuck you and fuck you and fuck you until neither of us can hold back any longer." He drove his over-heated penis deeper into her, and it seemed to swell and lengthen to a point where she could barely contain him. He felt the walls of her vagina beginning to quiver and tighten about him. The sensation it engendered within him made it impossible to hold back any longer. *"Now!"* he howled, and his tribute to her beauty began to pour forth as the woman beneath him screamed with her delight be-fore finally going limp beneath him.

When they had recovered themselves, he said to her, "I shall invite the caliph in Baghdad and the Great Khan to come to Sherazad to sign a treaty of peaceful coexistence between us all. And to seal this treaty, I shall share with them my greatest treasure: my Star of Cinnabar. When they have enjoyed your beauty and passion with me, we shall have peace between the four kingdoms."

Ohhhh, Tiffy thought. *A foursome! I've never had a foursome before, and none of them is going to have Joe's face. Gee, if I hadn't given my Sultan of Sherazad a differ-ent face, this would have never happened. Thank you, Carla, for making me see sense!*

Then she turned to her bridegroom. "If I may be an instrument of peace, my lord husband, then so be it. I will do as you command, and gladly."

"Your obedience pleases me well, Hestia," he responded.

Ping! Ping! Ping! The Channel is now closed.

Too bad, Tiffy thought as she rolled over in her own bed and fell asleep. But when she awoke the next morning, she realized that Joe was coming home. And if Joe was coming home, she was going to have a difficult time living out her fantasy of a foursome. Somehow she didn't want to hide out in the den. Joe hadn't been sleeping well lately. What if he woke up, found her down in the den apparently asleep, and turned off the television, which would just appear to be a snowy screen to his eyes? Would that end the fantasy and wake her up—or keep her prisoner in the Channel? She didn't know, and she didn't want to find out what would happen if she got stuck in the Channel. Damn! Why couldn't her husband be gone just one more day?

Carla called and wanted details of the previous night's adventure.

Tiffy supplied them, then explained her dilemma. "I just think about that foursome, and my clit starts twitching," she told her best friend.

"Oh, dear," Carla said. "What about hiding out in your craft room?"

"Same problem as the den. Joe wakes up and I'm not there, he comes looking for me. God, Carla, I want this fantasy! I feel like a kid who's just discovered sex. I want more and more and more! This is absolutely the best fantasy I've ever had!"

"Keep calm," Carla advised, "and let me think about it."

"Think fast," Tiffy said. "I gotta go. Joe wants to order the Friday pizza. Gah! I don't want pepperoni! I want a sultan, a caliph, and a khan plundering my body with their great big cocks. I want to be licked and sucked all over. I want to lick and suck! Damn! I'm twitching again."

Carla swallowed back the laughter that threatened to

overwhelm her. "I'll figure something out," she said. "Just stop thinking about it."

Then she hung up. Her laughter bubbled up now. Poor Tiffy! She had always been a reasonably sedate visitor to the Channel. She loved romance novels featuring harems. There wasn't one she hadn't read. Good or bad. Her fantasy had always been the same. It was simple in its creation. Tiffy was the beautiful slave girl who became the sultan's favorite. And the sultan had the face and voice of Joe Pietro d'Angelo.

She never felt guilty about her fantasy because she was actually having sex with her husband in the Channel and not some handsome stranger. It allowed her to keep her libido in check and not end up with a half dozen children, like her sisters-in-law. She and Joe had had fraternal twins, Brittany and Max. They were great kids now, grown and out on their own.

But now, Carla considered, he'd unleashed a tigress, and Tiffy wasn't going to be happy until she had gotten into bed with the Sultan of Sherazad, the Caliph of Baghdad, and the Great Khan of Samarkand. A foursome. Wow! Carla had to admire Tiffy's suddenly unleashed creativity.

I don't think I ever did a foursome, she thought. *A threesome, yes, but not a foursome. How the hell am I going to help Tiffy attain her dream coupling?* she wondered.

And then it came to her. For years the five friends who lived on Ansley Court had owned a big old summer camp on a lake in the nearby mountains. The past few summers they had been renting it out. The rambling summer house had been for their children more than for them. But their offspring were grown. They hadn't been up to Camp Cozy, as their kids had dubbed it, in a couple of years. The people renting it for the past two summers wanted to buy it. If she could get her Rick and Tiffy's Joe to go up to negotiate the sale, then Tiffy could have her one night to experience that foursome she wanted.

"Honey," she called to her husband, "I've had a sudden thought." And when Rick had joined her in the den, she said, "I know we've been discussing selling the place in the mountains for a while now, so why don't we do it? I could talk to Tiffy, Nora, Rina, and Joanne. We don't go up anymore. We take grown-up vacations now."

"I agree," Rick replied. "Paying for upkeep and the taxes and collecting one-fifth from everyone is becoming tiresome. Go ahead and speak to the girls. I know Dr. Sam, Joe, and the others will agree. It's past time we got rid of it, and the Chandlers love the place for their kids and their big family."

"I'll call Tiffy right now," Carla said. "Then you and Joe can start setting things up. You'll probably have to spend a night at the inn up there. It's too far for a day trip if you're going to do business. We don't want to be greedy, but we shouldn't give it away."

"You're a genius!" Tiffy said when Carla called to tell her the plan.

"Only if everyone agrees," Carla said.

"They will," Tiffy replied. "How soon can we get the boys up to the mountains?"

"Maybe next weekend if we can get everyone to agree," Carla said. "I'll make sure to be working at the hospital then, and you can say if I can't go, you don't want to go either. Let's hope the Chandlers are still enthusiastic, and if they are, let's close in mid-October. That way we can all have one final autumn weekend and maybe take one small personal item as a memory."

"What if the Chandlers want to negotiate over the telephone?" Tiffy asked.

"Rick already thought of that. He wants to go up unannounced with Joe so they can check out the condition of the house. There's a guy who does inspections up there, and they're going to meet with him first," Carla explained.

Carla called their friends the next day.

"It's time," Rina Seligmann said sanguinely. "Past time if you ask me. Hold on a minute. Sam! We're going to sell Camp Cozy. Okay with you?"

"About time," Carla heard Dr. Sam say.

"I heard him," Carla said.

"Everyone else in agreement?" Rina asked.

"Tiffy, yes. I've got to call Joanne next."

"They'll okay it. The Ulrichs want to buy a condo in Vero for the winter, and while the hardware store is still doing okay, that Home Depot at the mall has taken some of their business," Rina told Carla. "Where's Nora right now?"

"Thanks for the tip about the Ulrichs," Carla said. "I've got Nora's cell number. Who knows where she is right now? But I'll ask when I get her. Thanks, Rina." She next called Joanne Ulrich.

"We had great times up there," Joanne said, "but yes, we're on board to sell it. There's this condo in Florida we were considering buying. We trust Rick and Joe to get us all the best price. I know it won't be a fortune, but we might at least get our down payment for the condo."

"Rick says we can get at least two hundred fifty thousand for the place. It's got three acres with it, three hundred feet of lakefront, and the house is in reasonable shape. The guys will do the deal, and with no agent involved, we should each come out of it with fifty thousand," Carla responded.

"Sounds good to me," Joanne Ulrich answered. "As Captain Picard would say, 'Make it so!'"

Carla laughed. "You got it!" she said before hanging up. Then she dialed Nora Buckley. Nora actually worked for the Channel Corporation. Carla got her voice mail. God only knew where Nora was in the world. "Nora, it's Carla. We want to sell Camp Cozy. Everyone is in agreement, but we need your vote too. Call me, and where the hell are you anyway? You haven't been home all summer."

Nora Buckley called late the next day. "Hey, Carla," she said by way of greeting, "I'm in New Zealand. We're going to be opening up another resort here."

"The gorgeous Kyle with you?" Carla queried.

"Of course," Nora replied, laughing. "In fact, we're just about ready to go to bed."

"Too much information!" Carla told her, but she remembered when Nora had been her best friend in all the world and they had met in the Channel with their lovers. Kyle had a world-class penis, Carla recalled with a lusty little sigh. Then she got back to business. "So you vote to sell the place too, right?"

"I vote to sell," Nora said with a chuckle, for she had

heard that sigh and knew exactly what Carla was remembering. "Rick and Joe handling the sale?"

"Yep," Carla answered. "They can fax or e-mail the stuff to you at your office."

"That's fine," Nora agreed.

"Listen, we're doing one last weekend in mid-October. You know you and Kyle are invited."

"Thanks, but no. My kids loved Camp Cozy. I never really did," Nora said.

"I understand," Carla replied, "but I'll let you know anyway."

"You're still my best friend," Nora said softly. Then she rang off.

When Rick Johnson got home from his office on Monday afternoon, Carla informed her husband that everyone was in complete agreement. Camp Cozy was to be sold, with the Chandlers having the first chance to purchase it. "Tiffy says the office is slow right now, so why don't you and Joe go up this week?"

"Good idea," Rick agreed. "It's two weeks until Labor Day weekend. If the Chandlers are going to buy, this is the time to catch them. Make us a reservation at the inn for Thursday night. We'll go up first thing Thursday morning and be home Friday night. I've been checking out the real estate market up there, and despite everything, it's pretty good right now. The Baird place closed for three hundred thousand at the end of July, and they don't have as much lakefront or acreage."

"Is two fifty too low?" Carla asked.

Rick shook his head. "We bought the place for thirty thou, and while we kept it in good shape, we haven't put a whole lot into it over the years. None of us wants too much of a capital gain, considering we're all still working," he told his wife. "I've kept a strict record of everything we've put into the place. You know Johnson's Law number one."

"'Never mess with GOD or the IRS,'" Carla said, laughing.

She called Joe Pietro d'Angelo to ask if Thursday would be all right with him, and when he said it was, she made the reservation at the local mountain inn in the village near Camp Cozy. Then she called back to confirm it with him and talk with Tiffy.

"You are on, kiddo. Thursday night," Carla told her.

"Thank God!" Tiffy exclaimed. Then she lowered her voice. "I don't think I could hold out much longer. I tried to get Joe to give me a little action last night, but he said he was still tired from their trip into the city. I hope once I get him away this winter, he turns into the animal you claim Rick is now," Tiffy said wistfully.

"Getting away for a couple weeks does seem to prime a man's libido," Carla said. "Trust me, it's all going to work out. I got Rick started by some role-playing. He was the big bad pirate, and I was the helpless noblewoman whose ship he captured. He loved it. And eventually we didn't have to role-play. He just wanted to fuck me. In the meantime, you have your Arabian Nights fantasy to play with, sweetie."

"I'll talk to you on Thursday," Tiffy said and hung up. And to her relief, Thursday came quickly. She packed an overnight bag for Joe, gave him a kiss, and sent him off. "Drive carefully. Don't you and Rick forget you aren't kids in Camaros anymore."

He grinned at her. "You know what they say about boys and the cars they drive," he teased. "When I bring my Camaro home, I'll stick it in your garage, baby. I promise. I'm sorry about the other night, Tiffy."

"It's okay," she lied, giving him a quick kiss. "We'll make up for it when you get home. Don't exhaust yourself, Joey. It's been a while, and I'm more than ready."

"Gotcha!" he said, and then he was gone.

Tiffany glanced at the clock on the kitchen wall. It was just eight a.m. Twelve long hours until the Channel opened. The guys would get up to Camp Cozy by noon. If the Chandlers were still interested in buying, they would make the deal, but by then it would be too late to come home, and they'd stay at the Blue Hen Inn for the night. It was a nice place with a good little restaurant. They'd finalize everything in the morning, leave, and be home by sometime in the afternoon. It didn't matter when. She would have had her adventure in the Channel by then and be satisfied.

Carla called in midafternoon. "You ready?" she said.

"I have never been readier," Tiffy answered. "Just five more hours."

"Rick asked me to call you. They got there safely. They've spoken with the Chandlers, who still want to buy."

"Did they agree to the price?" Tiffy asked.

"Yep, and without even blinking. But I'll give Bill Chandler points for honesty. He asked the guys if they knew how much the Baird property went for in July and reminded them, as if two attorneys would forget such a thing, that the Bairds' Place had less property and lakefront," Carla said. "Rick said yes, they knew, but that the Bairds' house had been recently updated, and Quintet Corp. was content to take two fifty for Camp Cozy. They'll sign the papers in the morning, and Chandler will give them a check for fifty thousand to be put in an escrow account. They've agreed on a closing date as well. It's the Tuesday after the Columbus Day weekend."

"So it's all worked out," Tiffy said, almost wistfully.

"You aren't sorry we're selling, are you?"

"Nah. It was time," Tiffy replied. "Well, I'd better go. I'll call Joe about six so he won't call me when I'm not available to answer the phone."

"Call me in the morning," Carla responded. "I'll want a full report before the guys get back, and I'll expect every down-and-dirty detail, sweetie."

"I won't leave out a thing," Tiffany promised as she rang off.

Four hours, fifty minutes to go. She ate a light meal, then took a long, luxurious bath, using a new bath oil that called Night Blooming Lily she had seen at the mall. Then she called her husband. "Hi, honey," Tiffy said. "Carla said we've got a deal."

"Yeah," Joe replied. "We got a deal. The Chandlers are taking us to dinner to celebrate. They say there's a new restaurant halfway around the lake that's so hot you need reservations. Imagine that! Reservations up here. We're going at seven. I'm glad you called, but I was going to call you later and tell you all about it."

"Save it for when you get home," Tiffy said. "I'm taking this opportunity to watch the five DVDs of the Angelique novels. I'm turning off the phone because I don't want to be disturbed. They say that Michele Mercier and Robert Hossein are perfect as Angelique and the Comte de Peyrac. English subtitles, but who cares? I know the stories, having read the books."

"At least a hundred times," he teased her. "I'm glad you won't be lonely."

"Thanks for understanding, Joe. I don't often get a chance like this," she replied.

"I'll call you before we leave in the morning," he promised.

"Have a terrific dinner. I'll want all the details," Tiffy said. "Maybe we can all go there in October when we make our last visit to Camp Cozy."

"Let's hope the place lives up to its promise," Joe responded. "Have a good evening, Tiffy. I'll see you tomorrow afternoon. Good night."

"Good night, honey," Tiffy said and put the house phone back in its cradle. She sighed. If only Joe would be more like Rick was these days, she wouldn't need the Channel at all. Well, maybe now and again, but not so much. Carla had gotten Rick to stop and smell the flowers. If only Joe would too.

The clock in the hall struck the half hour. Thirty minutes to go. Tiffy went upstairs to their bedroom. If she was going to get a full evening of sexual pleasure, she was going to have to imagine that the Caliph of Bagdad and the Great Khan had already arrived at the palace in Sherazad. And that her husband, Ahmed, the Sultan of Sherazad, was even now explaining the treat he would offer them in exchange for a fifty-year treaty of peaceful coexistence. She climbed naked into her bed, and as the clock struck eight p.m., Tiffy eagerly pressed the B button on her Channel remote.

Hestia was standing at a spy hole listening to and watching the three men as they finished their meal. The treaty had been signed before the meal. She studied the two visitors. Rashid, the Caliph of Baghdad, was a tall, slender man who favored black clothing. His face was a long one, the look severe. He had a small, thin, dark mustache just above his upper lip. He was attractive in the traditionally handsome way. Balin, the Great Khan of Samarkand, was a totally different type. Of medium height, he had a stocky build with a broad barrel chest. His round head was shaved bald. Neither was as handsome as her sultan. She was curious as to the kind of lovers they would be, and she was soon about to find out, for the three men arose from the low table where they had been seated.

"Come, my friends," the sultan said. "We shall now go to my harem to enjoy the pleasures that my beautiful wife can offer us."

In her Hestia persona, Tiffy slipped from her hiding place and hurried to the harem. Her three young slave women were awaiting her. "They come!" she said as she hurried in to join them. "Is all in readiness?"

"Yes, Princess," they chorused as one.

"Remember, there is to be no shyness. You will obey the sultan and his guests without question," she reminded them. Her heart was rapidly beating now.

"Yes, Princess," they said again as one. They knelt about her.

The doors to the harem were opened by the eunuchs guarding her, and the sultan and his companions strode in.

Hestia, arms crossed over her chest, made her obeisance to her sultan and his two companions. Then, arising, she said, "I welcome you, my lord husband, and your honored guests. I am prepared in the name and cause of peace between our lands to serve you in any manner you wish." She bowed to them again.

The sultan indicated to the caliph and the khan that they were to seat themselves among the colorful cushions. Each man took one of the slave girls down with him.

"How would you have me begin, my lord sultan?" Hestia asked politely.

"First you will dance for us," the sultan said. "Then I would have you disrobe before us, Princess, and display your treasures for our eyes," the sultan ordered his beautiful wife. He turned to his companions. "She is a most graceful dancer."

"It shall be as you wish, my lord sultan," Hestia said, turning her head just slightly to nod to the musicians seated discreetly in a dim corner of the chamber. At the first note played, she began her dance. The music was heavily sensuous. She danced slowly, gracefully weaving across the floor, around them, behind them, before them. The bells on her ankles tinkled as she moved. The black-and-gold silk gauze of her garments swayed, tauntingly revealing and yet concealing her fair body.

And then Hestia began to remove the scant clothing that covered her. First she removed the black gauze that had allowed but a glimpse of her long hair, which now flowed like molten gold down her back. Next she tore away the veiling that covered her chest, reaching behind herself to unhook the silk-and-sequined bra that covered her breasts. She flung the covering aside almost defiantly, stamping her feet as she did so.

She saw the sultan smile faintly and lean over to speak with the caliph and the khan. His hand was absently fondling the slave girl in his lap, even as the other two men were caressing the women in their embrace. Hestia felt a stab of jealousy. The slave girl was obviously enjoying the sultan's attentions. *I wonder if she will enjoy the whipping I shall give her later for her presumption.* It was one thing for a slave to stay silent while her master touched her before his wife's eyes, but to openly enjoy it was intolerable, and Hestia would not stand for it. As further punishment, she would give the slave girl to her husband's soldiers for their amusement.

Now the dance was coming to an end. Slowly, slowly, Hestia discarded each of the dark silk scarfs that had made up the skirt of her dancing costume, until her only adornment was the thin gold chain lying on her hip bones to which the scarves had been attached. As the last note of the reed pipes sounded, she ripped the veiling from her face, a smile of satisfaction adorning her lips as she heard the caliph and the khan gasp with amazement at the great beauty of the Sultan of Sherazad's wife.

After giving them a brief moment to gape, Hestia walked forward to step up onto the low lacquered table that was placed before them. She turned slowly so they might fully see and enjoy the perfect body she possessed. Her back to the three men, she smiled when the khan remarked she had the fine flanks of a purebred mare. Turning back to face them again, she slipped her hands beneath her round breasts, displaying them to three sets of avid eyes. Releasing one breast, she licked the center finger of her left hand, then began to rub and encircle the nipple of her right breast with it. Her eyes closed as she enjoyed the sensation. A faint murmur escaped from between her lips. After a time, she ceased, freeing her breast from her hand. Her mons was smooth, as custom demanded. Hestia took a finger and ran it up and down the shadowed slit in her labia. Then, using both of her hands, she peeled the two plump lips open to the view of her spectators.

"She has a fine love jewel," the caliph remarked, eyeing Hestia's clitoris.

The khan nodded, his gaze avid with his growing lust.

Smiling, she released her hold on her nether lips, bending to hold out her hands so the two men might lick her fingers. The khan did so eagerly, but the caliph first inhaled the musky fragrance of her before sucking suggestively on her slender digits. "Shall I now join you, my lord sultan?" Hestia asked the sultan.

He nodded.

"Let me send the others away," she said, and at his nod of approval she dismissed the slave girls and the musicians. The chamber now contained but four people. Hestia stepped down from the low table and settled herself between the khan and the caliph. "I am so pleased that you have signed our treaty, my lords," she said to them. "We must celebrate your wisdom on the altar of the goddess of love."

The caliph put a hand on her shoulder. He caressed it, moving to her throat, and then down to a breast. "I should not disappoint so fair a sultana," he told her.

"You are kind, my lord caliph," she said. Oh, this guy

was smooth and sophisticated, unlike the khan, who was squeezing her other breast as if he were trying to get juice out of it. She turned to him. "Gently, my lord khan," she murmured. "My skin is delicate and fragile. You will bruise me, I fear." To her surprise, Balin Khan flushed.

"I apologize, Star of Cinnabar," he said. "You have aroused my lust as no female ever has. I want but to enjoy your beauty and fuck you into oblivion this night."

"In time, my lord khan," Hestia promised. Then, reaching over, she placed her warm hand upon his crotch, squeezing gently. "I can see you are already preparing yourself for me." The tip of her tongue slipped from between her lips to touch her top lip. "We will give each other much pleasure," she promised him. Then Hestia smiled into his rough face, interested to see that his small dark eyes held a full measure of intelligence.

He took the hand with which she had fondled him, and, raising it up to his lips, kissed the palm. "My weapon is large, and you are small," he noted.

"My cunt is expansive and will devour you, great khan," she promised him.

He nodded, satisfied, as the caliph drew her into his sole embrace, whispering into her ear, "It is your beautiful ass I would plunder, my princess, if you would permit me."

"I am yours at my husband's command to do with as you will," Hestia said. *Ohh,* Tiffy thought. *I never got ass-fucked before, but I can stop it if I don't like it. It is my fantasy.* She raised her head up to receive the caliph's kiss. His tongue plunged into her mouth, caressing hers, sucking on it. She felt his hand fondling her bottom eagerly and pulled her head away from his. "I think, my lords, you should dispense with your garments if we are to begin," Hestia advised.

Agreeing, the three men rose and put aside their robes so that they were all now naked. She looked to her husband, who sent her a smile of his approval. Hestia let her eyes wander over the male bodies. Ahmed's was, of course, the finest to her eye. Balin Khan had arms and legs like tree trunks and a smooth broad chest, but despite his size, he had no fleshy belly. His cock, however, was a marvel. It was indeed bigger than any she had seen before. The caliph, on the other hand, was slender but well muscled. His cock was long and thin. She had never seen one quite like it.

The caliph reached for her, pulling her into his arms to kiss her once again. Then he said, "I like to spank my women before fucking them. It primes them for my entry. Get on your hands and knees now so we may begin." When she had obeyed his command, he positioned her to suit his purposes and then put a hand on her nape. *What is it with these guys and necks?* Tiffy wondered. Then his palm descended on her plump bottom.

"Oh!" she squealed. "Oh! Oh! Oh!" She punctuated each spank with a cry.

Finally he slid his hand beneath her to ascertain if her juices had begun, and satisfied she was ready, he knelt behind her as her buttocks were drawn open by the khan and Hestia's husband, the sultan.

She felt something touch her anal opening and flinched.

"Easy, my beauty," he said. "I will go gently," he promised her as he moistened her with her own juices.

Pressure, and then the sphincter muscle gave way. "Ohhh!" she gasped.

" 'Tis just the head of my cock," he told her. "There is more to come." He pushed himself further into her narrow back channel. "My cock is thin, and made for this activity," the caliph assured her. Then, inch by inch, he pushed himself into her until he was well sheathed. "There now, my beauty, you are fully corked," he said.

She felt him quite distinctly. The long, thin penis throbbed within her. To her surprise she felt her clit throbbing too. And then her head was yanked up and a penis was pushed into her mouth. The taste was not familiar, and so she decided it was Balin Khan. Hestia began to suck on him. She hoped he wouldn't come in her mouth, because she was really eager to have him fuck her with that big dick of his. *Little chicks love big dicks,* Tiffy thought wickedly as she sucked the penis in her mouth, even as the caliph's member pulsed within her.

"We must take her together this first time," Tiffy heard the sultan say, and the other two men grunted in agreement. The khan removed himself from between Hestia's lips. He lay on his back amid the colorful pillows, the great penis sticking straight up. Still buried within her ass, the caliph carefully drew Hestia to enough of an upright position so she could be moved. Oh! My! God! They were both going to fuck her at the same time. She immediately aided their efforts as the three men carefully positioned her over and then pressed her down onto Balin Khan's massive cock.

Her eyes widened as she felt herself absorbing the khan's penis. To her amazement he was incredibly gentle as he filled her. Now she balanced on her hands as one man took her ass and the other her cunt. When her husband pushed past her lips with his own penis, the sensation was incredible. Then, as if there had been a signal, all three men began to move within her body's cavities. The caliph and the khan seemed to find a perfect rhythm for their members as they pumped her. Tiffy's head was spinning with the overwhelming sexual sensations buffeting her. *Can I die from this?* she wondered, but then she realized she didn't care. Her sucking matched the cadence of the two other men. She began to climax, but they weren't finished with her. They aroused her once again and she enjoyed a second round.

Then she heard the sultan say, "I think, my lords, it is time to release our mutual lust. Are you ready, Hestia, to receive our tribute?"

"Only if you promise to give me more later, my lords!" she gasped. She didn't know what was coming over her but she absolutely didn't want to stop. The cock in her ass, the one in her cunt, the third in her mouth felt wonderful, and like nothing she had ever experienced before. She wanted more. And more. And more.

"I promise," the sultan said.

"And I too," the caliph added.

"I could fuck you all night, my beauty," the khan admitted.

"Then let us come together, my lords," Hestia told them, and they did. Their juices flowed copiously as they spermed her, their penises jerking as they released their tribute to her. Finally they all collapsed in a heap, lying amid the pillows and gasping for breath with the ferocity of their exertions.

At last Hestia suggested that they go to her bath and

wash away the excesses of the last hour. When they returned, they found the pillows had been replaced with fresh ones, and there were wine and sugar wafers for them. Hestia poured them each a goblet of pale golden liquid, knowing it was heavily laced with aphrodisiacs so that her lovers could keep up the same pace the entire night. It wasn't long before the four were entwined again in another lustful bout. It was her husband's turn to have her cunt. The khan and the caliph watched avidly as the sultan brought his wife to a screaming climax. So aroused were the two men that they wasted no time in each mounting her in turn after the sultan had rolled away from her. So it went on throughout the night, and to her great surprise, Tiffy never tired. Indeed, she could not seem to get enough of the three men. Suddenly this was a fantasy she wanted to have forever. It wasn't going to matter anymore if Joe was too tired to have sex with her. What had ever made her think that just having a regular sex life with Joe again would be enough? With a fantasy like this, who cared?

Her breasts were sore from being sucked and nipped. She had allowed the caliph to ass-fuck her three times. His thin cock was indeed perfect for it. Balin Khan was a vigorous lover, and he loved sucking on her clit. Never, he declared, had he seen such a perfect one, or one of such a size. His tongue on that delicate bit of flesh had her shrieking a half dozen times. But then too soon, too soon the syrupy voiced called out that the Channel had closed, and Tiffany found herself back in her own bed.

Carla had the decency to wait until eleven a.m. to call her. "So," she said, "how did it go? Was it everything you hoped it would be?"

"More!" Tiffy said. "There isn't a part of me that wasn't licked, sucked, and fucked. I want more! I can't live without that fantasy. When I think of all the years I wasted on that dull old sultan-and-the-slave-girl routine. This was incredible. Three men. Three different penises, and each one perfect. The caliph had a long, thin dick, and he loves to ass-fuck. Not my favorite thing, but he's gentle and surprisingly nice. The khan is this big bald-headed guy with a cock that has to be ten inches at least. But he knows just how to use it. And then there's my sultan, who fucks like a dream. I've got to figure a way to keep Joe asleep so I can play in the Channel, Carla. Maybe I'll get Dr. Sam to check him out. If it's nothing serious, then maybe he can give him sleeping pills."

"Tiff, I've never heard you talk like this before," Carla fretted.

"You don't know what it was like," Tiffany said, "to have three cocks going at you at once. It was unbelievable. I need more of it."

"Did you ever make those reservations for a winter trip?" Carla asked.

"I don't know if I want to go now," Tiffy replied.

"You're starting to scare me," Carla said. "The Channel is fantasy, not reality."

"So says the woman who spent years playing a libidinous pirate queen on the Spanish Main," Tiffy shot back.

"I don't deny it," Carla replied. "But I knew when I had had enough, and canceled my subscription to the Channel."

"Well, I haven't had enough yet," Tiffy said. "In fact, I'm just getting started."

"I'm not suggesting that you do what I did, but you weren't so nutzo with your original fantasy," Carla pointed out. "You've gone over the top with this one. Make some reservations for a luxury winter trip with Joe, and get back to your reality."

"Yeah, yeah," Tiffy answered.

"Hey, Joe is just dropping Rick off. Your guy will be home in a minute," Carla said. "Gotta go. But for heaven's sake, think about what you're doing."

"Sure," Tiffy responded, hitting the OFF button and putting her phone back into its cradle.

Carla sighed. Tiffy had always been a little naive where the Channel was concerned, but Carla had always felt she was safe in her simple fantasy. This new fantasy, however, had turned her friend into a raving sex maniac. It scared her. Then she considered that Tiffy usually had a good head on her shoulders. When the twins had gone off to college, she had gone back to school and become a paralegal, and she now ran the law offices of Johnson and Pietro d'Angelo. She was going to calm down in a couple more days, and everything would be okay again. Carla laughed at herself for being such a worrywart.

In the next month, however, Tiffany began to look paler and paler. Joe insisted she see Dr. Sam, who prescribed rest.

"She's obviously been working too hard," he said.

"But she isn't," Joe Pietro d'Angelo said. "I don't think she's sleeping too good. I haven't been for a couple months now, but suddenly I wake up and Tiffy isn't there."

"You okay?" Dr. Sam asked.

"Yeah. I just had to cut the caffeine and stop eating after seven o'clock. Once I did that, I began to sleep better," Joe said.

"Make her stay home for a week or two," Dr. Sam advised.

"We're supposed to be taking a winter trip this year," Joe told the doctor.

"The perfect prescription for overwork," Dr. Sam answered. "In the meantime, keep her home. I'll stop by and see her in a few days."

"I'll get bored staying home," Tiffy protested.

"So be bored," the doctor responded. "You're showing all the signs of exhaustion, Tiffany. Stay home. Take naps. Drink wine. Eat chocolate. In other words, get some damn rest."

"You're playing out that fantasy every night, aren't you?" Carla accused when she learned of Tiffy's visit to Dr. Sam. "I'll bet you're hiding out in your craft room, aren't you? You are going to get caught."

"No, I'm not," Tiffy said. "When I get to the bottom of the cellar stairs, I turn off the lights in the stairwell. You can't see the door of my craft room from the stairs because it's around the corner. I don't turn a light on in the room, and I put a towel down so nothing shows through the bottom crack of the door when I have the television on. I carry a flashlight so I won't fall. I have it all under control."

"No one goes into the Channel every night," Carla said.

"How do you know?" Tiffy countered. "The caliph

has a new game. Instead of spanking me, he whips my bottom with a hazel switch. I get so wet so fast when he does that. The sultan and the khan tied me down last night and let my three slave girls make love to me. Then they forced me to watch while the three men fucked those little wretches until they were shrieking for mercy. Only then did they give me what I wanted."

"You're exhausted between work and the Channel," Carla said. She was really getting worried now. She had hoped Tiffy would get bored and let go of this particular fantasy. Instead her friend was becoming more and more involved with it. The fantasy was almost taking on a life of its own.

"Now that I can rest all day, I'll be fine," Tiffy assured Carla.

Early the next morning, however, the local emergency team came howling into Ansley Court. Carla's first thought was of Rina Seligmann, who was the oldest of the five friends. She hurried to the door, horrified to see the EMS guys entering the Pietro d'Angelo house. Opening the door, Carla hesitated. Should she go over? Before she could decide, Rina Seligmann walked quickly over to where Carla stood in her doorway.

"It's Tiffy," she said. "Joe found her unconscious and called Sam. Sam called the EMS when he couldn't get any response."

Carla leaned heavily against her doorjamb. "Oh, God, Rina, she isn't dead, is she?" She felt light-headed, as if she might faint, and struggled to fight the sensation.

"What happened? Does Sam know?"

"She was down in her craft room watching television,"

Rina began, and then she gasped. "That's her Channel telly, isn't it? She hides out from Joe there, doesn't she?"

Carla nodded. *Please, no,* she thought. "When did he find her?"

"He told Sam he woke up about three a.m. She wasn't in bed, so he went looking for her. When he didn't find her downstairs, he headed into the cellar and discovered her asleep in her recliner in front of the television." Rina's eyes grew wide. "Oh, crap! He turned it off," she whispered. "He turned the Channel off because he thought it was just an ordinary television channel. But he left her there because she had been having trouble sleeping too. Then he went back to bed. He got up, dressed, and fixed his own breakfast, thinking to give Tiffy a little more sleep time. When she hadn't come up by the time he was ready to go to the office, he went down to her craft room again and tried to rouse her. He couldn't. Poor Joe is all upset, to put it mildly. He keeps telling anyone who will stop and listen to him how much he loves Tiffy; how she takes such good care of him, not just at home, but she's so smart in the office. He says he can't, he doesn't want to go on if anything happens to her. This is just terrible! Oh, God, Carla, what's happened to Tiffy? Where is she?"

"In the Channel," Carla whispered. "She has to be in the Channel."

"She can't be!" Rina replied.

"Well, she is. Remember when that asshole Jeff Buckley was divorcing Nora and trying to take everything after all those years of marriage. Do you recall what happened? Nora was found unconscious in front of the den television. Well, she wasn't unconscious. She had made a deal with the guy who owns the Channel to remain there until she had time to figure out how to thwart Jeff, keep her house, and protect the kids."

"What?" Rina Seligmann was astounded.

"You can't repeat any of this, Rina," Carla said. "So you can remain in the Channel if you want to stay there and you have permission. However, that's not what happened to Tiffy. What's happened is that poor Joe turned off the television before four a.m. and stranded his wife there."

"What can we do?" Rina was looking very distressed. She was teary-eyed as the local rescue squad rolled the unconscious Tiffany Pietro d'Angelo out of her house and into the waiting ambulance.

"I'm going to call Nora now. Remember, she works for the Channel Corporation and is very tight with the guy who owns the whole shebang. She'll be able to help us out. In the meantime, they're taking Tiffy to the hospital. Sam diagnosed overwork, stress, and so on. They'll check her for stroke and other stuff. Hopefully, by the time they can't come up with a reason she's unconscious, she'll be conscious again."

"From your lips to God's ear," Rina said.

Carla slipped back into her house. Rick had signaled her from across the street that he was going to take his partner, follow the ambulance, and drive to their local hospital. With her husband out of the way, she could get to Nora Buckley quickly. Finding her cell, she punched in the number 6 and the phone automatically dialed.

"Carla," Nora Buckley's voice greeted her.

"There's a problem here, and you are probably the only one who can help us fix it," Carla began. Then she went on to explain Tiffy's new fantasy, how she had become addicted to it, and what had happened a few hours ago.

Nora listened. "I have been warning Mr. Nicholas that we were going to have to eventually make the remotes touch-sensitive only to the women who possess them. That way if anyone else picked up the remote when a customer was in the Channel, it would awaken her. This was bound to happen sooner or later. The dem . . . delinquents who monitor this sort of thing for us obviously weren't on the ball. There's been no report of an incident. I'll call Mr. Nicholas immediately and get back to you. Do you have Skype?"

"Yes," Carla said. "Rick likes to see people when he talks to them."

"Mr. Nicholas may phone you to hear this firsthand, Carla. He's a real charmer. Reminds me of that old-time movie actor Claude Rains. You'll like him, and you can speak freely with him."

"Okay," Carla said. She was actually curious about the mysterious Mr. Nicholas.

"I'll be back to you in any case," Nora said, and rang off.

In midmorning Carla's cell rang. A crisp, impersonal female voice said, "If you would be kind enough to turn on your Skype connection, Mrs. Johnson, Mr. Nicholas will speak with you."

"Okay," Carla agreed, and did as she had been bid. She immediately found herself facing an elegant gentleman, and he did look like Claude Rains.

"Good morning, Carla," the elegant man greeted her

in a faintly British accent. "I'm so sorry you have been distressed by this little glitch in our services. I want to assure you that it's being attended to as we speak. Tiffany will be regaining consciousness very shortly. Her condition will be put down as extreme exhaustion, but she'll be fine otherwise. I hope you will tender her my personal apology, although she will get a form letter regretting the incident and a year of the Channel free."

"This shouldn't have happened," Carla said bluntly.

"No, it shouldn't have," he agreed. "I am taking Nora Buckley's advice. New remotes will be issued as quickly as possible to our customers worldwide. They will have new built-in safety features. They won't work if anyone other than the female customer attempts to use them as they already do. If anyone else tries to turn off a television with them, their owners will awaken immediately. I suppose we should have done this years ago, but we corporations will nickel and dime everything," he said and chuckled. "I'm sorry we lost you as a customer, my dear. Julian has been punished, of course," Mr. Nicholas said. "He should not have invaded your fantasy."

"He suspected he would be," Carla answered.

"You were wickedly clever in your last encounter," Mr. Nicholas noted. "I could use a woman of your talents in my business."

"I'm happy being a wife and a nurse," Carla told him.

"Well, even I can't have everything," he said with a sigh. "Go and see your friend now. And reassure her she is safe, for her last few hours have probably been overstimulating. Good day, Carla, my dear. Perhaps we will meet again." And then he was gone.

Carla ended the connection. Her cell rang. It was Rick. "Tiffy's awake," he said.

"I'll be right over," she replied.

As soon as she had arrived at Egret Pointe General Hospital, both Rick and Joe left for the office. But not before Carla witnessed a tender little scene between her best friend and Joe. Holding her hand tightly, Joe told his wife how much he loved her and how he couldn't have gone on without her, had she not recovered.

"I'm going to cut back at the office, babe," he promised her. "We need at least two associates. Rick's been telling me that for the last few months, but I wouldn't listen. I'm listening now, Tiffy. We need more time together. What the hell has all our hard work been for if we can't take time to be with each other outside the office?" He kissed the hand he was holding. "I'll be back later. You get some rest now." Reassured his wife was going to be all right, Joe had said he'd rather work than go home while she was hospitalized.

Once the men had gone, Carla said, "I spoke with Nora's Mr. Nicholas himself. He wanted me to deliver his personal apology for what happened."

"What did happen?" Tiffy asked "I'm kinda blanking. I remember a very wild night that seemed to go on and on and on. And then I woke up here."

"Joe woke up and came looking for you. When he found you, he thought you had been watching television and fallen asleep. He turned off your telly before four a.m."

"Oh, my God! I was trapped in the Channel?" Tiffy grew pale and fell back onto her pillows. Could her crazy behavior have cost her everything? Perhaps her life? She shivered.

"Yeah, you were trapped, but it's okay. I called Nora. Nora called Mr. Nicholas, and voilà! You were sprung. And it won't happen again. Everyone is getting new remotes so no one but the remote's owner can turn off the television with it." She reached out and picked up Tiffy's hand. "You're going to be all right, sweetie."

Tiffy nodded. "I've had enough of foursomes," she said. "I think if I want a fantasy, I'll set up the trip I've been wanting to take with Joe next winter."

"Yeah," Carla said. "And you might want to delete the tale of the Star of Cinnabar from your remote," she suggested.

Tiffy giggled. She hadn't died. Indeed, she was very alive. "Oh, no," she said. "I'll delete the foursome, but my sultan is a pretty nice guy, and a girl's got to have more than one fantasy in her life."

"If you say so," Carla replied, laughing. "At least don't play when Joe's home. Another accident like this and we might not get you back."

Tiffy's expression grew serious. "You're right," she agreed. "I'll only play in the Channel when Joe is away." The color was already coming back into her cheeks. "Now, go find out, Nurse Johnson, when they're going to let me out of this place."

Carla stood up. "Yes, my princess," she said, and went out laughing.

Tiffany chuckled. The foursome might go, but Ahmed, the Sultan of Sherazad, was definitely going to stay for a while. It didn't mean she didn't love her Joe, because she did. She always had and always would. But she was none the worse for wear for her recent adventure, and as she had said to Carla, a girl had to have more than just one fantasy.

Especially when she was facing fifty.

ABOUT THE AUTHOR

Bertrice Small is a *New York Times* bestselling author and the recipient of numerous awards. In keeping with her profession, she lives in the oldest English-speaking town in the state of New York, founded in 1640. Her light-filled studio includes the paintings of her favorite cover artist, Elaine Duillo, and a large library. Because she believes in happy endings, Bertrice Small has been married to the same man, her hero, George, for forty-eight years. They have a son, Thomas, and four wonderful grandchildren. Longtime readers will want to know that Nicki the cockatiel flew over the rainbow bridge on December 8, 2010. However, they will be happy to know that Finnegan, the long-haired, bad black kitty, and Sylvester, the black-and-white tuxedo cat, still remain her devoted companions.